# Seen From
# A Distance

# Seen From
# A Distance

## A Novel

**Paul Hoffman**

Mill City Press

Mill City Press, Inc.
212 3rd Avenue North, Suite 290
Minneapolis, MN 55401
612.455.2294
www.millcitypublishing.com

ISBN-13: 978-1-937600-60-0
LCCN: 2011944713

Cover Design Alan Pranke
Typeset by Tim Parlin

*Printed in the United States of America*

*For it is a serious thing to have been watched. We all radiate something curiously intimate when we believe ourselves to be alone.*

**E. M. Forster**

# Part I

*The true solitaire is an extreme separatist,*
*an alien even at home.* *

# Chapter 1

Cusack stood at the window looking at the building across the street, his hand resting on top of a camera that itself rested on a tripod, the tip of its long, bulbous telephoto lens inches from the window. The rain had not gone on long enough and had left a yellowish film on the windows. It gave everything an appearance of something that couldn't be salvaged, like more rain wouldn't have helped and you wouldn't be any more energized with a clear view. It was still night but day was coming on, the darkness weakening in the sky above the building across the street.

Cusack had been in all of the second and third floor offices of the building across the street the night before, his first night on the job, although only the corner office on the third floor was on the work order. He wanted to be thorough and it had come off without a single hiccup. It was an uncomplicated business but he felt accomplished in the work, his first real work in nearly six months.

Thirty-six hours earlier, on the airport road driving in a light, steady rain toward downtown, Cusack thought he might have made a mistake accepting the assignment. The job was a tame surveillance project, a wired office mostly, the sort of thing Cusack had done

*Each chapter begins with a quotation from the works of W.S. Tyler.

many times before. The subject of the watch was a college professor named W.S. Tyler whose name Cusack had heard but couldn't quite place. Parsons had presented the assignment as routine when they met in Vienna, which made Cusack think there was more to it, something he believed he was supposed to think. It was why, in the end, he'd accepted the job.

Parsons had brought Cusack into the agency a few months after the end of the First Gulf War, a dozen years ago now. At the time, Cusack was unemployed and running out of cash. He'd decided against re-enlistment; there was nothing about the war he wanted to see again.

Parsons was Cusack's mentor at the beginning when Cusack's desk job was writing probability scenarios. Cusack and his co-worker, Ted Aanonsen were encouraged to be, alternatively, strictly logical and wildly fanciful. They worked together on scenarios that involved revolutions, economic meltdowns, genocidal wars, famine, catastrophic floods and earthquakes. Three years later, Parsons became Cusack's principal when he began field work and was there on their last job together, a disaster in Senegal, almost six years ago.

The condominium Cusack occupied was half of the fourth floor of a converted warehouse. The conversion was incomplete, a consequence of the original developer's bankruptcy. The second developer hadn't gotten much further before giving up. The original warehouse windows had not been replaced; it was drafty and the windows leaked in a hard rain. The floor planks were rough and gapped and the red brick walls had been inexpertly sandblasted. Cusack felt at home with its impending quality.

The place was barely furnished: an easy chair, two floor lamps, a large square pale green rug, a work table with a flex-arm lamp, two bookcases and a single bed. There was a kitchen of sorts with a butcher block island, a sink, refrigerator and stove on one wall and a bathroom behind the wall. Cusack had seen the other condominium on the top floor, which was unoccupied and even less prepared for occupancy than his.

Cusack continued to look at the windows in the third floor corner office across the street. There was nothing to be seen that early in the day but looking was what he did and this view was more pleasing than others in his past.

Cusack had had enough of flat landscapes in Iraq. Now he liked cities, only cities. Office towers, apartment complexes and parks where the trees were organized, tall and thick. He didn't like the horizon to be too far out. When that happened, things got thinned-out and indecipherable. It became the ultimate vulnerability.

Cusack could have refused the assignment Parsons had offered him. Even resignation or a medical retirement were theoretically available options, but the Saint-Georges investigation had been left open, the verdict suspended indefinitely. If he left the agency under those circumstances, they would never stop looking to him for answers. He, too, wanted answers though he didn't know whom to ask. The unique arc of the modern predicament: the people you ask are clueless; the ones with the answers are obsessed with other questions. It didn't help that his own memory of events was clouded and intermittent.

After six days in the hospital recovering from the injuries received at Saint-Georges, he was released and given limited office duty. His doctor told him at the time that his recurring headaches were common with concussions. A byproduct of the headaches in the early stages of recovery were lurid hallucinations complete with sound effects. Initially, they gave Cusack a sense of accomplishment: to be able to translate the experience into abstract smears of color - searing white and fiery orange - as well as operatic sounds - guttural screams and high-pitched whimpers. The difficult past assimilated by the art of hallucination.

"Over time," the doctor assured him, "the headaches should lessen in frequency and intensity."

"How long?"

"Hard to say. Come see me again - a month if nothing's changed." The doctor gave him a prescription and told him to take one pill at the first sign of trouble. "It will get better, I can promise you that. The headaches will occur less often. They will be less intense but you may have them for years."

Cusack was a dutiful, if skeptical, patient and as the appeal of hallucination quickly diminished, he was careful to take the pills as instructed. They weren't a cure. Cusack didn't have that kind of optimism. The headaches gave a warning, a kind of heat at the base of the skull and a thrumming in the ears before reaching full bloom but they were relentless and obliterating if not treated immediately.

He looked to the north over the office building across 4th Avenue and could just make out a few campus buildings and the clock tower of Old Main, three blocks away. To the west, across University Avenue, was an area of ruins eight square blocks in size. The northern end of it was marked by 4th Avenue.

The ruins were called the Washburn Redevelopment Area. The double-you-ar-ay. In the area were apartment buildings built in the 1970s by the Federal Housing Authority, blocks of small pre-World War I houses, warehouses, two hotels, office and retail buildings. The taxpayer paid to put up the public buildings and knock them down. There was a speculative boom and then the credit bubble that created it burst and everything stopped. On several modest ten-story towers, the top five floors were just girders. Most of the residential buildings were long-time squats, many of the occupants working in area restaurants and, in the summer, construction jobs. The cyclone fence encircling it had been up long enough to have been breached in places. Just inside the fence, an undergrowth of shrubs and stunted trees had grown wildly into a second, more effective barrier.

Cusack walked to the work table and shook a cigarette out of the pack. He took a kitchen match from a cluster he kept in a shot glass and struck it on a piece of broken concrete block that sat on the corner of the table. Half the size of a loaf of bread, blackened and smooth on one side, the block came from a building that had blown up in front of him. He kept it as a souvenir of Saint-Georges. It made sense to him as a souvenir. The match flared, lighting a thick pink burn scar that ran diagonally across his left palm. He held the cigarette between thumb and forefinger and inhaled deeply.

American cigarettes were the best, he thought. He exhaled slowly and the plume spiraled up and thinned and vanished. America offered the best of everything to the obsessive and the compulsive and the addictive and the mad. Why would anyone want to live anywhere else?

He tapped ash onto the saucer and went back to the window. He looked out at the steel gray sky and put the cigarette to his mouth. The smoke curled out and was suspended for a moment or two, then darted out the window. He felt transported for a moment into another place, a country setting deep in fog, which opened up to rolling fields and clusters of trees beside a narrow, winding road.

After returning to office duty, he was questioned about his activities related to the Saint-Georges incident. Two interrogators asked the same questions in different ways on different days. It was always done in the same small windowless room, next to the Human Resources office. There was a plain oak table and three chairs with padded seats and a double fluorescent in the ceiling that provided the only light. It wasn't as grim as it could have been and Cusack wondered if he was supposed to be grateful. The interrogators worked in rotation and each had a unique manner. One even apologized for, "going over the same ground again and again." His apology was not to be believed.

The questions began in a tight circle around the events at

Saint-Georges. What did you do when you arrived? Who did you talk to? Over time they spiraled out to include questions about Cusack's time in the First Gulf War, his early work with the agency, why he wasn't married and his attitude toward authority figures. They mentioned with an elaborate casualness that the two men in the van were Senegalese and did he have any insight into that? He said nothing and they moved on to the woman with him who was killed. Where did he meet her? When? Who initiated contact? Did he know she was married? Had they shared the same hotel room? How often? Was he acquainted with the husband? Why did he leave her on the patio just before the explosion?

Cusack had answers for all their questions but he didn't like them. They had a flat tone that belied the eerie quality of his own recall and were completely devoid of the crawling guilt he couldn't let out and couldn't get rid of. His affair with the woman, if such a brief coupling could be called that, had not meant much to either of them, he was sure, except that she had joined him for lunch just before he was to go to the airport for a flight home and was blown to pieces.

His interrogators never did anything unintentional. He was certain he would hear about the Senegalese again. The interrogators gave him a pass on the woman. It was a gift. Cusack had nothing to tell them and at that particular moment he didn't want to think about the woman or Senegal.

Cusack hadn't questioned his work at the agency before Saint-Georges - not at its core. He could see now that he'd always held himself a half-step to one side, a get-ready mechanism. It was another part of the modern predicament. The work itself became escape, and when the place to escape from disappeared you were nowhere at all, the ultimate bystander. But what was there to be done?

The Saint-Georges interrogation wound down without a marked conclusion. This absence of a verdict served its own purposes. Uncertainty promoted anxiety, a state of mind useful for inadvertent revelation. When you don't know what they think, you wonder what you're supposed to do.

Cusack had returned to his routine, was involved in the planning of several projects then was told he was being given a temporary assignment in Vienna. The abrupt nature of the reassignment might also have been a tactic of the interrogators, another prod to revelation. He advertised for a sublet and rented a garage for his car.

Before leaving for Vienna, he had to endure several sessions with a counselor, a routine procedure to determine his psychological fitness. They met in her office, which had a view of the Patapsco River and the far bank east of her office. He was fascinated by the woman, the language she used, the shape of her questions, and he found that he could focus wonderfully and not lose his temper if he just concentrated on a wisp of her curly pale hair, dampened by heat, that lay on her temple.

He recalled what one of the principals from his second or third field project with the agency used to say, "There is never a good reason to speak the truth." It was a cheap cynicism, which Cusack rejected. Lying was more effective if it was purposeful and calculated - the more limited, the more successful. The best lie was buried in a hundred truths and so, looking across the desk at the counselor, he considered the significance of every word he gave her.

"How do you feel about what happened?" she asked at the opening of their first meeting. She clicked a pen in her right hand above a blank notepad on the desk in front of her.

"It seems like a long time ago," said Cusack. He could see no recording equipment in the room but their meeting was certainly being videotaped. They liked to have a complete record.

"How often do you think about it?"

"When I'm asked about it." He looked just to the left of her face when he spoke, noting the leaves just coming out on the trees situated on the bluffs above the river.

"Do you resent the fact you have to go through this?"

"It's part of the job."

"I see your medical report has a diagnosis of concussion. Headaches that include hallucinations. Would you describe them to me?" She tilted her head when she said hallucinations, as if that word held some particular significance for her and should for him.

"Colors, shapes, sounds." Did she rehearse her vocal inflections and gestures? Interrogation was an actor's craft and she brought a worthy professional detachment to the interview.

"What kind of colors and shapes?"

"Like someone stirred the pot." He wanted a cigarette.

"And the sounds?"

"Screams, mostly."

"How do you feel about all that?"

He scratched behind his right ear. "I'm getting past it."

"It doesn't sound like you are."

Cusack was surprised that she expressed a judgment. He was pretty sure it wasn't in the play book. "I was injured. I'm better."

"Better," she repeated and began to write in the notebook balanced on her lap. She kept her head down for a minute, carefully tracing out some sort of judgment about his last answer.

He knew the trick of stringing out the silence. "You're sweating," he said.

"What?" she said, then looked again at her notebook.

"Are you nervous?" He asked. He was sick of them all.

She looked up then and brushed back a strand of hair from off her forehead. "How do you feel about the people who did this?"

"They were professionals." He could look at their work as precise and dedicated and possessed of that quality of "disinterested service" he'd heard used in reference to the term, "professional." He could look at it like that. There was no reason not to. Throughout their exchange she had made notes after each of his responses, meaningless scribbles, he was sure, all done for effect.

"Do you consider yourself a professional?"

"Do you?"

She paused without looking up, letting him know she wasn't there to answer his questions. "Who do you blame for what happened?"

"Blame is for politicians."

"How do you feel about those who were killed?"

"I can't do anything for them."

Although this first meeting was unsatisfactory for both of them, the next three went somewhat better. He was determined to return to work on his own terms. When something like Saint-Georges happened, there were some like his bosses who could not accept its unfinished quality and were determined that it fit into something. They were people who believed in the future and that made them dangerous to those, like Cusack who did not, in the same way the luckless are a curse on those who believe in hope. You could work around people like that, work around their presumptions, but you could not walk away from them.

In the end, the procedure went his way and the counselor sent him a letter full of condescension, saying he was fit to return to work. He didn't mind her tone. It was only malice if you cared. Appended to the copy that he and his boss received was a recommendation that he be limited to light-duty work pending a complete physical and psychological work-up six months down the road. Everything returned to normal, whatever that might have been or could ever be again.

After getting approval to return to work, the Vienna assignment was further delayed a month. In that time he tried to convince himself that the delay meant the assignment would be an intricate and involving piece of work. However, when he arrived he decided the extra time was made in order to create his Vienna work in the Baltimore office. It was a bland little package of exercises.

In the end, the Vienna assignment looked like a psychological fitness exam or, possibly, a test of loyalty. He put his head down and plodded through his days and even enjoyed, with his co-workers, the evening rounds of cafes and restaurants. They were a congenial enough group though he kept his distance.

Distance was a necessity; there was no help going to come from his co-workers. He was better but he was not the same; that was not possible. Somewhere he'd read that the only New Year's resolution you can't keep is to remain the same. He couldn't go back to the time before Saint-Georges. He felt himself on some sort of trajectory but he only knew what he was leaving, not where he was going to end up.

The flight from the States to Vienna included a lay-over in Amsterdam. There, he had time to visit one of Amsterdam's notorious cafes. He smoked two pipes of hashish, not something on the regular menu, and developed a substantial buzz for the hop from Amsterdam to Vienna.

Within a few weeks of his arrival, he took to solitary, leisurely, drunken lunches, which shortened the workday considerably. His office mates appeared not to notice. On the weekends, he took solitary trips by train to Salzburg, Budapest and Lucerne. With so much time on his hands, he went over again and again in his head the events of Saint-Georges looking for answers but found none. On those weekend trips, he thought he was being followed but without a careful, sustained piece of work he couldn't be certain and he didn't care enough to do that.

Most of his evenings were spent walking around the ordinary

neighborhoods and tourist zones of Vienna. The thing about European cities like Vienna, Cusack decided after a few months, was that their weary charm - a cracked patina of age that seemed deliberately applied like theater make-up - made you suspect after a while that it was, in fact, the mortician's pancake putting a glow on the dead. The thought didn't depress him but he didn't belong there.

Mostly, he realized, he wanted out, out of everything. He wanted to shed everything, to become a phantom, to be nowhere at all. In a way, the work had done this for him but it was no good now. He couldn't disappear into it anymore. And he couldn't leave it either.

Three and a half months into the Vienna job he was sitting at a sidewalk cafe at the corner of Neustiftgasse and Museum Strasse drinking what turned out to be his last cappuccino in Vienna when Parsons showed up. He took a seat across from Cusack as if he'd been expected and ordered a double espresso.

They heard the sound of motorcycles and two policemen rode into the intersection and stopped just ahead of the front end of a street protest. The police wore short, black leather jackets and helmets with smoked visors. They directed traffic with minimal, precise gestures that allowed the line of protestors through. The people in the cars delayed by the protest seemed indifferent to it all and listened to radios or talked on cell phones as if protest marches were as common as stop lights.

Parsons seemed in no hurry to explain his presence, content to watch the parade of several hundred people strung out in a column that stretched down Neustiftgasse and around the corner. Two twenty-foot wide banners on poles carried the protest message in German. The sun broke through the clouds just then as if offering a benediction. Several of the marchers broke away from the rest to hand brochures to spectators like Cusack and Parsons.

The brochure was printed in German but the photographs spoke the international language of horror: two bearded men were laid out as if in a morgue, their eyes open. Zipper-like stitches ran down the middle of their bare chests. No doubt part of the autopsy conducted by the Turkish coroners would tell the world they died of heart attacks. Above the photographs was: Der Turkische Staat Plan Ein Weiteres Gefangnis - Massaker!

Parsons put the brochure to one side. "The problem with the Viennese," he said, offering his own theory of Viennese deficiencies, "it's in their history. It's like that joke in the movie Amadeus when Mozart was told his composition had 'too many notes.' The Viennese have too much history."

"Americans have plenty of history."

"But the Viennese can't carry theirs anymore. That's the difference."

Parsons had theories; some played out better than others. Cusack, too, had theories and believed Americans didn't carry their history very well either except the cartoon versions they saw on television or in the movies. They didn't want to. They forgot what they wanted to forget. Amnesia in America wasn't a mishap, it was a plan. He sipped his coffee and crumpled the brochure.

Parsons asked if Cusack could remember the name Tyler.

"Should I?"

"He's your target. In particular, we want to know who he sees." Parsons offered no other information.

"Who am I working with?"

"I've decided to indulge your preference for working alone."

"An army of one?"

"I'll be around."

"Just surveillance?"

"Opportunity is our only limitation."

Cusack laughed.

Parsons made a show of a formal job offer then and Cusack thought this new project might lead him to something viable. Maybe work would make its claim, swallow up everything again, reassert the clarity of details, the oblivion of necessity. At least, he thought after accepting Parsons' offer, this was a real job, not like the sheltered workshop of Vienna.

*Freud tells us that we forget because we want to forget. It is much more than that. Forgetting is the only absolution.*

# Chapter 2

At the end of the First Gulf War, the unit to which Cusack was assigned was sent first to Frankfurt, Germany, then stateside. At Frankfurt, he stepped off the plane into a cool, needling rain. At first, Cusack was refreshed by the rain but then it just recalled sandstorms south of Baghdad. It put him into a loop that brought back things he wanted to forget. He needed a little more distance from Iraq, that was all. An old American school bus, painted olive drab, was waiting for them and everyone was taken to transient barracks and allowed to settle in. With nothing to do and nowhere to go, they blew off three days with German beer and opiated hashish from Pakistan.

Later, after a bouncy flight to Fort Dix, New Jersey, they moved into another set of ratty barracks and drank away an entire weekend while the soldiers' paperwork sat in the battalion clerk's IN box. Other members of the unit had been told they were getting a month's leave but Cusack's tour was over.

Home by then was only his father, restless in retirement, stumping around the two-story clapboard house with the paint peeling on the south wall and the sagging porch that overlooked a stretch of the Blackthorn River.

Cusack had thought about home while he was in Iraq but not in any organized way. It was moments from the past, images like his mother setting the kitchen table for breakfast on Sundays, the back yard covered in yellow leaves from the birch trees along the back of the property, the sound of the rubber ball hitting the garage wall when his older brother was working on his fielding skills and the curve of the river dazzling in the late afternoon summer light. All this was stitched together into something useful to hang onto in the hard days but something that could not be carried forward.

The Blackthorn River had figured prominently in the early history of the town. It meandered a hundred and fifty miles south from a lake in northern Wisconsin. The white pine forest that stretched sixty miles from Cusack's hometown to the north was cut and floated down the river. For a time in the years just after the turn of the twentieth century three mills were kept busy but the forest was mostly gone in twenty-five years and the last mill shut down not long after.

Like most of the houses in town, the Cusacks' house was built from lumber from one of the local mills. It was the only house Cusack had known growing up. It looked as it had during his last visit but he drew no comfort from its familiarity. It was a frame of reference and not one he could use anymore. His father belonged to the setting so Cusack was not disturbed by his presence. What belonged to a place required no precautions.

He re-occupied his old room, the one he'd shared with his older brother until he'd left for college. The air in the room was dry and musty and he struggled to open the window before emptying his duffel bag onto his brother's bed. It contained odds and ends, a canteen, a pair of boots badly worn at the heel, a knife fit for a serial killer, his dress uniform as crisp as the day he'd received it, a set of illegally expropriated night-vision goggles, a set of fatigues and his helmet with a few dings.

The things he brought back were attached to particular events and he kept them though he was not sure why since he liked to think the events themselves were not worth remembering. He folded the cammo fatigues and put them in the bottom drawer of the chest that stood between the twin beds. His dress uniform, with its three service medals above the pocket, was just a souvenir now and he hung it carefully in the closet. When he moved, he'd leave it for his father. He wasn't going back like the others from his squad to Fort Lewis or Fort Bliss or Fort Sill.

On the wall between the beds was a photograph that had hung there for as long as Cusack could remember. It showed his great-grandfather and mother standing in front of a two-story log house. A small boy and girl were standing to the left of the front door and another young girl sat on a horse to the right. Cusack's great-grandfather had cut the logs for the house himself, squared them, put in the windows and doors and the stairs to the second floor. He'd had a well drillled and the line brought inside, rare for the time and place. The black and white photo was taken in 1909. It had been shot from a distance and the facial features on the people were vague. It was a photograph meant for a high school history textbook, thought Cusack. Particular details but without the burden of useful precision.

After unpacking, he took a long shower, a luxury mostly unavailable to him in the desert. He tried to write a to-do list in his head, something to fill the time. Everything came down to leaving. He couldn't stay with his father. Cusack thought of Boston as a destination or Washington, D.C. Some sort of job in the security business. That had been the advice of his Commanding Officer, Lt. Colonel Burge. Cusack stepped out of the shower and dried himself. He looked down at his hands and thought about some of the things he'd done with them.

His father lived on a railroad pension and worked at the local hardware store on Saturdays, the busiest day of the week. He took the job after Cusack's mother died. Not for the money but someone to talk to, Cusack thought at the time.

After his shower, Cusack joined his father at the kitchen table. Everything looked familiar, but the smells of cooking and cleaning were missing.

"Hungry?" his father asked. "There's some chicken in the fridge."

"Naw, thanks."

His father took a heavy white ceramic mug out of the cupboard and poured coffee. He held up the pot and raised his eyebrows.

When Cusack said, "Sure," his father filled another mug, handed it to him, and sat down. The cups steamed and Cusack made a little ritual of getting milk for his coffee because he could think of nothing to say.

"I've heard at the store," his father said. "They say a Wal-Mart's coming," His father curled his fingers around the mug and lifted it to his lips. "That'll be the end."

Cusack had seen the end up very close in Iraq and didn't think it resembled Wal-Mart though he had no interest in offering his judgment. For weeks, even before Cusack had reached Fort Dix, he'd found it difficult to produce even the simplest speech. It had been a progressive separation from language; the further from fighting the less important it seemed. He still knew all the necessary words. It was their ordered arrangement that seemed impossible. Beyond expressing fundamental needs, speech seemed foolish, ugly. He began to develop a contempt for words themselves and so he looked for words that would stop talk.

"Yes, the end," he agreed.

His father took Cusack's agreement as encouragement to lay out the case against Wal-Mart. He did this at length, referring to details of Wal-Mart's employment and business practices in several articles he'd found on the Internet. Yet, with all of his father's passion, Cusack recognized, not in his litany of Wal-Mart evils but in his tone, a fatalism that was part of his own inheritance. His father was not going to lead or join a protest of Wal-Mart. As he went on, Cusack lost track of the details of his father's arguments and soon lost interest in the entire narrative, but he nodded agreeably. His father's chatter relieved him of any conversational responsibility and for that he was grateful.

Most evenings the two of them sat in near perfect silence in the living room. They would sometimes eat their dinner there, plates and glasses propped on tiny folding tables. The coffee table was usually covered with the dismembered sections of the day's newspaper. The only light in the room came from the television.

Sometimes his father would, during their meal or at a television commercial break, summarize the reporting on that day's more spectacular, grotesque or amusing stories. Occasionally, Cusack had his own information about an event, at variance with what was reported, but he kept it all to himself. He did not think his father was interested in other information. In any case, for Cusack, the truth was not a goad; enlightenment was not an obligation. He felt no more loyalty to the information he carried around than to the people who had put him in the way of that information.

Father and son occupied a matched pair of equally beaten easy chairs and let the television run. It was new since Cusack's last visit and much larger than the one before it. His father picked the shows; they tended to be crime shows. Cusack tried to follow the often complex story lines and keep track of all the characters but it was exhausting. It was all just noise and movement after a while.

Cusack took a beer when his father offered one. His father drank, though less than Cusack remembered. His drinking had bothered Cusack when he was younger but now it served to quiet his father and this made his company easier to take. Several days passed in this way with the two of them moving around in an amiable, nearly mute society.

Cusack settled into a routine. He had looked forward with intense anticipation to coming home and realized after a few days that the anticipation was just an eagerness not to be in Iraq. Though he didn't sleep very well, he stayed in his room until he heard his father leave. Then he would move down to the kitchen, fix himself a piece of toast or two covered liberally with honey, brew a pot of strong coffee and move out to the porch with all that and the newspaper. Occasionally, cars would drive by on their way to the bridge across the Blackthorn and, presumably, a few miles beyond to the interstate.

His father, too, had a daily regimen that kept him out of the house much of the day. His first stop was the drugstore for a cup of coffee and a visit with other retired locals, then the library for the out-of-state newspapers and pick up a movie and finally, the grocery store to get that day's needed items. A week and a half passed in this way.

However, even with the drinking after dinner, his father eventually asked about the war, which drove Cusack to the garage to find his fishing tackle, an excuse to revisit the Blackthorn River where he'd spent so much time as a teenager. There in the garage, home was fleshed out, a quality of existing separately from his own memories, his own determination of its place. There were the smells, gasoline from the lawn mower pushed into the far corner, firewood racked under the work table, a half-empty bag of mulch and turpentine inexpertly sealed in gallon cans. On the work table was the five gallon bucket that his mother used to carry her gardening tools around. There was a hammock on one wall. His mother always looked forward to hanging it though she seldom used it. She didn't believe in relaxation.

What came suddenly then were memories of his mother's illness and death, which occurred just before his deployment to Iraq. Death had worked a leisurely schedule with her, delivering a succession of debilitating illnesses. She went from doctor to doctor generously offering them a textbook of symptoms to analyze and treat. They responded generously, offering diagnosis and prescribing treatments. Generosity all around.

Eventually, Cusack's father could not care for her properly at home and she had to be admitted to the local nursing home. After a walkthrough, Cusack concluded that the name, Home of the Good Samaritan, was purely ironic, a joke by someone at corporate headquarters.

His mother was inconsolable for days when she was first admitted. After a week or two, however, she adjusted to her new setting and her decline resumed its gentle, hopeless progress. Then, one day in early summer, his father called Cusack and told him to come home. Cusack spoke to his commanding officer, received compassionate leave and was on a plane the same day.

Cusack arrived on one of his mother's "good" days. He offered to take her out and they went to the nearest park where he pushed the wheelchair around a small, man-made lake. The wide, asphalted path wound in among mature oaks and Norway pine. In line skaters and runners in colorful striped spandex raced by. She named things as they passed them: red bench, birch tree, white Cadillac, big dog and double-wide stroller with two children. Finally, she said, "I'm cold. Take me back." She'd had an accident and forgotten to wear her diaper but when he lifted her out of the wheelchair, he pretended nothing was wrong. She fussed with her bed sheets for a minute, and then asked him to get an aide for her.

She lost consciousness that evening after dinner but regained it the next afternoon and seemed to rally, even took meals with the other residents. The next day she slipped into a coma. She never regained consciousness and died two days later. He didn't cry at the funeral. He was glad she died then and avoided the fate of others in the home with their vacant stares and reflexive barking and other unimaginable miseries

The three Cusack children met at the wake. Cusack hadn't seen his brother and sister for several years; in fact, contact had been reduced to not much more than a Christmas card. At the wake Cusack was polite but vague in conversation. He had become unused to the ordinary intimate probing of domestic conversation and there weren't enough common childhood memories to carry small talk because he was a dozen years younger than either of them. His first thought when he saw them was that they could have been anyone. It was a shock of recognition only in the sense of understanding loss. He shook his brother's hand and gave his sister an awkward hug. Their children were introduced. Cusack wondered how long he'd have to stay.

When his sister had invited him to visit, Cusack said it would be difficult to get leave now that the war seemed likely. She seemed at a loss at what to say to that. He was relieved he had an excuse to put off a visit yet felt a pang of regret, too. He didn't like to think he was sentimental about the idea of family. Certain concepts were unattainable in the long run. He was home from the war now but a visit with his sister didn't seem any more likely.

Cusack climbed on the stool in front of the workbench, lit a cigarette and opened the tackle box. The inside was a knot of tangled, rusted lures, and he caught the dry, sour smell of fish when he emptied the contents onto the work table. He picked apart the mess of hooks, weights, bobbers, swivels, steel leader, plastic baits and brightly colored treble-hook lures. He could hear the television, a vague noise. The plastic baits that had melted together went into the trash. He found a rag, filled a small pan with hot, soapy water and cleaned everything. He smoked cigarette after cigarette and worked late into the evening until driven inside by the mosquitoes.

The next morning, Cusack walked alone to the hardware store where his father worked, although he was not working that day, to buy new line to put on the reel and collect some fresh plastic bait. Walking uptown to the central business district took twenty minutes. The neighborhoods he walked through seemed constricted and fixed in the past. He let it go. It didn't matter. He had a plan for the day.

The woman who waited on him was about his age and vaguely familiar. She ran each of his purchases across the bar code reader. He avoided her eyes. "You're Seth Cusack, aren't you?" she asked.

He nodded.

"You don't remember me, do you?

Cusack struggled for a moment, and then said, "No."

"We were in the same homeroom senior year. I'm Tina Biaggio. It's Tina Kimberley now, Tom's wife."

Cusack felt an extreme pressure, as if he'd been asked a complicated question in an unknown subject and the wrong answer meant everyone would die. No words formed in his head. His obligation seemed impossible to fulfill or even to understand. "Yes," he said finally, because agreeing with someone always worked. "That's nice," he added tilting his head at her, then looking over her shoulder at the clock on the wall behind her.

She looked as if he'd slapped her, blushed crimson and rang up his order without speaking again.

Cusack spent much of the next three days working his way up and down both sides of the Blackthorn River below the bridge. He took a thermos of coffee, a cheap folding chair and the newspaper. He tried a variety of baits, caught a large carp the first day and heaved it into the weeds. On the second day, he had no luck at all. On the third day he caught two trout of a satisfactory size and set them aside for dinner.

Later, while standing at the sink and fileting the fish, the blood smell made his stomach queaze but he pushed on. After washing the filets, he poured the bloody water on the flower garden by the side of the garage. It was something his mother would have done.

While Cusack worked at the stove that evening, his father talked about Cusack's mother. Busy with sauteeing the beans and microwaving the potatoes, Cusack paid little attention to his father's monologue. He set the table, then opened the oven door to check on the progress of the fish. His father seemed to need no encouragement to continue his reminiscence and finished a couple beers in the process. Cusack felt a serene satisfaction with his accomplishment on the river.

"What did you say to Tina Kimberley?" his father asked.

Only the difference in rhythm alerted Cusack to the fact that the subject had changed. "What?"

His father repeated the question.

"Nothing," Cusack replied.

"She said that when she talked to you, you looked at her like she was some kind of Martian."

Cusack removed the pan with the fish from the oven. Beautifully browned. He took the pot off the burner. The beans had a steamy gloss. He slid the fish onto their plates on the counter, then scooped out the beans.

"Yes," said Cusack. "I can see that now that you mention it. And I think she's right. She is a Martian."

"She's a nice girl," said his father.

Cusack pulled the potatoes out of the microwave, cracked them and put them on their plates. "Eat up before it gets cold. I think the fish is just about perfect."

Cusack sat down and forked a piece of fish into his mouth. His father took his time mashing his potato and spread butter liberally on it. He reached across the table, picked up the pepper shaker and tapped it over the potato and beans.

"I should have had you pick up a lemon at the grocery store when you were out but I didn't think I'd catch anything today."

His father pushed his beans around with his fork. "Maybe you should see someone, Seth."

Cusack chewed slowly and looked into the backyard, then turned his head slowly to look at his father. "See someone?" He put down his fork. "I've seen a lot of people since I got back, Dad." He paused, measuring his words. "They were all fucking Martians."

His father looked at Cusack and down at his plate. He began to eat steadily, saying nothing until he'd cleaned his plate. "The trout was good. Going out again tomorrow?"

"Not tomorrow."

Again that evening the two of them sat in the living room in front of the television. Cusack stared at the screen and began to see time as a seepage of distorted colors into a blackness that arrived at 3 a.m. In the war, in every day's action there was direction and scope. If you kept things in front of you, your environment was manageable. But the options were locked down. Not here.

He felt trapped by the lack of order in this life, trapped in a kind of chaos of choice. The answer, whatever it might be, was not here, for necessity was life's clarity and there was no necessity in this house.

*Expectation is an abyss which I examine endlessly and forever find something to be hoped for in the looking.*

# Chapter 3

Cusack's first move after arriving in town for the Tyler assignment was to pick up a car. The agency would have provided a rental but he preferred to have his own ride. At a local rental agency that specialized in older vehicles he chose a ten-year old Chevy Caprice, a model favored by his father and by the police. It was wide and long with a huge engine. It weighed a couple tons and he liked that it could take a hit. He ran it every day in the early morning.

The second morning while driving around, Cusack eased up at a stoplight and opened the window to get some air. To his left, across University Avenue was the Washburn Redevelopment Area. There was something appealing about the ruins, in the way the sunlight fell through them. It was as if in that light, it wasn't the cheap, crappy public housing and speculative commercial architecture of 1970s America but something very old and proud with a complicated and mysterious history. He realized suddenly that much of what he was looking at wasn't ruins but buildings half-built and abandoned. The cranes were still there, sentinels of failure quietly rusting away.

At the next stop light a smiling, homeless man wearing a long, black trench coat stepped in front of his car. He squirted Cusack's windshield with a water bottle, dropped it into his jacket pocket, then threw a large brown rag on the windshield, blocking Cusack's view. It was a confident move. The man continued to smile while he moved the rag around. Cusack noticed the two crumpled dollar bills on the dash, and decided the man must also have noticed them. When he'd thoroughly smeared the windshield, he tucked the rag under his arm, stepped up to Cusack's window and rapped on it. Cusack ran down his window and handed the bills to him.

"This is it?"

Cusack locked eyes with him; Cusack wasn't angry and wasn't going to get angry but a negotiation was out of the question. He hit the washer fluid button and the wipers, and still looking at the man, accelerated through the intersection. He'd experienced that sort of cleaning service in New York City years ago where the bums, often lacking a water bottle, spat on the windshield and wiped it off with their shirt sleeves before demanding money.

Cusack parked the car near the south entrance to the Washburn and crossed the street. He recalled bits and pieces from the local newspaper's three-part series on the Washburn. Cusack missed Part I, but II recapped the dreary 70s history of the place. Part III included the events that made it the mess that it was. In 2004, the city attempted to condemn and demolish all the public housing in the Washburn. It was half a success. A little later, a speculative real estate boom began. Developers tried to buy up the Washburn. Lawsuits slowed and eventually stopped the demolition of some of the public housing. The collapse of the credit market stopped the housing and commercial building boom. The county had condemned most of the buildings in zoning decisions that ended up in court, boarded them up even while the decisions were being appealed and squatters moved in repeatedly until the county gave up the fight. The city reluctantly left utility services functioning to the residential buildings in the Washburn.

Cusack was curious about the Washburn, wanted to know the dimensions of the settlement, its possibilities. He knew the agency had a contract here and was intrigued by Parsons' failure to mention it in Vienna. Surveillance of Professor Tyler might have been the job but Cusack liked to know the landscape where he worked. He didn't like to be surprised.

If you were desperate enough in the Washburn, what could you find? He wandered past two-story buildings, boarded up, with makeshift chimneys coughing up a thin, white smoke. Children eyed him from makeshift playgrounds of abandoned pick-up trucks, discarded furniture, bathtubs and refrigerators without doors. Women watched their children and him, too. They stood in twos and threes and smoked. There were no men visible anywhere.

Cusack sat on a bench that fronted a park with a fountain that no longer worked. He lit a cigarette and tried to guess what the building at the end of the block had been originally built for. The first five stories were complete then another five that were only girders. A few buildings had been demolished but the wreckage had been left sitting where it fell. The Washburn could never acquire the independent, parallel, social quality you could find in a blasted Third World country, where complete societies existed within larger ones. This was America, after all. Here a place like the Washburn had distortions but they were recognizable as part of some larger, clarified pattern.

According to the local newspapers, there was a plan in the works to clean out the Washburn and finish the redevelopment. The squatters were to be removed, by force if necessary, with bulldozing or implosion soon thereafter of any buildings not judged salvageable.

Student-led rallies on behalf of the squatters were held on the campus and Cusack had seen numerous signs of protest.

Some buildings stood next to the rubble of those already knocked down. It looked to Cusack like several cities in the old Yugoslavia early in the war before the artillery work had progressed. Like it was there, people lived in the ruins, though it wasn't really a place to live. He stopped occasionally in his walk around the Washburn and spoke to residents, peeked into buildings to get a sense of things but carried his pistol, a 9mm Beretta, as a precaution. You never knew.

There was no garbage smell, just smoke and a dry dust suspended in the air. As he passed an apartment building with drapes on the windows and small, neat lawn in front, eighties rock and roll and country and western dueled from neighboring windows on the second floor. He hadn't seen a grocery store or a drugstore, a doctor's or dentist's office, or, for that matter, a Wal-Mart. Not even a lawyer's office. The area was without an identifiable center, like an early video game world, a platform where you had to fill in the critical human details from your own imagination.

The residents appeared reluctant and avoided eye contact. They seemed to carry a notion of the outsider but no palpable feeling of solidarity. One for one, none for all. In that sense the Washburn didn't seem, to Cusack, all that different from the prevailing tendency in the rest of America. The WRA was a backdrop and the squatters just sketches against that backdrop.

He left the Washburn at the next block, stopped at a store called Tobak and News and purchased a pack of cigarettes and both local papers. Next door was a coffee shop where he ordered a large coffee and a raisin bagel and sat in the shop reading until he'd finished the bagel. He liked this part of the day, the morning light and the distractions of the newspaper.

Cusack recalled his meeting in Vienna with Parsons when he was hired for the Tyler assignment. Parsons said little about their shared past; he was not nostalgic. His reference to Saint-Georges was limited to the remark, "You look good."

Parsons' own physical appearance had altered little in the six years since Senegal. He was six-two and thin. He had large, bony hands and he never gestured with them. He had a habit of drawing parallels between the work and something historical that was important and written about. At the end of their meeting, he said, "You believe there is a moral dimension attached to everything we do, don't you, Cusack?"

"I don't take that line." Parsons was fishing for something but Cusack couldn't guess what.

"I think you do," said Parsons. "We all do."

Cusack wasn't going to argue the point. He wanted out of Vienna and this job would do that and everything else didn't get into the play.

Parsons spoke during the interview of the stations he'd headed - Rome, Jiddah and Panama City, but only bland details and a timeline - date in, date out. They were all places where Cusack had worked but, curiously, never at the same time as Parsons' tenure as station chief.

Parsons told Cusack he was back from Cairo and trying to settle in. His office space wasn't ready for occupancy but he was getting right to work. Yes, he'd changed all right if only to the extent that his existing tendencies had become more intense. "A moral dimension attached to everything we do." Cusack put the grasping for justification down to one of the inevitable failures of aging.

There didn't seem to be anything about the Tyler assignment that would be historical and written about. After he'd finished his coffee, Cusack returned to the condominium. On the floor next to the camera was a suitcase-sized tape recorder. Occasionally, the device planted in the office across the street was activated by a door opening or the slam of a file drawer or a voice and then the reels would turn. Cusack spent the rest of the day going through the newspapers a second time and listening to Tyler's meetings with students.

Cusack would listen attentively for a short time, keen on something Tyler had said, then lose interest and turn on the radio. Occasionally, when he heard a new voice in the office, he would adjust the Nikon and snap a photograph or two. Cigarettes piled up on a plate that lay next to the tripod.

The front page headline in the newspaper was Computer Virus Has Worldwide Impact. The subhead - Wall Street Shut Down. Further down the page another headline that read, Telecomm CEO on Suicide Watch and below that, Earthquake Kills Hundreds in Japan.

Tyler's voice suddenly boomed as if in a lecture hall, trying to reach the students in the back row. Startled, Cusack walked to the window and saw Tyler at the lectern reading from pages in front of him and marking the text.

"All of our difficulties can be resolved by doing nothing. It is that simple. It is that impossible. We have been raised to believe in the moral imperative of action. Not to act is failure."

The blinds in Tyler's office had been removed for cleaning although they had been cleaned just six weeks ago. This was arranged before Cusack's arrival and allowed him a clear view of the office except for a corner by the door.

Tyler wrote a few lines then stopped, the pen poised above the page. "All of our difficulties have been brought into existence only because of our actions and can be unmade only by stillness." He was circling the same thought. He turned a page, glanced at it and turned another. He flipped several more pages before apparently finding what he was looking for. Cusack guessed he was seeing Tyler at work on his next book and not in preparation for class.

Tyler marked up another page and, after a minute, Cusack returned to the newspaper. On the front page of the second section was an article about a protest against tuition price increases at public colleges across the state. He turned to the editorial page. The editors expressed an on-the-one-hand, on-the-other opinion about plans for the Washburn Redevelopment Area.

Cusack had hoped for a little more entertainment from the newspaper. Most days, America was a coast-to-coast freak show and out of that would step an American of interest, someone with dimensions. But not today. Today, America was trying out for normal, like it was tired of all the excitement. He reached for his pack and lit another cigarette.

Tyler began speaking again. "Let's see. Not to act is failure. (In the West, the central redemptive act is the crucifixion of an upright man. As Cioran reminds us, we should by now have come to an understanding of the mechanism of our errors.) Yes, that's better." Tyler began to wheeze and nothing came through the speakers for a minute.

Cusack let the newspaper drop to the floor and froze, his head turned toward the speaker on the tape recorder.

Tyler picked it up again. "We fall into habit but it is not by accident." Tyler's voice echoed in Cusack's room. It was an eerie presence. "Consider, what is it for any of us, this intoxication with routine, but a subconscious pursuit of immortality." He'd moved suddenly on to something else. Cusack couldn't follow the thread of his thoughts but maybe there was no thread to follow.

After another period of quiet, Cusack picked up the Tyler file that had been left for him at the airport. The precautions and hurry-up quality of the project didn't fit with what he'd seen after he'd arrived. On site, nothing looked urgent and nothing matched up with the hype. Cusack knew the agency was working with the State Bureau of Criminal Apprehension on plans for the Washburn. He wondered why he hadn't been folded into that operation. An appetite for melodrama might be the reason and another aspect of Parsons' aging. Worse yet, this might be another fake job like he suspected of Vienna and boring, dead-end assignments might be all he'd ever see again.

Cusack opened the file looking for any useful clue to the Tyler question. He was born on August 4, 1931, in Carbondale, Illinois, and raised in Scranton, Pennsylvania, and Portland, Maine, but mostly in Madison, Wisconsin. He enlisted in the U.S. Army in 1950 just weeks before the Korean War began. He lost a couple toes on his left foot to frostbite during a long retreat before overwhelming numbers of Chinese. He and the rest of his division were involved in several engagements with the Chinese and he won the Distinguished Service Medal.

After his discharge from the Army, he completed an undergraduate degree in English at the University of Wisconsin at Madison. Five years later he earned a doctorate in humanities from the University of Iowa. He taught at more than a dozen universities in the United States, including at Madison and abroad. He married Anne Burgess, the daughter of a carpenter and a librarian and a daughter, Lauren, was born three years later. Ten years after that, he was divorced. His wife had suffered from depression her entire adult life and, after consultations with several doctors and numerous hospitalizations, successfully committed suicide on her second try. Tyler never remarried.

Tyler had damaged lungs, something else he brought back from Korea. The prognosis was indeterminate. It was noted that he had been a long-time smoker, which was a contributing factor to his condition. Cusack smiled at that and lit another cigarette.

His daughter married a Senegalese national, Philippe Ogbemudia, in Lyons where her father was teaching at the time and where Philippe had requested and been granted political asylum. The family returned to the United States when Tyler was offered and accepted his present teaching position.

Philippe, a political dissident and human rights activist, remained active from a distance in Senegalese politics, supporting the opposition party even after he came to the United States. A little more than five years ago he had been deported; the reason given by U.S. Immigration was his association with the Front for the Liberation of Senegal, tagged as a terrorist organization. Three days after his return to Senegal his body was found floating in the waters of the Ile de Gore ferry port at Dakar. Englishmen spotted the body while waiting to embark on a deep-sea, sport fishing day trip.

Cusack looked at the date of Philippe's death. Nine months after the helicopter crash near Matam in northern Senegal which nearly killed Cusack. Nine months after the story broke about the three villages wiped out near Matam. The agency had spent years dealing with the fallout from Matam. As the agent in charge, the greatest burden of justification or exoneration had fallen on Parsons.

Cusack resumed his examination of the file. Tyler, with little previous history of political activity, stepped out of character (at his daughter's urging?) and accused the CIA of arranging for or condoning the murder in order to curry favor with the authoritarian regime then in power in Dakar. This charge received brief play in the local and then national media. The CIA refused comment and the government in Dakar said it was investigating Philippe's death. The file contained no further mention of the incident.

Tyler's daughter, Lauren, and granddaughter, Sarah, moved in with Tyler after the death of his son-in-law. The next year, Lauren entered the graduate program and became his assistant.

Cusack didn't believe what he'd read. Nowhere in the file was there a real justification for why the file had been created. The CIA accusation might have gotten someone to work up a jacket on Tyler but that didn't carry much weight. What you aren't told can make what you are told a lie. Someone like Tyler, if Parsons was to be believed, would have a more substantial history. Cusack was disgusted. Saint-Georges might have happened because someone was given a file like this. Details without weight. Facts without context. It was like what you'd get in bad fiction. He closed the file and dropped it hard on the floor.

Cusack knew Parsons hadn't given him the Tyler file in Vienna because Parsons knew, if Cusack had seen it, he would have demanded more. Parsons wasn't telling him everything and Cusack never expected he would. The question was how long he'd maintain that separation and what sort of moves Cusack would have to make while not having the full picture. It began to be a worry. Cusack was curious now about the timing of Philippe Ogbemudia's deportation. Cusack had been reluctant while recovering from his injuries to examine all that had happened surrounding the incident at Matam. Then he got busy and there didn't seem to be much point in going back over it. Things were different now. He had an ambition for knowing the connections.

The day wore on and the air in the room warmed. Cusack switched on the fan, which sat across the room on the floor near the bed. It had bright blue plastic blades and as it pivoted back and forth, the loose sheets of newspaper on top of the stack lifted, moved in a tight circle and fell.

By mid-afternoon, he was looking forward to his meeting with Parsons, if only for the chance to get out of the building. The meeting time and place had been pre-set in a message left in his luggage at the airport. This action, like the Tyler file drop, showed what seemed to be an excessive caution or an appetite for melodrama, the surveil of a decrepit college professor and his daughter and granddaughter.

He felt a stiffness in his shoulders and pain began to crawl up into his head. It recalled for him the early days at the hospital where the pain started out as white with an accompanying metallic taste in the mouth. Then colors from the rest of the palette were added as the pain became a large uniformed creature inside his head who tramped around, heavy-booted. Cusack stood and the pain sharpened as the creature inside tried to cut an escape route through his right eye. He walked to the bathroom, found his bottle in the medicine cabinet and shook out two pills. He bent over and sluiced them down with a mouthful of water directly from the tap.

Earlier in the day, Cusack had visited the location of his scheduled meeting with Parsons, a bar called Stub's. It was located a few blocks off-campus on a street with a small grocery store, a used bookstore, another bar, and a flower shop whose frail scents were overwhelmed by exotic spices, turmeric and curries from a Thai restaurant across the street. The inside of Stub's reeked of beer and the walls were covered with sports photographs. The visit was a reflexive precaution; he didn't like to walk into any meeting cold.

There was a knock at Cusack's door. He went to the work table, took out his Beretta and jacked a round into the chamber. He stepped to the door and, looking through the peep-hole, saw Parsons on the landing. He slid the door open.

"What's wrong?"

"The bar is a dump so I thought I'd see what you've done with your place." Parsons was wearing a dark blue, double-breasted suit, a blazing white shirt and a red tie. The uniform of a politician. He walked past Cusack, swinging a thin, tan leather valise, made a quick circuit of the room and dropped the valise on the chair by the window. He turned to face Cusack.

Parsons had lost weight since Vienna and now seemed almost wasted though he'd retained his silky manner. The fact that Parsons, too, had been at Saint-Georges working a security crew just days ahead of Cusack's arrival as chauffeur/bodyguard, nagged at Cusack. Senegal, Saint-Georges and Tyler. Too many things in the same loop without the satisfactory tie-up.

"Your accommodations agreeable?" Parsons leaned back against the window frame and crossed one foot over the other.

"Nice view," said Cusack, who looked past Parsons at the sunset beyond the buildings in the Washburn across the street.

"That's what sold us on it."

"Newspapers, Cusack?" Parsons said, toeing the pile of newspapers on the floor. "You're still getting the newspaper? Nobody gets the newspaper anymore. That's what you have a computer for."

Cusack walked to the work table and returned the Beretta to the drawer.

"What do you have for me?" asked Parsons.

Cusack took a camera disk and an audio tape from his jacket pocket and slid them across the table.

Parsons looked at them but didn't move from his place at the window. "Anything interesting?"

"Interesting wasn't really the point, was it?"

"What do you mean?"

"This isn't a proper surveil."

"Again?"

"We have a full complement of staff and equipment working with the state BCA on the Washburn six blocks from here. We could have had Tyler's office wired up like a Hollywood sound stage. Lights, camera, fucking action. Instead, I'm here by myself with a sound-activated tap and long-distance Nikon shots. It's like seventies nostalgia. What's that about?"

"Do you have anything to drink?"

Cusack took his time lighting a cigarette. "Bourbon."

"With ice."

Cusack rounded up two bourbons with ice and handed one to Parsons.

"Have you made anything of the photos I emailed yesterday?" asked Cusack.

"They're in the system. In due time."

"Great."

"One more thing," said Parsons. "Tyler isn't the only reason you're here. The Washburn operation is at a delicate stage. We're advising the mayor and governor but we have no operational authority."

Cusack waited for elaboration.

Finally, Parsons said, "It's important we know who visits Tyler. Keep the photos coming."

"Am I looking for anyone in particular?"

Parsons turned slightly and nodded in the direction of Tyler's building. "Been in there?"

"The first night I got here and you know it." Cusack looked where Parsons was looking. The building with Tyler's office was full of small commercial and professional enterprises and university faculty offices. On the first floor were two restaurants, an espresso shop, a children's toy store and a used bookstore/tobacco shop. "Been through the upper floors. All look to be straight up."

"Except our friend in the corner office, third floor?" said Parsons.

Cusack looked at Tyler's office. With the lights off inside, the windows were impenetrable. Cusack thought about the file on Tyler he'd read earlier. "He could be what he seems."

Parsons leaned back and let his eyes slide to the left as if he could read something in Tyler's darkened office windows. "No one could be that droll." He finished the cigarette, dropped it on the floor and put his toe on it. "A bit stark here. Need anything? Another lamp, cable TV, a couple chairs?"

"Will I be staying that long?" Cusack was looking at the room but his mind was elsewhere.

"The daughter knows something. That's for sure."

Cusack wondered where he'd gotten that idea. "Presumption, Parsons. It can blind you to the possibility of innocence." Cusack walked to the work table and dropped into the chair. He picked up a piece of wire and twisted it into shapes: a horse, a peace symbol and a rabbit face. He didn't like the tendency of things. The Tylers should have been obvious and they weren't. Parsons was aiming at something in particular and that was how you got things wrong.

Parsons repeated, "Innocence," drawing out the word.

"Do you have anything more on Tyler for me?" asked Cusack.

"Did you look at the file?"

"Pretty thin."

"You're going to fatten it up for us." Parsons stepped over to the chair, picked up his valise, extracted a large manila envelope and handed it to Cusack. "You're going back to school."

Cusack tipped up the envelope and the contents slid out. The first item was a college class registration card with his name on it and his signature. Always the extra touch on the shoulder, the faked signature that said, "You can count on us," a calculatedly two-edged reassurance. Beneath the card were several sheets covered in close print, which described university policies and services.

"Don't you think I'm a little old for this?" They were changing up the game and Cusack was trying to take it in stride, trying to see where the wrap-up would put him. It was a given that Parsons had this ready to go from the beginning but Cusack wasn't going to get angry. This back-to-school trick had to be better than snapping random photographs and listening to college students talk about their scholarly ambitions. Parsons had withheld information and had misrepresented the assignment and that meant what he said was suspect.

Cusack wasn't surprised. It was a practice that wouldn't win friends.

"Not at all," Parsons said with a short laugh. "Colleges are full of adult students now. Lifelong learners, they call them."

"Who takes classes in philosophy now?"

"The meaning of life holds no interest for you?" Parsons took a big drink out of his glass.

"Am I supposed to leverage his family to get at Tyler somehow? And what am I looking for? Exactly."

"You say family like it's some sort of exotic jungle animal."

"The target looks wrong to me."

"Professor Tyler knows some things. He needs to be persuaded to share."

"Persuaded?" Cusack was getting the beginning of a bad feeling. He recalled a man, only vaguely identified as "working with us" during his weeks in the old Yugoslavia. He, too, liked the word persuaded. Cusack never turned his back on him.

"Do you remember the Front for the Liberation of Senegal?" asked Parsons.

"I do." The Front was attempting to overthrow the Senegalese military rulers. Almost six years ago, Cusack was part of an operation that involved a "secret" trip to Matam in the north of Senegal near the border with Mauritania. It was a night flight by helicopter into a disputed area and he thought it oddly similar to his chauffeur assignment in Saint-Georges. Cusack was the leader of a mismatched security team that accompanied a Senegalese deputy minister to a meeting with insurgents to discuss a cease-fire. It seemed to Cusack to be all for show and it ended very badly. Parsons was the agency's principal liaison for the operation and the agency in charge. Cusack was brought in at the last minute to Dakar from Johannesburg.

"You read the file. Tyler's son-in-law, Philippe Ogbemudia, was a member of the Front." The last bit of dying sun highlighted the deep lines in Parsons' face.

Cusack rattled the ice in his glass. Parsons was enjoying the story and wasn't going to be hurried.

"Tyler is the key."

Cusack looked out the window and caught a glare from the sun setting behind one of the abandoned apartment buildings across the street. "Why didn't I get this upfront?" In certain situations, glare did the same thing as shadows, making it hard to get a read that didn't tire the eyes and take everything off center. In Iraq it was just another hazard and became everything or nothing in the long run.

"I almost forgot. Here's your phone." Parsons put a cell phone on the table. "Speed dial is set. One-two-three and you get me." He palmed the digital camera disk and the audio tape.

"What if you can't be reached?"

Parsons looked at the floor. "You don't need to worry about that."

"You understand," said Cusack, "I like to see the full scope of the landscape. That way, I don't end up spending time and energy being alert to things that don't matter."

"This is the way it works."

"Do we have a timetable?"

"I can't say."

Cusack started to count up the things Parsons wouldn't talk about. It left him thinking about the loyalty track and where it could let you down. "Does all this go back to Tyler's son-in-law?"

"The son-in-law is dead."

"Who's responsible for that?" That was something else Cusack wanted to know. It was a big deal whoever it was that decided someone had to die.

Parsons lit a cigarette and blew a cloud toward the ceiling. He pointed at the registration material. "This will give you a chance to meet with Tyler, visit his office, make contact with his daughter."

"I don't think you should come here again," said Cusack. "It's not a good idea."

Parsons made a show of looking around the room again as if he was ready to leave and had misplaced his keys. "I think you're going to like college. Meet new people, expand your horizons."

Cusack gave Parsons a long, steady look and Parsons returned the look without blinking. Parsons finished his drink, put the glass on the floor and moved toward the door.

"Hey, look on the bright side." Parsons grinned over his shoulder, readying the punch line. "Maybe you could finish your undergraduate degree."

After Parsons left, Cusack waited a minute before walking across to the work table and dialing a number on the cell phone. He hesitated a moment before hitting send.

"Aanonsen," said the voice at the other end.

"Cusack."

"Been a while."

"I'm working with Assistant Director Parsons." He walked to the work table and tipped a shot of bourbon into his glass.

"Your concern?"

"I'm on the job and I don't know him anymore." Aanonsen and Cusack started with Parsons when they came into the agency.

"What do you need?"

"We're surveiling a professor named W. S. Tyler. I have a file but I'd like to know what else there is on him."

"I thought you were in Vienna banging the hausfraus and getting fat on the pastries."

"I was. Now I'm here."

"I'll let you know if I get something."

"We'll have drinks when I get back."

Cusack snapped the phone shut. He and Aanonsen had worked for Parsons for almost three years. Then Cusack went into field work and Aanonsen went into research. Cusack wondered if this job was the best choice he could have made though it was beyond recall at this point. He didn't like to be so far out with men he didn't know or didn't trust but sometimes you just have to make the best out of what you've got.

*I wonder if the ape, smiling as he looks through the bars of his cage at the "more successful" experiment in evolution, ever thinks, "Given half a chance, I could have done better."*

# Chapter 4

Cusack stepped out of the elevator on the third floor in Tyler's building and turned to his right down an empty corridor. Cusack's most recent face-to-face work was a brief role as a reporter meeting a jailed embezzler named Eberhard. The meeting had not gone well. That was then. Now, Cusack took a deep breath and stepped off quickly toward Tyler's office. He passed students, a janitor pushing a cleaning cart and a priest who looked preoccupied. The floors looked freshly mopped and there was an antiseptic tang in the air. On the wall between the office doors were bulletin boards covered with notices: ads for local bands, foreign language tutors, calls to join political protests, yoga classes, apartments for rent, and ads for discounted health supplements and their magical results. On each of the office doors was a small printed sign. Doctor Indira Phukan. Doctor Kevin Dugan. Doctor Samuel Beckett and, penciled in parentheses, No kidding! And Doctor Stephanie Newton. The door to Professor Tyler's office was ajar. Cusack stopped in front of the door and listened to Bob Dylan declare that he was not going to work on Maggie's farm no more.

Cusack waited until the song concluded, then knocked and was invited in. Tyler's daughter, Lauren, was standing on a chair retrieving a book from a shelf near the ceiling. She was wearing blue jeans and her thick black hair was pulled back into a ponytail.

"Professor Tyler?" asked Cusack.

"No, he won't be in today." She looked at him for a moment as if trying to place him, then stepped down and around the podium near the window. She waved him into a chair on the far side of a broad oak desk, which occupied the middle of the room. "I'm his assistant, Lauren. Can I help you?" She touched a button on top of the boom box and Dylan was silenced. The next song on the disc, It's All Over Now, Baby Blue, had started and he almost asked her to let it play. She remained standing as if unsure how long the meeting was going to take.

"My name is Seth Cusack. I've registered late and the registrar says I need this form signed so I can get into Professor Tyler's class." Cusack was just beginning to work into his role and felt awkward. He guessed that might look authentic to Lauren. What was the old joke? Sincerity was difficult. Once you could fake that, you were all set. Lauren lifted a pile of books and black three-ring binders off the desk chair, set them on the floor and sat. "Late registration, did you say? Sorry, I'm not tracking very well today. A long night. Had five of my daughter's eight-year old friends for a sleep-over."

Cusack was unprepared for chattiness. He'd expected quiet, reserve, even sullenness. There was no basis for thinking that; there was nothing at all in the file to indicate her personal qualities. Reserve was his expectation, something he'd concluded from the severity of her features in the photograph in the file. It hadn't gotten her right.

"Is it too late to get into the class?" Cusack tried for a plaintive tone.

"No, not at all. Father needs at least eight students or they cancel the class."

"Father?"

"Yes. I'm his daughter. And yes, nepotism is alive and well." She smiled, conceding a throwaway line.

"Nepotism is fine so long as I get in the class."

The poster on the wall to his right showed a prison door with a red circle around it, a slash mark through it and beneath it the line, The Homeless Need Homes Not Prisons. On the floor next to the desk were more signs. Feed the Needy Not the Greedy. No Corporate Welfare. Leaning against the wall was a bundle of four-foot laths and stacks of pamphlets with matching slogans.

"You'll be welcome, for sure. He gets tired of classes full of twenty-year olds. Youthful enthusiasm only goes so far."

"Funny thing for a teacher to say."

"Honestly, sometimes he likes to teach and sometimes..." She made a dismissive gesture with her hand. She considered the remark as if the thought was new to her. "He thinks he ought to like to teach."

"I suppose a lot of people like what they think they ought to."

"Too many."

Cusack nodded, not sure what to do with that remark.

"Let me see that form, get this out of the way."

Cusack pushed the form across the desk to her.

She took it and said, "I'll sign this. Don't worry, I've been forging his signature for years. Even the FBI lab couldn't tell the difference."

While she examined the form, he took the opportunity to get a thorough look at her. Flawless skin. Icy blue eyes. A face with strong angles, high cheekbones, aquiline nose. It was a face that would wear well over the years.

She reminded him of a woman with whom he'd been involved ten years ago. Nothing comparable in her appearance, more a similarity in the projection of personality.

"I can't keep doing this," the woman had said after they'd been involved for a year. "Live only in the present, like everything good just disappears down the drain. I have to see something ahead, someplace we're going together."

Cusack had no language to reply to this. She was referencing an ambition that he did not recognize. He said nothing and let her draw her own conclusions.

At the time he told himself he could take the punishment if she stayed. What he couldn't take was the relief if she walked. He realized later it was the sort of clever-sounding thing you said to get past something you didn't want to look at too closely.

The telephone on the desk rang and Lauren lifted the receiver. "Hi," she tilted her head to pin the receiver to her shoulder while she finished signing Cusack's request. "Yes," she said, "I'll take care of it." She hung up the phone.

"I haven't had many adult students lately," she said. "Philosophy doesn't usually fit in with career transitions. What do you do for a living?"

"I'm not working right now."

She was not that easily put off. "When you were working, what did you do?"

"A research firm near Baltimore." The agency did research and it was located near Baltimore. He had answered her question. Whoever said that the facts speak for themselves?

"What kind of research?"

"Government contract work. Very boring."

"Not very good at it?"

Cusack laughed. "I did get laid off."

Lauren had made a clear space on the desk to sign the form, nudged a file and exposed a book titled, Palmistry: The Art and Science of Reading Palms. She noticed what he saw and laughed. "My daughter's school's fall festival. I'm the palm-reader, Zelda. Tarot cards, too."

"No one is interested in the consolation of philosophy?" Cusack liked her laugh.

"If you know the future, do you need any consolation?"

"More than ever, I would think."

"Well," she said. "It seems what they want the consolation of, I'll quote my father, 'is a comprehensive sedative delusion.'"

Cusack considered that remark for a minute. "What are the sedative delusions he has in mind?"

"The usual: politics, religion, art."

"He covers the board."

"That's my dad."

"And you're doing your bit with the palm-reading."

"What we do for money." She shrugged.

"Well, at least it goes to a good cause."

"The ends justify the means?"

"Has class started already?" Cusack felt himself struggling to keep up; it was always easier to be the one controlling the questions, when he knew the agenda of the person in front of him.

People loved to talk about themselves, their natural tendencies fitting perfectly into his own professional interests. When the situation was well-crafted, the conversation could be shaped and pointed. And if done right, it could be economical; it could be about what it was supposed to be about and nothing more. Cusack could see from only a few minutes with Lauren that the Tylers were going to be a different kind of work. He wasn't liking the prospects for any kind of success.

"You talk to a career counselor yet?" said Lauren. "Employment prospects for philosophers are pretty bleak."

There was a knock at the door and Lauren excused herself. She stepped into the hallway to speak to the student who seemed to want permission to deliver an assignment late. Lauren closed the door and Cusack didn't hear her answer.

Cusack walked across to the bookcase. On the shelf next to the boombox was a pile of CDs including Dylan's and one of the Senegalese singer Youssan D'Nour. He moved to the podium next to the window and could see the windows of his condominium although the dark tint made the camera behind them invisible. On the street below, the merchants were still moving items onto the tables on the sidewalk. Half the sidewalk was in the sun, half in shade and shoppers appeared and disappeared as they moved in and out of the shade. Cusack returned to his chair but several minutes passed before Lauren stepped back into the room.

"What were we talking about?" asked Lauren.

"Employment prospects."

"The college does have a placement office."

"I'm not in a rush to get back to work."

"You're in the right place then." She pushed the form back across the desk.

"What all do you do here?" he asked, trying to move the subject of the conversation to her father.

"What a teaching assistant usually does. Grades papers, tests." She pointed toward the door where she'd dealt with her supplicant. "Counsels students," she added.

Cusack looked at an oxygen tank in the corner near the door and she followed his look. "My father has early stage emphysema."

"Sorry."

"Oh, he still gets around pretty well."

"The class bulletin says that your father taught at a number of universities, here and in Europe."

"Growing up like an Army brat. We moved just about every year when I was a kid."

"They say travel is a broadening experience."

"They say a lot of things."

Cusack put the form in his bag and pointed at the floor. "What's all this?"

"The protest?" She pointed over her shoulder. "We're trying to keep the homeless from getting totally screwed. Squatters getting evicted from the Washburn Redevelopment Area, over there."

Cusack nodded.

"Do you know anything about the philosophers you'll be studying?" asked Lauren. "Cioran and Pascal and Ekelund?"

"I had a teacher in high school who liked Pascal," said Cusack. "And we read *The Pensees* but that was a long time ago."

"Is this class part of a degree program for you?"

"I don't know if this class fits or not. I never finished my undergraduate degree. Took a lot of history classes and English lit. I think I need about a year's worth of credits to finish."

Lauren leaned back in her chair, appearing to relax. This, she seemed to accept, was a reason for him to be there. Someone in mid-life drift. Most of the time that was probably a more accurate term than life-long learner, Cusack thought, although the college made money either way. Mid-life drift just didn't have the right tone.

"Can I get a syllabus and a textbook list, too while I'm here?"

She turned around and pulled a file folder off the credenza that sat under the window. After a minute of sorting through the folder she produced several sheets of paper. She ran her eyes over them before passing them across the desk.

"This will tell you what you need." She stood. "Anything else I can do?"

Cusack also stood. "No, thank you." He left the building and returned to his place by a meandering route that showed him the campus layout.

Cusack's professional opinion was that it was more efficient to observe from a distance, collecting information through the detached, neutral device of the camera or the ghostly voice-only audio device. Personally, involvement with an assigned target was for Cusack both tiring and difficult. It required playacting, being someone other than yourself while collecting impressions from the target. Inevitably, distortions occurred that on both sides changed everything. During the next few hours he stepped to the window occasionally and looked down on Lauren, sitting at the desk marking up papers.

Even given his limited exposure to the Tylers, Cusack thought he could detect tension between father and daughter. It was understandable. She'd had to move back in with him after being on her own for years and he'd almost certainly used his influence to get her in the graduate program and the job as teaching assistant. Gratitude and resentment were inseparable twins. Useful leverage there?

Tyler appeared at his office at 2:30, greeted Lauren and asked her about visitors. She referred to Cusack as an "adult student." When he and Lauren left the building an hour later, Cusack hustled down to his car and followed them. Lauren got behind the wheel of the late model Volvo, and Cusack wondered if Tyler's physical condition barred him from driving.

They collected the granddaughter, Sarah, from her school, Lincoln Elementary, located about three miles north of the campus. The flag on the pole in the school yard snapped in the wind. Cusack parked two blocks away but could still see the girl between the rows of yellow buses parked in front of the school. She chatted with her friends, a bright purple backpack slung over her shoulder. The school yard was full of children, some clustered in earnest talk, others running around and screaming. When Sarah saw her ride, she skipped down the sidewalk and climbed into the back seat.

The neighborhood where the Tylers lived, five miles from the university campus, was populated by older, mid-sized, well-made homes of brick and stucco on lots with large oaks and maples. Leaves were beginning to accumulate on the lawns and in the gutters. To Cusack, the street looked like a television advertisement for life insurance or minivans with good crash ratings or political ads selling fear.

He marveled at people's eagerness to belong. He understood it as a kind of ambition but he knew his own habits of mind and felt himself always moving in another direction. There was too much in the wind now. Clarity was missing and calculations had to have a more precise starting point to mean anything. After Saint-Georges his starting point had become indeterminate and not to be relied upon.

Lauren parked the car on the street in front of the house, and the family made its way up the sidewalk, Tyler trailing with his oxygen tank. It looked like a small bomb. Cusack drove down the alley behind the house, took note of the size of the garage and its distance from the back door of the house and then drove back across campus and parked the car on a side street a half-block from the condominium. He turned off the engine but didn't move. He let his window down and lit a cigarette.

From his vantage point he could see the alley and the front of the building. No one entered or left the alley and he saw nothing that concerned him among those who entered or left the front of the building. He continued to sit and watch for ten minutes. It was a habit, nothing more. When he finished the cigarette, he left his car and walked down the alley.

Back in his room, he threw himself into the easy chair without bothering to remove his jacket. He lit another cigarette, took a drag and followed the lazy drift of the smoke until it disappeared sixteen feet up amidst the gray steel girders. He felt edgy like when he took an extra hit of speed to make it to the end of a twenty-four hour surveil. There was no reason to feel that way now. Any momentum there was on this project was out of his control.

*The most difficult task is to set ourselves into the habits of freedom, to reject habitually the comfort of intellectual and emotional routine, to practice the unfamiliar.*

# Chapter 5

Cusack was a light sleeper and awoke several times during the night, the last time at four a.m. He gave up on sleep then and slipped out of bed. At the open window he stood listening and looking but the street below was quiet and empty of traffic. Then there was a sudden rush of air and it began to rain, the drops smacking the window.

He thought of the woman who died at Saint-Georges. Kristen Pedersen was the bored wife of a professor at the local college. Cusack was full of resentment and boredom at his bodyguard assignment and thought that might have been, in some way, what brought them together - an unspoken yet shared resentment. Thinking of her didn't make him feel guilty, but the memory worked on him. It made him feel involved even so long after the fact and that was harder.

She and Cusack hooked up at the hotel bar his first night in Saint-Georges and then went back to his room. "No pressure," she said but it seemed to him that she worked everything over into something that couldn't be taken just for itself. It was expectation turned inside out. To her credit, she tried to make the best of things. She made herself the butt of sly jokes. It made her likeable even with the bitterness. Everything she did in bed was infused with urgency not because Cusack thought it mattered to her but because she wanted it to be on the record as something she'd done. He figured she was storing up details to reveal later to her husband. "And then, you know what I did? And then, you know what I let him do?"

Cusack was in Saint-Georges, a town in northwestern Oregon, providing security for a Health and Human Services Department assistant undersecretary named Minette. It was a penance. Minette was given a minder to satisfy his vanity. The guy was an asshole but he had to be way down the assassination list.

However, it was the Pedersen woman's face that kept coming back to him and he didn't like that. There was no necessity in her death except in the larger working out of some kind of indifferent fate. Thinking about it months later, he decided that wasn't enough of an answer. He believed in fate but it just wasn't enough. Bystanders shouldn't get blown to hell.

He cranked open several more windows to get air moving and, looking down, was hypnotized by the rain, invisible until it fell below the street lights where it turned silver. The stop light turned from green to yellow to red. A sour, woolly smell was carried on a chill wind into the room.

Cusack had gone for years without a stake in much of anything. It had looked like a winning strategy, but seeing something as an asset rather than a frame of reference also had its attractions and after Saint-Georges he felt a yearning to own more than just a vantage point. However, once set on a trajectory, would he be able to fix its destination or would the end become random and not a destination at all?

Late the next morning, carrying the class textbook list that Lauren Tyler had given him, he left the condominium. The merchants along

4th Street and University Avenue were organizing a sidewalk sale, setting up long folding tables, snapping out brightly colored plastic table cloths and pinning them down with merchandise that no one seemed to want when it was inside their stores. Still, some people slowed to take a look. The sales clerks, who were college girls, smiled as if they were in on the joke. At the far end of the block, several tents were being set up. From the coffee bar on the first floor Cusack had what he wanted, a coffee and a newspaper. He sat at a sidewalk table on the corner; it was warm enough in the sun.

Later that morning he walked to the student bookstore in a mall that was located a block from the eastern border of the campus. It was a single gigantic room with a high ceiling. The fluorescent lights gave off an indeterminate fluttery glare that made colors both harsh and inaccurate. On his way in, Cusack passed a girl who was pawing through a bin of maroon colored sweatshirts decorated with the university's logo in gold. The bookshelf next to the bin held notebooks, giant coffee mugs, t-shirts and desk accessories all with the university logo.

He walked down several crowded aisles before finding the books for his class. He was struck immediately with the fact that, with the exception of the grossly overweight man behind the cash register, everyone in the place was half Cusack's age. Where were all the lifelong learners?

It was at the checkout that he noticed the security cameras on the wall behind the cash register and above the exit and on several pillars among the bookshelves. There were several students in line ahead of him. He paged through the introduction to *Second Light* by Vilhelm Ekelund and overheard the conversation of two girls who stood behind him in the line.

"I let a guy talk me into that once before and I could hardly sit down for a week afterwards."

The other girl giggled.

"Of course, I was drunk at the time."

Cusack could smell the perfume or shampoo of the girl closest to him, a rich, complicated scent.

"I am such a cheap drunk," the second girl boasted. "Two beers and I'm asking strange men if they'd like ..." then a giggle. "Of course, they deliberately misunderstand me and start to unzip their pants. It's disgusting."

"Disgusting is what they are."

"Yeah, but Brian's okay."

"Whatever you say."

"No, really."

Was he intended to overhear this talk, old man that he was? Girls trying to shock. He wanted to see what they looked like.

The man behind the counter, his head rolling slightly on a thick, soft neck, looked past Cusack and said, "Can I help you?"

Cusack laid his three thin paperbacks on the counter. Compared to the armfuls of books that others had dropped on the counter, Cusack's pile made him feel like a fraud. He smiled. He was a fraud.

"Cash or credit?" The man swiped the back of each book with a wand.

"Cash." Cusack paid, took his bag and walked out.

The entrance to the bookstore was located on one side of a broad interior courtyard where light streamed from a vaulted glass ceiling three stories above. Skinny trees with equally skinny branches sprouted from massive concrete planters and the leaves shattered the light, making everything serene like a day remote from consequences.

There were five kiosks in the courtyard selling wedding photo services, hot dogs, costume jewelry, ice cream and cell phone plans. Pungent odors drifted out of a hair salon next door. A young woman pushed a stroller while talking on a cell phone. Directly across from the bookstore was an espresso shop called Brewberry's where tiny, high, round tables and chairs of brushed steel were clustered on either side of the entrance. As Cusack approached, a potent roasted coffee smell thickened the air.

Cusack bought a cappuccino, went back outside and set his bag on a table. Cameras looked down from each of the eight pillars that circled the courtyard. Above the pillars shoppers leaned over a railing and scanned the tables below. He touched his lips to the cup, steam fogged his glasses and he wiped them on a napkin.

He pulled out *Second Light*, by Vilhelm Ekelund, translated by Lennart Bruce. It appeared to be a compilation of quotes from the many books published by Ekelund, a kind of greatest hits retrospective. He flipped pages and the book fell open on a quote by Bakunin. "Only he who can forget himself has strength." He turned back to the Introduction and began to read, all the time aware of the eyes of someone from the second floor railing. Cusack thought he had seen the man before but couldn't recall where or when.

Cusack sipped his coffee and examined the shoppers passing in front of him. They seemed ordinary. It was pointless to resent the presence of the watcher although the project had been sold to him as routine. He hadn't taken Parsons' words at face value but he'd no reason to think they needed backup when the project was a decrepit college professor. Maybe the watcher was Parsons' idea of building overlap into the project and that, thought Cusack, was exactly Parsons' style. Security meant keeping your own people under observation and in the dark until the last minute.

The second book out of the bag was, *The Pensees*. Brother Christopher had assigned it in religion class during Cusack's senior year at De La Salle High School. Cusack skimmed through it while sipping the last of his cappuccino. What he read had a dried, preserved aspect to it. That was about right, he thought. The fixed, dead quality of the past. The last book out of the bag was titled, *The Temptation to Exist,* by E.M. Cioran. In the Introduction, Cusack discovered that Cioran was in the modern tradition of Kierkegaard, Nietzsche and Wittgenstein. His philosophy was personal, aphoristic, lyrical and anti-systematic. Good for him. Cusack returned the book to the bag, stood and walked back inside Brewberry's.

A sandwich board next to the cash register had the day's specials written in a precise hand with chalks of various pastels. Wild rice soup, lemon tarragon chicken salad on Irish potato bread, roasted turkey with provolone on foccaccio. He looked into a glass case of desserts including caramel apple empanada and white chocolate cookies with macadamia nut that were the size of dinner plates. He ordered the soup and another cappucino.

As he returned to his table, he scanned the second floor railing but the man was gone. If he was one of Parsons', this showing was just another of those ambiguously comforting reminders, "We're here for you." A more sinister possibility existed - that someone else was interested in Tyler - but Cusack couldn't list it seriously, not yet anyway.

Cusack opened the Cioran book and tested the soup. Too hot, he put the spoon down and went quickly through the Introduction again. He'd finished that and was about to begin on the book proper when he sensed someone else's presence.

"Mr. Cusack."

He looked up into the pale blue eyes of Lauren Tyler.

"Ms. Tyler, it's nice to see you."

"Getting right into the books, I see."

"Have to. Rusty study habits. Would you care to join me?" He pointed at the chair opposite his own.

"Thanks, yes." She put a small paper bag imprinted with the

Aardvark Card Shop on the table. "Let me get some coffee." She stepped into the shop and returned a minute later with coffee in a to-go cup. She perched on the other chair. "What do you think?" She pointed at the Cioran book.

"Too early to tell. The woman who wrote the Introduction seems to think he's special."

"Is this your only class?"

"I thought I'd ease back into the school thing."

"Hmmm."

Cusack sipped his cappuccino and watched two Middle-Eastern men arguing in front of a shop at the far end of the mall.

"What made you decide to come to Ashland?"

"I dated a woman who graduated from here. What made you come here?"

"When my father first started having... trouble, I came for a visit." She lifted her cup. "I decided he couldn't be on his own."

"You said you all bump along pretty well."

"Yes, well...." She pried the top off her cup and blew on it. "He blames the war for everything now. He lost a couple toes to frostbite in Korea and believes the two winters he spent there affected his lungs as well. I tell him he smoked for thirty years and he's seventy-nine years old and he should be grateful for what he's got. It's emphysema, coming on for ten years or so. But the oxygen tank is recent."

She talked fast and seemed nervous to Cusack. He dipped his spoon in the bowl and ate.

"That smells so good. I wasn't going to eat but I think I'll get a bowl and join you, if you don't mind."

"Not at all."

While she was collecting her soup, Cusack thought he would have to step carefully given the Tyler's history with the CIA. Cusack was prepared to humor Parsons but there was no way this job was going to run out on any schedule. Lauren returned and settled into her seat.

Just then a young woman approached their table. "Ms. Tyler?" she said. "Excuse me."

"Yes, Susan, what is it?"

"I just wanted to know if you're coming to the rally tomorrow."

"Yes."

"Should I stop by your office to pick up the signs?"

"Sure. Eleven o'clock?"

The girl nodded and gave Cusack a quick, appraising look and left.

Cusack dipped his bread in the soup and chewed it. After a minute, he said, "It must be nice for your dad to have you around."

"Nice might be a stretch." She spooned up the soup and blew on it. "But we bump along, as you say. How about you? You have any family?"

"My father's been retired for a while. I have a brother and sister but they live out West." He dipped into his soup again. "I checked out one of your father's books at the library. The Introduction mentioned he'd gone to jail. A little unusual for a professor, I thought. What was that all about?"

Lauren tried her soup, too. "Politics. It was all about my husband who was Senegalese. He worked for the creation of a free Senegal and raised money for a rebel group fighting the Senegalese government. They labeled him a terrorist. Our government, in its wisdom, sided with the Senegalese military dictatorship. He was deported and they killed him."

"Really? That's ... incredible. I'm sorry to hear that." He sipped his coffee. "How was your father involved?"

"He raised hell and the local D.A. thought he could make political points off the radical professor attacking American values. Pro-terrorist activist. Dad said Philippe was fighting for freedom and accused the CIA of complicity in Philippe's death. Some radio talk-shows and local politicians all saw a chance to make points. Still, there was a protest march on Dad's behalf at the college and then things got a little out of hand. The media, of course, overreacted. Big surprise. Anarchy. Violence in the streets, according to the DA. Then Dad spouted off to the judge and got thirty days for contempt of court."

"You make it sound almost routine."

"The cops and the usual assholes kept it from being routine. Threatening phone calls at all hours, slashed tires, a cop car around all the time. And that, the cop car, was not at all reassuring. Protect and serve, my ass. Graffitti all over the garage. Dog shit in the mailbox."

"Is that why your Dad finds twenty-year olds uninteresting now?"

"Young people didn't have anything to do with all that shit. That was all grown-ups." Lauren looked away as if regretting her plainspokenness.

Cusack spooned up the last of his soup. "When I signed up for this class, someone told me I'm what they call, 'a lifelong learner.' I'd never heard that expression before."

Lauren smiled. "Oh, they have labels for everyone they want to sell something to."

A little later, she excused herself saying she had to finish her shopping. Cusack watched her until she disappeared into a shop on the far end of the mall. Later, out on the street, he stepped up to a newspaper kiosk and handed a couple bills to the vendor. He folded the paper and tucked it into the bag with the books. He lit a cigarette and looked around. There were cameras on top of the street lights and that always raised a question. Who was reassured by being watched - those doing the watching or those being watched?

Cusack passed a set of newspaper boxes in the block before his door. They included the student paper and Washburn Protest was the headline.

Back at the condominium, Cusack stepped inside the door and examined the room in the reverse order he had before leaving. Nothing appeared out of place. He put the bag of books on the work table and walked across to the camera and recording equipment on the wall under the window. The tape recorder had ticked over. Someone had visited Tyler's office. Cusack leaned down and looked through the camera. The office appeared to be unoccupied.

He sat at the work table and put the books on one corner. He lit a cigarette. Had the watcher at the mall been there to keep an eye on him or Lauren. If it was for her, what did it mean?

*Give up your questions and everything makes sense.*

# Chapter 6

Cusack had another routine bad night's sleep. By midafternoon of the next day he was feeling groggy and tried to nap. He made himself comfortable in the easy chair with an extra pillow under his lower back. Leaving the television on with the sound at a whisper, he dozed. Eventually, he slept deeply enough to dream.

He was riding in a helicopter, the pock-pock sound of the blades deafening even through the doors. He felt the engine vibrations through the soles of his boots. The soldiers sat shoulder to shoulder on hard benches across from each other. The smell of old sweat was mixed with gasoline. The night air was cool and Cusack could see only the outlines of the men sitting across from him, a darker darkness.

He looked at the floor and waited for the change in the tempo of the vibration, the shift downward. It occurred to him after several minutes that there was no chatter in his headphones. They started getting ground fire and Cusack heard the pinging as rounds hit the chopper. Vasquez was the team leader and would ordinarily be running through the routines in the set-up. Everyone got ramped-up in his own way but it was Vasquez's job to hold the focus. Cusack turned and tapped his arm but Vasquez ignored him. Cusack grabbed his arm then and Vasquez sagged toward him, gore oozing from a blown eye socket and his jaw moving as if air needed to be chewed before it could be swallowed.

Cusack stared at the mess that was Vasquez' face and said calmly, "It will be okay. Hang in there."

Cusack looked around for a medic but couldn't speak because he didn't know which of the figures across from him was the medic and all the faces might look like Vasquez if he reached across for help. Blood dripped onto Cusack's hand and he pushed Vasquez away.

The ground fire intensified and still no one reacted and there was silence in his headset. He looked at his watch but the face was blank.

Then Cusack was on the ground with an Iraqi soldier in front of him and Cusack struck him in the throat. The soldier went down and, in the purple-black darkness between a barracks and a munitions shed, the only sound was the high-pitched whistling as the soldier tried to bring air through his crushed larynx into his lungs. Cusack looked around for someone else to kill but there were only the two of them and while he looked around the whistling stopped.

Somehow, Cusack had lost the rest of the squad. He was alone in the darkness and it worked away at his nerves. The darkness had a palpable quality that concealed an unknowable yet terrifying menace. He held himself very still, strained his eyes and ears but could detect nothing. Fear made it hard to breathe.

The wind came up and sand bit into his face. He knew he was forgetting something urgent but couldn't remember what it was. It was right behind him and it was making a knocking sound but he couldn't make himself turn to see it now. He tried and tried but he couldn't turn.

Cusack awoke with mechanical abruptness in a freezing panic and looked at the television screen where a man and woman in extreme close-up were murmuring at each other. He couldn't tell what they were saying and the knock came again, someone at his door. He jumped up, grabbed the pistol from the work table drawer and glided across the room. When he slid open the twelve-foot-high steel door, no one was there. He stepped across to the top of the stairwell and looked down but there was no one there either.

He went back inside, slid the door shut, dropped the bolt and returned to the living room. Sound from the television droned on. He poured himself a double shot of bourbon and lit a cigarette.

Cusack hadn't been bothered about the mission into Matam for years. Now, it looked like his dreams were becoming a concoction of disastrous Iraq missions with the one in Senegal. Working with Parsons, that's what brought all the bad memories back. In Senegal, there had been a hurried need to put together a team. The team Parsons assembled made Cusack nervous and the Senegalese chopper pilots were reluctant and that made Cusack take Parsons aside and ask him to delay the action until they could get their own pilots. Parsons had the final word on sending Cusack in.

This dream was new, mixing elements of Iraq missions with parts of the assignment in Senegal. If the purpose of dreams was to mend the past or predict the future, his dreams weren't getting the job done.

It was the middle of the day and going back to sleep was out of the question. The tinted windows dimmed the sunlight and the only light in the room came from the television, which gave the room an underwater look like he'd stumbled into an aquarium. The watery distortion made everything look worse than it was like a setting in an alternative universe with no way to get back into real time.

He left the condominium, walked out the front of the building and turned south on University Avenue. He crossed the street at the southern entrance into the Washburn Redevelopment Area and walked through the open gates. A half-block inside was an open square, which must have been a crowd-pleaser years ago. In the center were the remains of a fountain. Traces of a walking path remained; stumps of trees edged a narrow section around the fountain itself, which may have been devoted to flower beds.

Several four and six-story buildings, in various stages of decay, overlooked the square. Cusack was reminded of what he'd seen during his brief stay in the old Yugoslavia. There, buildings were bomb shelters, minimal protection against artillery barrages. Here people milled around in front of one of the buildings, which looked to have been a hotel, though not recently. This was the part of the Washburn with the public housing projects and the older neighborhoods that were scheduled for early demolition. The newer and incomplete construction was mostly on the north end of the WRA.

As he approached the former hotel, several of the men abruptly disappeared inside. When he reached the sidewalk in front of the entrance, only women and small children remained. Some had the look of illegals. The fact that the men vanished at his appearance reinforced his judgment. "Marginales" he recalled from his Spanish. Usually a term used on the Indians of Mexico. Marginal people, treated as invisible or worse.

He thought he had no stake here and should just turn and leave but instead walked up to a woman and said the first thing that came into his head, "Any room here?"

She shook her head and looked down at her feet. He glanced over his shoulder and realized he wasn't the reason the men had ducked inside. Two police cars crawled by. As they passed, Cusack asked, "They come often?"

"Every few days. Sometimes there are three or four cars. Then they come in and look around."

"What do they say they're looking for?"

The woman shrugged.

"INS come with them?"

She shrugged again.

Cusack took out his pack of cigarettes and held it toward her. She hesitated, then picked out just one. He lit it for her. Over her shoulder were the office buildings, condos, shops and restaurants beyond University Avenue, another world to these people.

"You have water, electricity?"

"Sometimes."

"Any room in any of those?" He pointed at the other buildings that fronted the square.

"Did someone send you?"

Cusack shook his head and glanced at the other women who got busy suddenly with their children. The children endured their mothers' fussing and kept staring at him, giving nothing away, their eyes as flat and unreadable as stones. A variety of pleasant cooking smells issued from the open windows above.

A young man stepped through the front door, looked up and down University Avenue and approached Cusack with confidence. "You interested in a place to stay?" The man was Cusack's height but thinner and his skin was very black. He spoke with an accent, which Cusack guessed first was Jamaican but then reconsidered. Nigerian, maybe.

"I have a place for now," said Cusack. "But, who knows, maybe in the future."

The man's eyes went first to Cusack's face then everywhere else. "Now is good, yes. But," he held his hand out palm down and waggled it, "the future, it's a bitch." Then he smiled because even when life was a bitch you might as well smile.

It was time to get moving. The Washburn wasn't his assignment.

Getting oriented to his location didn't require in-depth interviews, social problem research or making friends.

"What's your name?" asked the young man.

"Call me Russo. And you?"

"Call me Victor."

One of the women near Cusack bent down and picked up her child. The other women followed suit and all went inside leaving Cusack alone with Victor.

Cusack offered Victor a cigarette but he declined.

"The police," Cusack pointed to the place where the police cars had cruised by. "What are they after?"

Victor continued to smile but changed the question. "Who are they after? Criminals, yes? They look for them in poor neighborhoods because the rich do not commit crimes, yes?"

Cusack laughed. "That's right, Victor. Exactly right." Victor had a point of view. It arranged the elements of the world for him. Cusack had seen that before and he didn't mind. "I understand they are going to knock down these buildings. Where are you going to go then?"

"I think we may not go. People have to have a place they call their own." He pointed at Cusack. "I'll have that cigarette now." After he took his first draw, he said, "You cannot just move them around like furniture."

"Will there be violence?"

Victor looked thoughtful. "Violence begins sometimes from the smallest thing. It starts out small then it becomes ... promiscuous. Then, it's just the way things are. I know this, yes."

Cusack heard a threat in Victor's remark. It wasn't a personal threat, more like a description of an atmosphere. Cusack couldn't place Victor's accent for sure but his point of view came from everywhere - Bosnia, Sudan, Sri Lanka, Gaza and Bolivia...

"Mr. Russo, if you decide you need a room in the future or anything else, ask for Haley."

"Not you?"

"Just Haley." He turned and entered the building, closing the door behind him.

Victor wasn't offering Cusack help but a warning. As he walked away, Cusack tried to guess where Victor got his status in the Washburn. Maybe because he was a social critic and a comedian.

*What is the purpose of education but to introduce
complication and obsession to the innocent?*

# Chapter 7

On his first day back in college, Cusack was awake early. He made
a pot of coffee and drank it while reading from the Ekelund book.
He was a student now and wondered how he was supposed to feel.
An hour later, he packed his bag with the three textbooks he'd purchased, a notebook and several pens and slung the bag over his shoulder. An early childhood memory intruded from his days at St. Mark's
Elementary. The teacher said something about what a good student
he was and then ruined it by adding, "Just like your sister."

He opened the work table's drawer looking for cigarettes but it
held only his gun. He considered moving the gun as a precaution
against a possible intruder but there was no place to hide it that a
thorough search wouldn't discover so he left it. He glanced at his
watch and headed for the door.

At the drugstore in the building across the street, he picked up
cigarettes and felt ready for the day. On his way out of the store Cusack passed a sales clerk looking glum and carrying merchandise to
tables on the sidewalk. One of the tables he passed had a scattering
of items – oven mitts and refrigerator magnets, meat thermometers,

can openers and more. He passed three blocks of mostly restaurants and bars, then student dormitories named Pioneer and Kellogg. Occasionally, he halted, pretended to an unfamiliarity with the area and looked around. The mall-watcher was off the job or being careful.

On campus, Cusack passed several metal posts with two-way speakers and red panic buttons and signs that promised help and safety. If you feel endangered or wish for a security escort, push this button and identify yourself. College security staff will respond immediately.

Cusack angled across a student commuter parking lot. The kids' cars were mostly new and sleek and expensive. Lexus, Audi, the occasional ecologically friendly Toyota or Honda. The American cars were all tricked out sports cars - Mustangs and Firebirds. Money appeared to serve its usual purpose - sorting. Still, the students Cusack had seen seemed a little anxious. America was well into an anxious century.

The Ashland campus had two dozen buildings, the original nine built just after World War I. Seven of the original nine were clustered around the quad, a grassy, tree-covered square divided by broad sidewalks. Students occupied benches beneath the trees talking on cell phones or tapping away at laptop keyboards. The wind blew abundant leaves across the sidewalks and the carillon located at the top of the student union rang the hour.

The quad he saw would make the sort of picture that ended up on recruiting materials and course catalogs. Walking under the trees on the quad, Cusack felt neither sad nor resentful. He was past caring about what hadn't worked out twenty years ago. The past, he conceded, was never dead but it was sure as hell buried.

His class with Tyler was located in Ford Hall, one of the buildings that fronted on the quad, its granite face done in neo-Classical style. At the top of the outside steps, he held the door for several girls while he looked out over the grassy square. He saw nothing that concerned him.

The stone steps to the second floor and the dark oak railings were well-worn and the building hummed with young voices. At the top of the stairs, Cusack stepped left quickly and put his back to the wall. He let the anonymous tide of students move past him. He'd sensed something impending like a blow to the head and when nothing justified the sensation he became angry. He pulled open the door to room 212 and stepped inside.

Only four chairs of he chairs in the room were occupied. Three women, one man, all late teens or early twenties. The women sat near the front; the man sat in the middle near the far windows, which were tall and wide. The light pouring in was filtered through the trees and made Cusack feel calm and well-placed.

He slipped into a seat on the aisle near the door, where he would be the first to see anyone who entered. He unloaded his bag and leafed through Cioran while occasionally taking a look at his fellow students. Three more students filed in - two boys, one girl. Several of the girls appeared to know each other and began talking about other people identified only by their first names. For a moment, Cusack was disappointed that the mall-watcher hadn't registered for the class.

At a quarter past the hour, Tyler entered. He had a silver, metallic briefcase in one hand and dragged a silver oxygen canister on a two-wheeled cart. He walked with an odd gait, the result, Cusack guessed, of the lost toes of his Korean frostbite. His white hair was thin on top but thick and long on the sides and brushed straight back. He wore black pants, a white shirt and tan sport coat. He stepped behind the wide table at the front of the room and laid his briefcase on it.

"My apologies for being late," he said and wrote his name on the whiteboard. He hauled a sheaf of papers out of his briefcase and said, "I'll pass out the syllabus and give you other pertinent information in a minute. Office hours, phone number and email address. I hope you all have your books with you so I can begin immediately."

He looked around as if challenging anyone to disparage his hope and continued, "This is an undergraduate class so my expectations for it are somewhat diminished." He looked at the ceiling. "What am I saying? My expectations are totally diminished." The student who sat by the window snickered. "However, that does not mean you can skate through this class. If you learn nothing else from me in this class, it is that despair can be as disciplinary in its effects as hope for some people. It has been that for me. Maybe it can be the same for you."

Two of the women who sat near the front of the class gave each other a quick look.

Tyler said, "As open-minded as the chairman of this department claims to be, my own declaration to him of a committed belief in the utter futility of things did not impress. He answers to parents who want their children to exit this school in four years with a diploma of some sort and enough hope to get a job. But the survival of hope and the dubious achievement of employment are not part of my purpose. You are students in, and I am a professor in, the College of Liberal Arts. I am supposed to open your minds to possibilities and that is what I intend to do.

"As to the requirements of the class. Pretty simple, really. You will have to write a brief essay on each of the three philosophers we'll be discussing. Your final assignment will be to write a five page paper in imitation of one of the three. They say, 'Imitation is the sincerest form of flattery.' I think it's a helluva learning experience as well."

He put the oxygen canister on the table. It got everyone's attention, as it was intended to.

"I have the class list here. I will take attendance every class. And there are only eight of you." He paused as if considering what to say next. "One unexcused absence is allowed. Shit happens, as they used to say many years ago. Two or more absences will have a serious negative effect on your grade. Be advised." He took an obvious breath, perhaps to highlight his next remark. "You are perhaps curious about my friend." Tyler pointed at the oxygen canister. "I have a medical condition and may occasionally have need of some oxygen. If I can make it to this class dragging this thing around, and huff and puff through a two-hour class, then so can you.

Tyler pulled more papers from his briefcase and handed them to the girl nearest him. She separated the stapled packets, took one and passed the rest. Eventually, one came to Cusack. It looked like the one he'd collected at Tyler's office but he tucked it into his bag anyway. He craved a cigarette.

"I've taught this class at the post-graduate level and to undergraduates like you. No matter what your age or depth of knowledge, I believe instruction in the art of the aphorism is a good thing. I believe aphorism is the poetry of argument. There are a number of great writers in this tradition but this semester, we're going to look at Pascal, Ekelund and Cioran. I suppose I could as easily have selected others in this tradition, such as Nietzsche, Kierkegaard and Chamfort."

He studied the canister as if weighing its need, then continued, "Nietzsche is regarded by many as the modern stylist par excellence of the aphorism. Examples abound. One of my favorites is, 'Objections, digressions, gay mistrust, the delight in mockery are signs of health: everything unconditional belongs in pathology.'

"I think this quote summarizes some of the salient aspects of the modern tradition. We might also see in it any number of related... applications. For instance, many people believe that the man of fixed ideas is the most dangerous of all creatures. But I think it is the man of fixed realities who must be most feared. The facts in front of him make no impression. He is everywhere a tourist in the sense that a tourist is a mere shoplifter. And because he will learn nothing, he can do anything." Tyler picked up the oxygen mask and breathed into it for a minute.

"As you might have guessed," he continued, "I've just attempted to give you an observation in the style of one of the aphorists we're going to study."

When Tyler paused again, several students who had been taking notes at high speed since he first began speaking, looked up. "Now, more particularly, to what you're facing in this class. Every writer is of his time and it is certainly true of the three we will be looking at this semester. But great writers also transcend their time. Blaise Pascal appears new and fresh to us because he is that sort of writer.

"The other writers you will read in this class may be somewhat less accessible than Pascal even though they are both of the 20th century. E.M. Cioran has a style which might take some getting used to. I would recommend you read him in short bursts. In fact, all three should be read that way, at least in your first read-through. Vilhelm Ekelund may be the most difficult of all to appreciate. He developed his own lexicon and simple comprehension, let alone appreciation, may require considerable effort."

Near the end of the class period, Tyler said, "I'll tell you that I have written several books in a style that some critics have said is reminiscent of Cioran. One critic went so far as to say it was too reminiscent and accused me of plagiarism. Of course, I rejected that charge. Gore Vidal once said of himself, though I think it describes in many ways the contributions of critics of all times, "I have nothing to say, only something to add.

"A few years ago, one of my students submitted as his 'in the style of' assignment a word-for-word lift from one of my own books. He may have assumed the onset of Alzheimers. He may have read that critic. While I applaud such chutzpah, he got an F. A word to the wise."

When the class ended, two of the students stepped to the front of the room to ask Tyler questions. Cusack packed his bag slowly and waited for Tyler at the door.

Cusack introduced himself and said, "Professor, I wanted to thank you for letting me register late for the class."

"Nonsense. You made up for the drop-out." Cusack held the door open as Tyler pulled the canister into the hallway. "Saved the class. Less than eight and I'd be home right now."

"I've looked a bit into your books. Are you working on another?"

"My agent thinks so."

They moved slowly down the hallway, noisy with hurrying students, to the elevator. Tyler worked to draw breath. "The obligation of teaching a class gives me an excuse for a lack of progress that my editor is polite enough to accept."

"I met with your daughter."

"She mentioned it." Tyler gave Cusack a sidelong look.

"I've been out of school a long time."

"That's not a drawback, in my opinion. Some life experience could help in appreciating these guys."

"I think it's their hostility to systems that I find appealing." Cusack thought his awkward student role was working pretty well. "Do you ever teach a class on your own works?"

"Yes, I did once and nobody enjoyed it."

They stepped onto a crowded elevator and rode down. Cusack didn't like having anyone behind him. Someone bumped him and he flinched high up in his gut. He realized he wasn't over some things and he didn't like it. Outside, Tyler put the oxygen mask to his face for a minute while Cusack stood awkwardly nearby. After a minute Tyler took the mask off and hooked it to the handle on the cart.

"I'm fine. You can go."

Cusack nodded and turned away. He wondered what had happened in the elevator full of harmless college kids. He recalled how the counselor responded when he said he was getting past it. "It doesn't seem like you are.

*To want to be perfectly free is to want to
be someone else.*

# Chapter 8

At the time of the bombing, Saint-Georges was a college town of 50,000 set on a curve of the Saint-Georges River a half-mile from the Pacific Ocean. Fishing was the business of the early settlers who'd come west lured by the California Gold Rush. After fruitless years scrambling after rumored gold in the mountains east of San Francisco, they looked for a more dependable sort of income and headed north. For generations it had come from the sea. By the 1980s, however, overfishing by Americans, then the Koreans with their deep-sea vacuum cleaner systems, finished off the business for good.

By the time the Koreans showed up, the town had been diversifying for years. Town leaders had been, unlike leaders in many other places, vigilant about the future and had tried to get out of the way. The town had promoted a mix of businesses - light manufacturing, retail and tourism. However, Western Oregon University and its research facility, located on the north side of the river across from downtown, had become the city's biggest employer.

Cusack's assignment was to play minder for Louis Minette, the undersecretary in the Emergency Response Division of the U.S. Department of Health and Human Services. It was the short straw: bodyguard was the worst assignment on the agency's list. Cusack was only going through the motions for Minette but even that, he figured, was more protection than he needed.

Cusack arrived in town the day before Minette and checked out their rooms at the Harrington Arms Hotel. He did an electronic sweep of Minette's room looking for bugs, talked to hotel security and the city's deputy police chief. The hotel was an antique but had an attentive staff. On schedule, Cusack collected Minette at the Saint-Georges airport, located on the high bluffs across the river east of town.

Minette was chatty from the back seat. "This is big. This facility will be doing very important work in disease prevention and control. Applications both civilian and military. Fantastic technology."

Cusack nodded and turned on the radio. The reception was poor and he played with the channel selector. The drive into town was slow going; heavy fog had come in early and the sun had been too weak to burn it off. The airport road ran mostly along the river and the fog shifted across it. He rolled the window down and a cool mist settled on his face. He squinted into the swirls of white. In the face of indifferent nature, Cusack was philosophical. No point in getting annoyed about fog when the entire assignment was a penance.

"The flight in was ridiculous," said Minette. "I have my security pass so I got right through check-in but there was some disturbance with a couple of the passengers so we were delayed a good forty-five minutes. I think they ended up knocking them off the flight."

Cusack yawned and lit a cigarette.

"Would you put that out?" asked Minette.

Cusack took one more draw and tossed the cigarette out the window. Minette opened his briefcase and began to read from a file. Cusack recalled what he'd read on the flight from Baltimore about Western Oregon U. It had long-standing relationships with several large public health research hospitals in the Northwest. The research facility was awarded to Western Oregon, in part, because a large pharmaceutical and medical supply corporation named DSM Inc. put up half the construction money. The rest came from the U.S. Departments of Health and Human Services and Defense. It was a lucrative package for the university: construction of a new state-of-the-art facility and operational funding for three years with additional funding possible. The strings attached were not usually examined too closely. Money, in Cusack's experience, trumped an awful lot of ethical quibbles.

Car lights appeared suddenly out of the fog and Cusack tensed and tapped the brakes.

"Hey, can you pick up the pace here?" said Minette without looking up from his file. "I'd like to get a shower in before I go to the college."

Cusack swallowed several words and pressed slightly on the accelerator, then after a minute, eased up again. The centerline was invisible, and although there was a guard rail, he didn't want to test it. He was not going to risk death for this self-important putz. The road turned away from the river, then back again to the bluff at that point, high above the river. Suddenly, the lights of the city appeared spread out along the curve of the river. The fog swallowed everything again as the car descended steeply toward the bridge. Cusack speeded up again when they crossed the bridge whose lights were haloed in the fog.

Cusack had complained about his assignment to his boss, Arthur Rupp. Rupp told Cusack to enjoy himself, that the assignment was more like a vacation. "Go to the beach. That part of the Pacific coast is spectacular and the asshole will be in meetings at the college all the time anyway. Just get him back and forth from hotel to college to airport. That's it."

Before Minette's scheduled arrival, Cusack wandered around the event venue. The college buildings were built in the fifties and sixties in a mess of architectural styles. At the administrative office he had to wait an hour to meet college security staff. They told Cusack there had been no recent security incidents and background checks on student activists produced unexceptional results.

The buildings of the research facility were newer, all three-story blocks of red brick separated from the college by 300 yards of lawn and a high fence. At the facility, Cusack spoke to the director of security who told him a six-member team from Cusack's agency had been there for three days performing a security review before the facility became fully operational. The team leader was someone named Parsons.

Arriving downtown with Minette, Cusack wheeled the car into the parking ramp next door to the Harrington Arms and escorted Minette into the hotel. He waited in the lobby while Minette unpacked, showered and changed clothes. Cusack took a position on a sofa in the lobby, which allowed him to see the front door, the front desk and the elevators. Just going through the motions.

After ten minutes on the sofa, he stepped outside, stood under the awning and smoked a cigarette. The fog had cleared off and the sky was brilliant blue but clouds were stacking up to the west. Across the street was a three-story building, the first floor occupied by a Vietnamese fast food restaurant, a copy shop, a drugstore and a travel agency.

Cusack was disgusted with himself. The assignment was a warning and a punishment for a foolish lapse of judgment on his part. Rupp was not a bad guy but he wasn't going to take a hit because Cusack couldn't keep his mouth shut. The good soldier, Rupp had said, is the soldier without questions.

Cusack wondered what Rupp would have for him after this assignment when he returned to Baltimore. Cusack pitched his cigarette into the gutter and Minette appeared in the lobby wearing a suit of deep blue and a white shirt that glowed. Cusack drove him to the research facility in silence where a uniformed guard relieved Cusack of responsibility for him. As he walked away, Minette told Cusack to return in two hours to collect him. Cusack found a coffee shop a few blocks away. He inventoried the customers, most of whom looked like students, and scooped up a copy of the International Herald Tribune. What drew his attention was a front page article about the ethnic Kurds in Turkey, the subject of the protest he and Parsons had witnessed in Vienna. It mentioned that European protests had drawn the world's attention to the conflict.

Cusack had, in his career as a watcher, become expert in killing time. It was a profession that demanded such a skill. He folded the paper carefully and read steadily and when he was finished, walked around the neighborhood, noted the location of an all-night drugstore, a twenty-four hour clinic and the police station. After that he drove back to the research facility.

Allowed in the front door, he made no effort to get beyond the security station, which was manned by two young men in gray uniforms with yellow epaulets. They strained at the effort to appear tough and settled for the mannerisms of Hollywood hard men. Cusack dropped onto a sofa and flipped through an old Sports Illustrated. Minette finally appeared in the lobby accompanied by a young woman. They smiled at each other until Cusack joined them when Minette shook hands with her and said goodbye. Cusack took Minette to the hotel and stayed with him all the way to his room.

"I'm next door," said Cusack. "Here's my cell phone number. Put it on your speed dial."

"I'm fine," said Minette. "Go get dinner or whatever."

"There are a couple restaurants on the first floor," said Cusack. "I'll be in one of them."

Cusack picked the restaurant he thought Minette would not choose. It was the Blue Tulip, written in an iridescent blue script next to the entrance. It occupied a single small room and offered a limited menu. The young woman who seated him gave him a pitying smile. Alone at dinner. She had a generic prettiness, the forgettable, regular features of a magazine cover and he smiled back, returning the pity.

He ordered a bowl of white chicken chili that came with a small baguette and coffee and milk. He was finishing his second cup of coffee when Minette appeared in the doorway of the restaurant and crooked his finger. Cusack put a ten-dollar bill on the table and walked Minette to the car.

Cusack drove Minette this time to the president's house, which had a large sloping lawn, a view of the river and a wide sweep of the valley. Minette didn't speak during the ride but looked at page after page from a file on his lap.

Cusack drove the car onto the graveled driveway in front of the president's house. The moon, gigantic and yellow, cast an arbitrary light, making some things sharply visible and dismissing the rest into an atmospheric darkness. It made him feel vague and cut off from the center of things. Everything he was doing seemed pointless and yet he felt only resignation. It didn't amount to a philosophy. It was one of those moments when he couldn't get the work in front of him, couldn't make it significant.

"Wait here," was all Minette said as he stepped out of the car.

Cusack cracked all four windows and smoked. He craved more coffee and, as if by magic, a young woman came out of the house with a sandwich and a mug of coffee.

"This is very thoughtful of you," said Cusack.

"You're welcome."

"I'm greedy, though. I could use something to read. Any chance of a newspaper?"

"Just the local."

"Anything."

A little later the woman brought out a copy of the Saint-Georges Sentinel and a second cup of coffee. Cusack pointed at the coffee and said, "And she's psychic, too." By the time Minette appeared, he had read the entire paper twice. The school board had a controversial new member arguing for the teaching of intelligent design in the science classroom. The mayor and the city council were at odds over allowing a big box retail store inside the city limits.

After returning Minette safely to his room, Cusack adjourned to the bar at the top of the hotel and ordered a bourbon and ice. One wall of the bar was all glass and the view encompassed the bluffs and the bridge he and Minette had crossed on their way in from the airport. He found scraps of the Los Angeles Times. Better than nothing. He'd worked his way through a second bourbon when a woman asked if she could look at his newspaper. He waved it away.

After a minute perusing the paper, she asked, "Here for the conference?"

"Yes."

"You a presenter?"

"No."

"Not a talker, huh?"

Cusack looked at the woman again and realized he hadn't been with a woman for four months and hadn't been involved with anyone for nearly three years. He had gotten into the habit of not wanting and, as a habit, it was progressive and intensifying. He felt a twinge, something like loneliness, and smiled at her.

The woman was looking at him with her head tilted to one side.

"You think I'm drunk?"

"No." Cusack wasn't sure he wanted company but he wasn't sure he didn't. Time would tell. He was distanced from any urgency and that made decision-making an untroubled exercise. He sometimes thought this quality was what women found attractive in him. "Are you here for the conference?" he asked.

"My name is Kristen Pedersen. I work at the college."

"I'm Seth Cusack. I'm here with the Department of Health and Human Services undersecretary." Cusack saw no reason to lie about his assignment; there was nothing secret about Minette's presence.

She smiled. "What is someone who works for an undersecretary?"

"Someone at the bottom of a very short stack," said Cusack.

She asked him a series of questions in a tone that reminded him of a job interview. To those question he responded with thick slices of autobiography, mostly lies. He let himself go, inventing extravagant things just to see how they sounded. He stitched his family into it and turned them into the freak show that he sometimes wished they had been. He thought the extravagant details gave the whole thing a gloss of plausibility. He was pleased with the sum of it and imagined it was how a short story was written.

To one of her questions, Cusack admitted he hadn't completed college and asked her opinion of the university, as if he might be interested in attending. He'd been at the agency for twenty years and it was then that he realized he was interested in returning to school. Unintentional self-revelation. Surprise.

"How do you like your undersecretary?"

"I just met him."

She had by then finished a second drink and was getting quieter. In response to his question, she gave the university a passing grade but advised against taking any classes from her husband. Cusack could see the outline of trouble there and dropped the subject. She asked him how long he was going to be in town and he told her just the one night.

"Do you have a room here?"

"Yes."

She held his eyes for a moment, then said, "Let's go."

He left money for the bill.

After she left the room, Cusack lay staring at the ceiling. The intense sex exhausted him and he was grateful for that. Still, her commentary about her husband was part of an unnecessary drama.

Cusack would be back in Baltimore in twenty-four hours and he wanted no part of any complication. He thought about that and wondered if he was losing all sense of proportion. No one he knew lived like he did. They operated in a field of options that he could barely acknowledge let alone consider. They made calculations that never occurred to him. For him, things happened, he made choices and after that things fell out a certain way and then he made more choices. That was it. He showered, poured himself a drink and went to sleep.

The next day, Cusack took Minette to the college and was told to be back at three to drive him to the airport. With time on his hands, Cusack reconsidered his earlier indecision, called Pedersen at her office and asked her to lunch. He would drive. She suggested one of the restaurants on the plaza in the center of town. He thought he'd be nice. A lunch by itself, self-contained, no expectations. He picked her up at the college and headed for downtown.

"No sex, today, I'm afraid," she said with a brittle smile.

"Mmmmm."

"Disappointed?"

Cusack had no clever answer, no charming come-back. "Yes," he said but he'd waited too long.

"I can sure pick 'em."

"What kind of restaurant are we going to?" There was no percentage in a fight.

"It's called Chan's Italian Restaurant."

"That's a hybrid I've missed," he said.

Cusack stopped at a corner and looked onto the plaza, a broad open cobblestoned area surrounded on three sides by stores, restaurants and bars. "I don't see any open spots. Why don't you go get us a table and I'll park the car."

Restaurants fronting the plaza all had tables on a broad common dining area. She stepped out and he drove the car to a parking spot a block away. He returned to the plaza and spotted her under the sign for Chan's Italian Restaurant carrying a glass of wine in her hand. Cusack went inside to the bar, returned with a bourbon on ice and took the chair on the opposite side of the table.

"How long have you lived here?" he asked.

"Forever."

"That long?"

"Oh, hell, no reason to take it out on you." She gave him a half-smile. "You're just the guy I slept with. The prick I'm married to is the real problem."

"Are you edging toward a compliment?"

She laughed like she thought she wasn't supposed to laugh. "I don't know you well enough for that." She emptied her glass.

The waitress brought menus and Pedersen ordered a half-bottle of wine.

"How did you get this assignment?" she asked.

"Bad luck."

"Washington D.C. must be an exciting place to work." She seemed to want something from him but Cusack was just killing time. They'd slept together by mutual consent. Gratitude didn't enter into it, though on some level, he thought he owed her this.

"Not really," he said. "Everyone is always taking an angle. It makes you think things are being kept from you."

"Maybe that's what they want you to think."

"Yeah, I suppose so."

There was a minute of silence until the waitress reappeared to take their orders.

"You know, I don't think you're a chauffeur," she said.

"Everything is more complicated than it appears." He lit a cigarette.

"I'll bet." She looked across the plaza as if she expected to see someone she knew.

"You aren't really a driver, are you?"

"Why not?" Cusack thought it was a self-esteem question. She didn't want to think of herself as someone who had casual sex with a chauffeur.

"Something about the way you move, the way you look at everything. Are you an ex-cop, FBI?"

Cusack was impressed. "I used to be a researcher."

She nodded.

He poured half his drink down his throat and felt immediately better. He thought about what Minette might be getting up to just then but felt not the slightest flutter of worry. Remembering the woman he'd seen Minette with at the research facility, he guessed the only one who'd want to kill Minette was his wife.

"Do you think it matters whether you're happy or not?" Pedersen asked.

"I never think about it."

"Then you must be pretty happy."

"It just doesn't come up."

"I wish I could be like that."

She tossed off what was left in her glass. The sun was bright, the air was stoked, and she stood to shrug off her small waist-length jacket then looked around for the waitress. "How long does it take to get a drink around here?"

Cusack thought that pity was what he ought to feel but he couldn't entertain it. "She sees you."

Pedersen sat again, brushed off her skirt and took a deep breath. "Maybe this wasn't such a good idea."

She was talking more or less to herself. For Cusack, it was okay. She was working through something and he was just a presence, someone to talk to. The waitress brought the wine then and Cusack declined another drink. They said nothing for a few minutes and then the waitress delivered their meals.

Pedersen had ordered a complicated salad. She took occasional stabs at it between visits to the wine. Cusack had ordered haddock and ate greedily. He realized there would be nothing on the plane back to Baltimore and considered getting a sandwich to go. Had to be better than anything available at the airport. The waitress fussed around Cusack's table before hitting her other tables and returning to the kitchen. Cusack and Pedersen continued to eat steadily in silence.

Cusack finished the haddock, chewed the last bit of the hard roll and washed it down with a sip of water. Most of the tables in the dining area were occupied and there was a steady buzz of conversation. Cusack looked to the south where the windows of high-rise apartment buildings were molten with sunlight. "Are you finished?" Cusack pointed at Pedersen's plate.

"In a hurry?" She put her fork across the plate and looked out across the plaza.

"I have to take the undersecretary to the airport."

"So you're leaving now?"

"Fortunately, we're on different flights. He's kind of a pain in the ass."

"I know the type."

He stood up. "I'll get the car." He walked out of the plaza. When he reached his car, he unlocked the door, turned and saw a brown cargo van turn onto the plaza. It seemed to be heading toward the tables at Chan's and picking up speed.

The van disappeared into a brilliant orange and yellow flash and Cusack could see nothing. Then he was blown off his feet and everything went black. When he came around he struggled onto his hands and knees, grabbed the car's mirror and pulled himself up until he felt able to stand.

He was faced away from the plaza, looking down a long, empty street. There was a ringing in his head and when he put his hand to his head, it came away bloody. He looked down to see if there was any other damage, then turned toward the plaza but it was as if he was fighting the force of several Gs like an astronaut at liftoff.

Fire roared a hundred feet into the air. Cars were on fire and debris floated in the air as if tossed there by a parade crowd run amok. Fiery streamers drifted in the air and settled slowly to the ground. Thick white smoke blocked his view for a moment and he moved uncertainly toward the plaza. The air was hot and smelled of burnt metal. When the air cleared he saw a chair from the dining area on the roof of a car and, with fire pouring out from under the engine, it looked like a float from a Fourth of July parade. People were running in his direction their faces streaming with blood but he didn't recognize Pedersen among them. The man leading the group was on fire and swatted at the air around him before falling to the ground.

Finally reaching the plaza he saw two bodies on the ground. The first was a man, his shirt blown off and the skin on his back roasted pink and charcoal black. The exploded sheet metal of the van had acted like shrapnel. Pieces were embedded in his back and legs. The second body was of a woman lying on her back whose white hair appeared perfectly coifed and with her forearm raised as if she were blown up at the exact moment she'd gestured to the waitress for the check.

Cusack started having trouble breathing, bent over and put his hands on his knees. He felt nauseous but it was stupid to be sick. He straightened up and realized he could hear nothing. To his left, a storefront window blew out and brilliant yellow and orange flames billowed. He turned quickly and felt as if something had gone off in his head. He staggered and caught himself on a piece of railing.

One of the cars that was on fire exploded silently, its rear end lifting a bit off the ground. He was approaching the place where the restaurant tables had been when a second explosion knocked him down. A gas pipe had been shaken loose from the first explosion and the gas buildup was swift in one of the buildings fronting the plaza. The explosion blew out the walls and the roof pancaked into the basement. These precise details were provided later to Cusack by newspaper accounts. In the hospital he had time to read all the newspapers.

Cusack nearly stepped into a crater ten feet across and four feet wide. Smoke. Silence. Not quite silence. A continuous hum.

Someone grabbed Cusack's arm and pulled him along. There were small fires everywhere on the plaza. With several other men, Cusack helped lift wreckage off people on the ground. He stepped away for a moment and took several breaths but couldn't drag enough air into his lungs. When he knelt down, he saw Pedersen's jacket wadded up under a piece of concrete. He was suffocating then and when he put his hand on a chunk of concrete, it burned him. Then he really couldn't breathe and passed out.

He remembered the ambulance ride and the emergency room, the fussing, hands everywhere, the silent mouthing of unknown words. They pumped sleep into his arm and he awoke the next day to a different world.

# Part II

*To see and not understand is perfect serenity.*
*To will oneself against the automatic actions of*
*the mind is real freedom.*

# Chapter I

After leaving Tyler outside Ford Hall, Cusack walked up the quad, and passed the Boland Administration Building with its statue of Arthur Boland out front, his right arm fully extended forever making some point in a long-forgotten argument. Cusack passed a row of shrubs still green and a parking ramp on his right that blocked the sun. He came around the end of the ramp and crossed the street. In the next block there was an art supply store, a sports bar, a Vietnamese restaurant and a cookie shop.

Cusack continued down the street thinking of Tyler and Parsons' interest in him. There was something not right about it. Parsons wanted a score and he seemed to think the daughter, Lauren, could make it happen. Saint-Georges put a stain on Parsons' record but Cusack wondered if anything the Tylers had could help. Parsons' ambition looked like desperation and that just bent your judgment. There was something else, too, about the current version of Parsons that made Cusack reluctant. It was the way he saw things, chose what he saw in a way that left too many things to one side. Cusack figured that way of seeing was all motivation and no second-guessing. There was no arguing that it produced results if you didn't get killed very early in the day. You and everyone around you.

Like others Cusack had known, though of lesser abilities, Parsons could have used some fundamental consequences in his life to help him see what was necessary and what was just optional. That was always the problem in the lives of people like Parsons. An absence of fundamental consequences.

Even after Saint-Georges, Parsons kept his title though he was moved off certain kinds of projects. News of the fallout from Saint-Georges passed through the agency and followed Parsons from assignment to assignment. Parsons' possible promotion to director was no longer a subject of speculation. Cusack wasn't sure what Parsons' exact role at Saint-Georges had been but he recalled that the research facility director told him of a security check that Parsons ran just days before the bombing. His failure to pick up on the bombers must have been why he took a hit when the town blew up. After his own recovery, Cusack was reluctant to revisit the incident in any detail and no one in the agency was forthcoming on the subject. Now, that history seemed to have some immediate relevance and Cusack could see value in a look back.

Cusack shifted his bag from his right hand to his left. A group of runners from the college stampeded by and he flinched. The noise of a passing truck had covered the sound of their approach. He took a breath and watched them race on to the next block before turning a corner.

First in the elevator, now in the street. This was new. It was the bite of panic that came out of nowhere just before you were lifted out of a hot zone, the fear of being the last one taken down, of just missing getting out safe. It was a long time, not even at Saint-Georges, since he had felt that undisciplined. He was beginning to think that Saint-Georges had been a point of departure for him. He just wasn't sure what that meant.

He thought it would reveal itself to him in time. Maybe that was what the counselor, in her own way, had been trying to get him to see. Maybe he shouldn't have been so hard on her. Thinking about Saint Georges, he considered all the winners and losers. First, there were all those dead and maimed to be considered. The dead had, of course, gained the advantage of a dubious afterlife. The maimed had their scars and, presumably, a check from their insurers. The medical research and supply corporation, DSM, which had pumped a load of money into the research facility at the college, must have lost some traction. The bombers emulated celebrities where any publicity was good publicity. They had killed nine people and planted terror in others. Their return on investment involved a calculation of profit that worked in no other business model on earth. Finally, for the people in the security business, Cusack's business, there were more lucrative contracts, more anti-terror.

Catastrophes almost always had their upside for someone; it was just a matter of perspective. It was a shitty point of view but there it was. Distance in time or space flattened out the location of things until the urgency was gone and everything could be seen for what it was, or for what someone wanted it to be. Those usually immune from consequence, like Parsons, were often fans of the long view.

It was bad luck, not catastrophe which resulted in his bodyguard assignment to Saint-Georges. Cusack was involved in an incident at an agency party at a fashionable Washington, D.C. hotel. An agency project in Panama for the U.S. Department of Defense had been concluded successfully and the agency's principal on the project, a man named Clayton Straub, said something smug about it and Cusack, half-lit, said, "You were the party planner for that? What was the round-up, eighty-two dead civilians, more or less? Kudos all the way around."

Straub sneered something and Cusack stepped in close to emphasis his point but others crowded around and Straub and Cusack were led to different ends of the room. Even though it happened off the job, Cusack was convinced it made it into his personnel file. It accounted for certain facts. His original assignment was canceled but there was no lecture from his boss Arthur Rupp. Cusack thought he had worked for the agency too long for it to result in any formal action but the bodyguard assignment was a clear message from management.

Cusack walked into the lobby of his building and took the elevator to the fourth floor. He showered, put on jeans, a white shirt and a blue and red striped tie. He was going to scout the Moravia Hotel bar before the meeting with Parsons.

The Moravia Hotel bar occupied the top floor of a former warehouse and office building of the old Keillor Flour Company situated on the Mississippi River waterfront. The elegant facade of light gray slate stonework and tall, narrow windows was complemented inside by highly polished, wide-plank floors and narrow stone columns. Across a thin strip of the river from the Moravia was Donnelly Island, whose nineteenth century factory worker row houses had been converted into upscale condominiums. A marina for luxury boats was built where barge traffic had originally docked to collect wheat and iron ore. Now it was all high-powered cigarette boats and two-story luxury cruisers. Upstream, more boats, just offshore, bobbed at anchor. A refurbished wooden-beamed bridge connected the island to the rest of the city.

It took him fifteen minutes to find his way to the Moravia. Standing in the entrance, he could see into the bar to the left. On the right wall were booths. Small round tables filled the center. The bar which had a polished brass rail was on the left and ran the length of the room. Through the windows straight ahead, Cusack could see lights on the river.

Cusack ordered a drink and carried it while he walked around. He took note of all the exits and checked out the men's room. A door in the near corner appeared to lead to the basement. He sat at a table near a window while he finished his drink.

On his return from the Moravia, he stopped at a drive-in espresso shop on University Avenue, collected a cappuccino, and parked two blocks from his place. He pried the top off his cup and drank. There was little traffic and few people on the street. He finished half the coffee, re-capped it and stepped out of his car. He ducked into the alley next to his place and climbed the three flights of stairs to his rooms. At the top landing he saw that his door was narrowly open. The pistol was in the belly drawer of the worktable. It was stupid to have a gun and not carry it. He toed open the door and stepped inside.

"Come in. Come in," said Parsons from across the room.

Cusack closed and bolted the door. Parsons was sitting on the leather wingback chair with his legs crossed at the knee, reading a book and sipping a glass of white wine. The bottle, chilled and dewy, was on the floor by his feet.

This visit, Cusack realized, was how Parsons had to respond to Cusack's demand that he not return. Parsons had to enter Cusack's place uninvited, make himself comfortable, leave the front door open. He had to talk to Cusack as if Cusack were a guest. It was a management style.

Cusack looked at him for a moment, then walked to the worktable, put down the coffee and opened the drawer. The pistol was there, in its holster. Cusack closed the drawer, pried the top off the cup and drank.

"How's school?"

Cusack looked over Parsons' head through the window at the

dark top of trees in the Washburn Redevelopment Area. "I sat through a lecture and a brief history and summary of the worldview of a modern philosopher. What would you like to know about him?" Cusack dumped the rest of the coffee into the sink and pitched the cup into the wastebasket. He took a mug from the cupboard and picked up Parsons' bottle. The label had a white unicorn standing on its hind legs. Cusack poured a healthy slug into the mug, drained it and tipped in more.

Parsons rose from his chair and walked to the windows that looked down on University Avenue. Taller than Cusack, he had to tip the window to get a clear view of the street below. He looked at the street then turned around and leaned against the window frame. His face was lined, gray stubble on his chin. He wore a long black coat, black pants and a black shirt and he looked, appropriately enough, the part of a dissolute cleric, a man of faith whose faith, Cusack was pretty sure, had lapsed.

"I walked around the area before coming up." He pointed at the Washburn with his thumb and licked his lips. "It looks like someone dropped a bomb." He took out a cigarette. "And should have dropped a few more."

"The real estate people call it a transitional neighborhood."

"I'll bet they do." He lit the cigarette. "Doesn't it remind you of Sarajevo?"

"People live in those buildings."

"Of course they do. People will live anywhere."

"Are you worried about them?" Parsons might know what he, Cusack, knew. He liked games, an insight into Parsons' character that had come to Cusack suddenly.

"It's just a situation." He drew on the cigarette and blew smoke straight up. "If you look at them, you can see they can't be taken seriously. They're incapable of coherence." Parsons liked theories;

they seemed to please him.

"You don't think people with nothing to lose can be dangerous?"

"People with nothing to lose are nothing." Parsons looked at the mug in Cusack's hand as if it held something distasteful to him.

"And Tyler?"

"The agency has business here. We're working with the mayor and the state Bureau of Criminal Apprehension on the Washburn."

Cusack said nothing.

"DSM and the agency are consulting," Parsons continued. "We're looking for more but the mayor is reluctant. He thinks he can negotiate his way out of this."

"What's Tyler's connection?"

"The good news is the deputy mayor is on our side."

"Divide and conquer."

"We're fighting tradition here, the mayor's attachment to negotiation. He's a politician, after all. And the BCA – old-style cops. They don't understand that the other side knows all their tactics and how to beat them." Parsons no longer appeared to be talking to Cusack but to some inner audience.

"And Tyler?" said Cusack. Tyler was Cusack's assignment. He didn't want to hear about the big picture unless Tyler was in it.

"Tomorrow night at nine. The Moravia Hotel, second floor bar." Parsons looked away, worried his lower lip with his upper teeth. "I'll have some information for you then. Maybe you'll have something for me."

"What about my study schedule?"

"The daughter," Parsons continued as if Cusack hadn't spoken. "You've seen her twice now, right? The visit to the office and the mall?" He took another drag on the cigarette and pointed the smoke out the window. "What's your take on her?"

Cusack resented the question and wondered why. "She's not

an easy read. When I met her in Tyler's office, she had a book on palm reading for her daughter's school festival. She was going to play the gypsy psychic. She came off like a naif but ..." Cusack recalled her laugh.

Parsons pointed at Cusack's hand. "Why don't you show her that and have her tell you what it portends?"

Cusack looked at the burn scar and turned slow eyes toward Parsons. "Fuck you."

"Yes, well ... events, as they say, are in the saddle."

"Again?"

"There's a certain time pressure now." Parsons again blew smoke at the ceiling.

Cusack took his time absorbing the implication. Was the squatter problem coming to a head? "What could that be?"

"Tyler is a sick man. It's now or never."

Parsons was hiding something, a linkage of some sort but Cusack couldn't be sure what it was. "Out in the mall at the bookstore, there was a guy watching me. One of yours?"

Parsons tilted his head as if he'd heard a sound through the open window that he couldn't quite identify. "I know all about your paranoia." He finished the cigarette and tossed it out the window. "No one is watching you."

"I bumped into Tyler's daughter there, you know." Cusack smiled. "Maybe she's running a network."

Parsons ignored the sarcasm. He seemed intent on conveying a lesson of some sort. "The daughter matters here. Some people don't know what they know. They need to be moved toward that knowledge."

"Is that supposed to mean something to me?"

Parsons turned to look at the building across 4th Street. "Saint-Georges was a disaster for the agency. We've been taking a beating in the media all the way back to Senegal. Tyler's had a part in that. And then Saint-Georges gave the wrong people an excuse to continue what they began with Senegal."

The wrong people were people like Tyler. Parsons was talking about villages near Matam in northern Senegal where Cusack had gone down in a helicopter. "I'm getting interested in what happened at Matam again," said Cusack. "Six years but I'm finally ready for some answers."

Parsons had his own read of Cusack's remark. "I've been sidelined since Matam and I want back in. This is our chance for that."

An unknown number of people, though estimated at two hundred twenty, had died near Matam. Nine people died and dozens were injured at Saint-Georges and somehow Parsons' stalled career was the disaster. Cusack resisted saying anything, refilled his mug again and joined Parsons at the window.

"Your mall-watcher," said Parsons, "what did he look like?"

"Like everybody. Like nobody. Like they're supposed to look."

Parsons shook out another cigarette and appeared not to hear Cusack or not to be listening, as if the question had been raised only to appease Cusack. He took his time lighting the cigarette.

Cusack didn't appreciate being strung out on a job. Saint-Georges had made him put a lot of things to one side. It made him reluctant, for one thing, which was as dangerous as enthusiasm. His recent brush with Pascal had reminded him that the Catholic Church, too, was no fan of enthusiasm. It couldn't be monitored properly and that made prescribing it dangerous to the faith. The Church was a long way back in Cusack's history. He was no longer any kind of believer and danger for him was all in this world.

Cusack wasn't going to explain anything to Parsons. He wasn't paranoid and he didn't like the condescension. Cusack took another heavy slug from his mug. He was beginning to think that, under current circumstances, no matter what he said, it would be beside the point for Parsons, who heard only what he wanted to hear.

"Tell me about Saint-Georges," said Cusack. "I've got some distance now, so I'm curious."

"Anything in particular?" Parsons had always had a way of asking questions that took everything the long way around, like you were better off for seeing the landscape around the answer. In the end, it was self-indulgence, an insular event, a way of being content with any answer at all, or none.

"What was that research facility about? There was too much security for what they were pretending to be."

"People's idea of security can end up as big as their worries. The research facility work is still top-secret." Parsons wanted Cusack to know he wasn't entitled to an answer.

Cusack wasn't put off so easily. "Indulge me. I'm a lifelong learner."

Parsons picked a bit of tobacco off his lip. "They are working on delivery mechanisms." He seemed to want to say something very specific. "The public health people and DSM, the pharmaceutical company, wanted a better way of mass inoculation. Not just for the bird flu, for instance, but possible biological weapons attacks. We can spray pesticides on fields of corn, why not the same methodology for mass inoculations? Spray people on a shopping mall parking lot or a football field. Where and when an attack comes – we're not going to have a lot of warning."

"And the Defense Department?"

"Battlefield applications. If they knew the troops were going to be exposed to some toxic shit, it would be extremely valuable to be able to deliver a counter-agent to as many troops as possible as fast as possible. Spraying our own troops from the air in response to an attack would have been a tremendous breakthrough."

Cusack had a flash on what had gone wrong at Matam. He could see it, a helicopter coming in over the villages and letting loose some godawful shit. Not an inoculation. The wrong dosage maybe. The application fucked up. Something like that. And that was why, later, when Cusack and the Senegalese diplomat had arrived in a helicopter, it was shot down. "But the DoD people had to be thinking about offensive weapons applications, too. Right?"

"They had a neat little device designed for use in low-level insurgent situations. The scenario involved capture of a few insurgents. Implant a biological agent in a computer chip. Let them escape and track them. When they're back with their own people, activate the agent. No symptoms for a week while they're infecting everyone, then something that looked like flu only something that would completely incapacitate them. Everyone rounded up without a shot being fired. A brilliant concept but the technological barriers proved to be too much."

Cusack recalled the rumors he'd heard out of Senegal months after he'd returned to Baltimore. Technological barriers. Two hundred deaths.

Parsons exhaled and the smoke raced out the window. "I'm curious myself. What's in this for you after, what, twenty years? This ... watching?"

"Field work?" Cusack smiled. "I like it."

"The excitement?" Parsons waved dismissively at the room.

Cusack had a sudden impulse to punch Parsons in the face. Flatten his nose, see a nice spray of blood. Cusack didn't get violent impulses so much anymore. He had learned to substitute control for violence. He saw it as a progressive development, a sign that he was becoming more civilized. That was the difference, wasn't it, between civilization and all other cultural experiments? It was like that bumper sticker, Chose Hope, the one he'd seen the other day in the mall parking lot. Chose Hope. Chose Control.

*The true dichotomy in the soul is not that
between truth and falsehood but that between
anguish and clarity.*

# Chapter 2

After Parsons left, Cusack went into the bathroom and swallowed two pain pills. A headache was coming on strong now, traveling up from the base of his skull, starting to bloom with giant petals of an excruciating darkness. It was a mistake to have waited so long to take the pills but he hadn't wanted to show weakness in front of Parsons.

After taking the pills, Cusack moved around the living room, dropped the blinds and turned off the lights. He lay on the bed and tried to think of nothing at all. He closed his eyes but he couldn't find the kind of pure, blank nothing that he wanted. There was, instead a constant flicker behind his eyelids of moments without coherence. There was violence, usually seen after the fact and pain in the present. Finally, he opened his eyes and stared at the ceiling. After a time the pressure on his eyes, so extraordinary at first that he felt they would be pushed out of their sockets, began to recede.

He gave himself another twenty minutes before rising from his bed. He shuffled to the sink and poured a large glass of water from the tap as cold as he could get it. He emptied the glass standing at the sink, and paced the room. The more he knew, the less he liked his options. He felt himself getting sucked into an untenable situation and tried to think of what would get him out. Looking for angles had gotten him here in the first place. Finally, tired of his thoughts and the four walls of the condominium, he collected his keys and his jacket and walked out. At the college library he showed his student id and signed up for a computer terminal.

He sat for several minutes staring at the screen before beginning his search request. A dozen years after his discharge from the army and several weeks into his stay at his father's house he borrowed his father's car and drove to Eau Claire. In the main library, he read about the war.

He'd been deep inside the war but that wasn't enough; he wanted to know it from the outside. Understanding, after all, was just perspective. He read stories of American and Iraqi families. The Americans from Dubuque and Oakland and Buffalo, proud of their husbands and daughters. Iraqis from Mosul or Basra, fearful, grieving, defiant. There were photographs, too, a cascade of images: Americans saluting caskets, widows receiving the folded flag, Iraqi women wailing, plucking at their clothes, bodies wrapped in sheets in front of them; Iraqi children of various ages, their faces blank, eyes fixed on some blasted inner world.

A majority of the articles in magazines expressed support of the war. An absolute necessity. Rule of law. The critical importance of national sovereignty. A tyrant defeated or at least, caged. There were anecdotes about Iraqi atrocities in Kuwait, later debunked as war propaganda.

Now, a dozen years later he was searching for information about the incident of the helicopter crash in Senegal that nearly killed him.

It had been newsworthy at the time because a Senegalese diplomat had died in the crash. There were column inches on it here and there in various newspapers and magazines but they dealt mostly with the death of the diplomat. Other pieces about the reported deaths of civilians in the villages around Matam appeared weeks or months later and mostly in the foreign press. They all mentioned the government's refusal to allow an independent investigation.

After recovering from his own injuries in the crash, Cusack let the incident remain a jumble of moments, unprocessed. No one in the agency wanted to talk about it much either. Over time, he'd let it become a piece of work gone bad, something to be filed away under experience. Now, it needed to be brought forward and hooked up. He thought he needed it so he could work the job in front of him.

Additional searches brought up stories of Tyler's lashing out at the CIA for the death of his son-in-law and Philippe Ogbemudia's charge of U.S. collusion in war crimes at Matam. The articles contained insufficient detail. Other articles included photographs from a French news service photographer who'd sneaked into the area. There were dozens of bodies laid out near a collection of huts. However, the date, location, and cause of death could not be independently verified because only the Senegalese Army had access to the area. For months after Philippe's accusations, rumors circulated about those killed in the villages east of Matam. As Cusack moved forward chronologically through the files, interest in the story and reporting on it petered out.

Cusack logged off, found his car and, after a meandering half-hour drive, which included a pass through the college campus, ended up parked in front of Tyler's house.

There he switched off the car's lights but left the motor running. The badly tuned engine gave off a noticeable gasoline smell. It pleased him somehow, reminding him of trips when he was just a kid with his father in their old pickup to the lumberyard in the next town over. Home improvement projects that were begun enthusiastically enough but often were never quite completed..

The basement was full of half-empty cans of paint, recycled plastic containers full of screws and nails, a rack of tools that occupied half of one wall and stacks of leftover lumber. Evidence of his father's serial absorption in fix-up projects. For all his determined work, however, the house didn't look like those he saw now across the street.

On Tyler's street, the yellow, gauzy illumination produced by the streetlights was filtered through the trees and cast vague shadows all down the block. Cusack lit a cigarette, cracked the driver's side window and let the smoke race out. The only sound was crickets and there was in the whole setting, in its unguardedness, a nonchalant, unexpressed sense of permanence. Cusack, an outsider and locked in a pattern of drift, admired its weighted-down quality.

The drapes in Tyler's living room were wide open. The room was bright but showed no sign of an occupant. There were lights on in two rooms upstairs but again not a shadow of a soul anywhere. For a moment, Cusack wondered if he had the wrong address. He couldn't stay long. A strange car parked on a suburban street with the motor running would get a neighbor calling the cops pretty damn quick.

Tyler appeared suddenly on the other side of the street and at the far end of the block. His face was clearly visible although the street light gave his face a gray and sickly cast. He was moving slowly, drawn forward by a small black and white dog on an invisible leash. Tyler wore a long black coat and a hat with a brim. As he passed under another streetlight, his face was lit again and then fell into darkness.

Cusack eased his hand up onto the column and cut the engine. He shifted lower in his seat and cupped his hand around the cigarette. His eyes went back to the windows of the house. Lauren and the granddaughter must be inside. He took another drag on the cigarette and blew smoke toward his feet.

Tyler continued to move forward steadily, the dog not wandering as some did to investigate smells here and there. There must have been something better waiting in the house that pulled him along. Dog and master stopped in front of their house and Tyler bent over to mutter something to the dog and rub his head before they moved toward the front door, the dog now straining a bit at his leash.

The front door opened as if by remote control and light splashed onto the steps. Lauren was framed for a moment in the doorway with a mellow, caramel light around and behind her. Tyler let the leash go and the dog darted inside. Lauren said something to Tyler that Cusack couldn't hear, then stepped back as Tyler entered and closed the door.

Cusack tried to see something significant in what he was looking at. There was plenty of potential for treachery in the ordinary but he was having difficulty putting the Tylers in the box where Parsons wanted them to be. Cusack accepted the possibility of an organized lifetime deception. The British turncoats who stole the atomic bomb for the Soviets were one example. There was that American woman who lived for years as a housewife and mother, even acting in local theater and who was, in her youth, a member of the gang that kidnapped Patty Hearst. But the Tylers didn't look to be playing out that way and that meant Parsons might be holding out on him. That wouldn't be a surprise but it was a proposition with no useful center for Cusack.

He finished his cigarette and pitched it out the window. At the same moment, the passenger side door opened. Cusack turned and saw the mall-watcher step into the car.

"Tyler's got a nice dog, don't you think?" he said as he tugged at his trench coat. He said this as if they were long-time partners and had been sitting there for hours making small talk.

Even though Cusack didn't have his gun, he felt no anxiety. Something about the way the man leaned forward with his hands between his knees. "Russell terrier, don't you think?" said Cusack.

"Sure. Why not?" He gave Cusack a quick smile.

"You have a name?"

The man reached inside his jacket and produced a generic identification card that could have come from anywhere. "I'm a consultant to the State Bureau of Criminal Apprehension, F. Peter Storti."

It was no coincidence Cusack had pegged the guy for a peer when he'd seen him at the railing. Consultant. "What does the F stand for?"

"Let's go for a ride," Storti said, pointing straight ahead.

Cusack started the engine, put the car in gear and pulled away from the curb. "Any place in particular?"

"Just drive."

Cusack drove in a leisurely manner, taking lefts and rights with no specific intention. They left Tyler's neighborhood and passed along the edge of the campus. Lights on the quad showed students returning from or heading toward the library.

Cusack said, "What's your interest in Tyler?"

"We have an interest in the Washburn Redevelopment Area."

Cusack waited, paying close attention to his driving.

Storti continued, "The squatters are being moved out. The exact date and time is, as they say, yet to be determined. Unfortunately, the students don't appear to need much of a reason to stir up trouble."

"I'm just watching. I'm the Invisible Man."

"The Bureau received a communication saying that you guys, 'pursuant to national security interests,' were surveiling one W.S. Tyler, college professor. Sounds like someone is stirred up."

"We're gathering information. That's all." The silence stretched out while Cusack considered Storti's approach and exactly how much Parsons had left out of his briefings "We have no fixed ideas," Cusack added, thinking he'd throw a little Tyler language into the mix. The Bureau was sharing some high-level information with this consultant.

Storti abruptly changed the subject as if he'd committed himself to too much. "College towns make nice places to retire."

They passed under a street light and Cusack glanced at him. He was clean-shaven, had a large, square face, a small blunt nose, and straw-colored hair in tight curls. He was somewhere in his forties. He wore a black trench coat, the collar twisted up on one side. "It seems a little run-down to me," said Cusack, "more like an old mill town than a college town."

"Maybe higher education is a dying industry, too." Storti settled back in the seat, getting comfortable for a long story. "I grew up on the Iron Range in northern Minnesota. Towns dying right and left. High quality ore ran out but those people were hard to discourage. Taconite was going to save them, then China boomed. After every revival they ended with less than before." Storti stopped talking and stared out the window.

At a stop light Cusack punched the cigarette lighter and lit up. He thought of his father knocking around his house and waiting placidly for Wal-Mart to deliver the end. Discouragement just wasn't in some people's make-up.

"Been back there lately?" asked Cusack.

"Not in years. Too depressing."

"They say, you can't go home again."

"They say a lot of things," Storti said repeating Lauren's remark from earlier. "Let's go to your place."

A few minutes later Cusack was leading the way up the stairs. At the door to his place, Storti stepped back while Cusack worked the lock, letting Cusack know his intentions were benign.

Cusack marched across to the worktable while Storti closed the door and made his way to the easy chair.

"Have you talked to my boss?" asked Cusack.

"Parsons? Several times and I'm seeing him tomorrow."

"The Moravia?"

"How about a drink?" asked Storti.

Cusack poured out two large bourbons on ice and they sat by the windows, which were tilted out to let in a breeze. An indeterminate sour smell filtered in. The tallest buildings were all lighted as if to reassure. Cusack figured Storti was talking to him because Parsons had tried to keep his, Cusack's presence, secret and somehow Storti had found out.

"How long have you been watching the Tylers?" asked Storti.

Cusack looked out. There'd been a fat slice of moon above the Tyler's house when Tyler brought the dog home but by the time Cusack reached the condominium, the clouds had poured in, piling darkness on darkness. "A few days." Cusack saw no reason to lie.

"The Tylers don't look too dangerous to me." Storti sipped his drink. "Except for the daughter, maybe. You know what I mean?"

There was a discrete rumble of thunder; the sky trying to clear its throat without calling attention to itself. Fat drops of rain spotted the windows.

"You at the mall to watch me or the Tyler woman?" Cusack wanted to ferret out Storti's purpose and didn't figure he was going to volunteer much.

"Pure coincidence." Storti rattled the ice in his glass before taking another sip and offered Cusack a big grin. "I was shopping for a tie."

"Parsons bring you into this?" said Cusack. "Why?"

"What's Tyler done to get your people worked up?" asked Storti.

"He's a deep thinker." Cusack tossed off half his drink.

"That is annoying." Storti looked steadily at Cusack while inhaling the fragrance of his bourbon.

"Why aren't you housed with the rest of your agency people?"

"I'm special."

Parsons was holding something back, something significant. He wouldn't introduce complexity for no reason. The Washburn, Storti, the state police and Tyler were all connected somehow.

Storti held his glass out. "More?"

Cusack brought the bottle, tipped a couple inches into Storti's glass and put the bottle on the floor between them.

Pure coincidence, that was a good one. It wasn't Storti that bothered Cusack but Parsons. Was the Tyler assignment just a blind, a cover for some larger action?

*It is the shimmer of inebriation that we pursue, illusion by chemical or belief. Hangover is reality concentrate.*

# Chapter 3

Cusack arrived for his meeting at the Moravia a half-hour early. He wanted to see Parsons enter the bar and know who, besides Storti, entered with him. It was nothing special, a reflexive caution. He parked his car two blocks from the Moravia, locked up and walked by the restaurant entrance and onto the Donnelly Island Bridge. He leaned on the railing and made a routine of lighting and smoking a cigarette. Dark whirlpools in the channel gave him the creeps.

He shifted a few steps over to a spot under a bridge beam that blocked the streetlight and left him in deep shadow but with a clear view of the entrance to the parking lot, a half block away. He leaned back against the railing and observed passersby on both sides of the bridge. It was a minor task what he was doing but it soothed him. From where he stood it was possible to detect only the barest pulse of the city; it seemed a natural thing, as if the city were dozing.

On the island, a young woman pushing a stroller talked on a cell phone. Trailing the young woman was an older couple. The man had a thick white beard and was cutting the air with the blade of his hand as he talked. His companion was ignoring him. They passed out of range. Imitation Victorian gaslights lined the streets on the island. Two cars passed Cusack, a red Corvair convertible with its top down and a forty-year old Mercedes sedan. There was a noisy rumble as they passed over the bridge planks. Incomprehensible human chatter drifted down from a rooftop bar a block away.

He was feeling an edge now, an undisciplined anger rising. It was worse because he couldn't be sure who to be angry at. There were too many players. DSM and the city cops. The mayor and the squatters. Storti, too, was a complication which should have been anticipated, and something Parsons should have mentioned. And Tyler seemed to be about as dangerous as one of Santa's elves.

Parsons arrived at the Moravia in a nondescript Chrysler sedan. Parsons was in the habit of making statements and Cusack thought he would have come in a big Lexus, at the very least. He parked the car on the far side of the Moravia and a minute later walked in the front door. Cusack waited to see if anyone else of interest showed up.

Cusack lit a second cigarette and waited while two more cars entered the restaurant parking lot. It was a weeknight and business seemed a little scarce. Five minute passed, then two young couples, talking and laughing, went in. Cusack looked for a single man in a suit and tie, someone who resembled everybody and nobody. That would be Parsons' minder, if he had one.

Finally, when it was past the time for him to join Parsons and no minder had shown himself, Cusack wondered if he had lost his knack. Storti should have been inside but he'd gotten past Cusack somehow. He threw his cigarette into the river and strolled back across the bridge through light and shadow, the sound of his shoes loud on the planks. Inside the Moravia, he skirted a crowd waiting to be seated in the restaurant and climbed the stairs to the bar.

Parsons was seated at a table by the window. Storti sat to Parsons' immediate left and that was expected although he wondered again how Storti had slipped inside without being noticed. There was a third person at the table and Cusack held back to get a good look at her. She smiled at something Parsons said, showing off a lot of teeth. She had very dark skin and large eyes and she held a glass of red wine in her hand while she talked.

Cusack stepped quickly across the room and took the chair farthest from the window. He turned it slightly so he had a view of the bar's entrance. He'd lost the knack for sure - he'd missed the entrance of two of the three people at the table. Now, if anybody else was coming, he wanted to see them first.

Parsons introduced the woman to Cusack. "Christine Beaupre, this is Seth Cusack. Ms. Beaupre is the Deputy-mayor." They nodded at each other. "I believe that you've met Mr. Storti. He works for DSM."

Cusack settled a look on Storti. DSM had been in Senegal and worked under contract, like Cusack's agency, with the Senegalese government. There was a DSM employee on the helicopter that crashed. DSM was the corporation money behind the research facility at the college in Saint-Georges. A consultant to the BCA was how he'd identified himself. Not the whole truth and nothing but the truth.

A waiter, in black pants and a white shirt, appeared next to Cusack. "Sir, what may I get you?"

"A bottle of Newcastle and the opener."

"I'm sorry, I didn't catch that."

"I want a bottle of Newcastle and I want you to leave the cap on so I can open it myself."

The waiter betrayed no reaction to Cusack's request but only said, "Yes, sir," and turned back toward the bar.

Parsons sipped his martini and eyed a woman at the bar, a middle-aged brunette showing off a lot of thigh. Cusack took his eyes off Storti and examined the room. A buzz was in the air, impossible to identify beyond a techno-rhythmic beat, not loud enough to defeat conversation but appreciable at the brain stem. The crowd, such as it was, was mostly twenty-somethings, well-dressed and trying to spend their money well.

Finally, Parsons leaned toward Cusack and said quietly, "Maybe you thought this operation was not well-thought out. We came to some critical information unexpectedly and had to act quickly. You needed to get a feel for Tyler's life, thus the set-up across the street from his office. Somewhat unsophisticated but effective."

"When I get a feel for his life, what am I supposed to do with it?" Cusack didn't appreciate Parsons talking in front of outsiders of his doubts about the operation or Tyler. For Cusack, agency business was closed up.

The waiter returned, put the bottle of beer, a glass and the opener in front of Cusack. Cusack lit a cigarette and placed the spent match carefully in the ashtray near Parsons' hand.

"I've caught up with your reputation since we last worked together, Cusack. But we're going to play this as it lays."

"What's the link between Tyler and Saint-Georges?" This was important to Cusack. It went to the reason for being there.

"Nothing that absolute," Parsons appeared to relish the words as he spoke them. "Tyler hangs out with certain kinds of people and attracts a certain kind. That's his track record. So, we're looking to cast the net wider than the Tyler family. But evidence?" He looked away. "More like suggestions. Implications. Coincidences. Circumstantial parallels."

"Tyler looks like any old college professor," Cusack said in a tone as flat and bored as he could make it. "His media shot at the CIA over the death of his son-in-law was perfectly understandable."

Parsons considered his drink for a minute. "You've already made contact with the daughter. But we can't really call that work, can we?" He smiled at Beaupre and Storti.

"This set-up," said Cusack. "The way it lays. Suggestions. Coincidence ... and what else? Where do you end up when you start with that? I'm just curious."

"There are complications here, Mr. Cusack," said Beaupre. "My boss, the mayor, is very concerned about the possibility of violence when we clear out the Washburn."

"That's where DSM could offer some options," said Storti. "Our Civil Disorder Resolutions Program ..."

"For now," said Beaupre, cutting off Storti, "we've settled on a policy of persuasion with the squatters."

Cusack snapped off the bottle cap and upended the bottle, taking in half the contents before putting it back on the table. He hadn't realized how thirsty he was. He could take a pitcher now, but not with this group. "I'm missing something."

"Tyler is at the center of both our problems," said Parsons. "He's connected to Saint-Georges and those who perpetrated it. And here, he's supporting the squatters' cause."

"This is it," said Storti. "Tyler and his daughter are well thought of by the students. You take some action against him and they might see a conspiracy. A little trouble with the squatters and a little trouble with the students could feed on each other. We could have trouble on two fronts. Negotiation is always an option. But you can't lock yourself in to just one."

"The mayor is going to use staff from the Human Services Department to try to talk the squatters out," said Beaupre. "He's committed to a peaceful resolution."

"DSM is ready to offer its services just in case," repeated Storti.

"You get to know the Tylers," said Parsons to Cusack. "Maybe we can manage both problems." He sipped from his drink. "The women can't resist you, Cusack. And the student card gives you a perfect entree into Tyler's life. We need to see what he sees. We need to meet whomever he meets."

Beaupre said, "We have no reliable informants inside the Washburn …"

"The daughter can be worked," said Parsons, "because of her dead husband. Obviously. One more thing," he added, taking an envelope out of his case. He extracted a photograph from the envelope and pushed it across the table.

Cusack glanced at it. "What am I looking at?"

"It was one of yours from the first day."

It was a picture of Tyler's office. The woman in the picture was Lauren. The man had been in the frame only long enough to snap one shot. "Who's the man?"

"You said you thought the daughter was a naif."

Cusack said nothing.

"Victor Ogbemudia. He's the brother-in-law."

"And?"

"Like his brother before him, he's a member of the Front for the Liberation of Senegal. Our information was that he'd left Senegal a year ago and was seen recently in Montreal. We think he's here for a family visit. If he is, he's illegal. We have some reason to believe that he may be in the Washburn. Members of the FLS are, as you know, on the terrorist watch list." Parsons leaned back, glanced at the brunette and drained his glass. "You still think your girl's a naif?"

"To her, he's still family." Cusack recognized the Victor in the photograph as the Victor from his tour of the Washburn but he was going to keep that item to himself for the time being.

"And," interrupted Parsons, "if Victor went to ground we might never get him. You know Philippe Ogbemudia married Tyler's daughter while he was teaching in Europe. We think Philippe may have found in Tyler a sympathetic listener, even counselor." Parsons sipped from his drink. "There is a Senegalese thread running through this, as I'm sure you've noticed, from our own work six years ago in Senegal to Tyler's demands for an investigation of those stories about Matam to the identity of the bombers at Saint-Georges." Parsons' tone was somber but his eyes kept drifting back to the brunette.

"I still think he's a harmless philosophy professor."

"We justify with words."

Storti said stiffly, "The job at hand, please."

Beaupre looked at Storti. "As I said, the social workers are going to get first crack at getting the squatters out. That is the mayor's decision. "

"And what's your preference?" Cusack looked at Beaupre who ignored him. He turned toward Storti. "DSM ready to do its bit for world peace, too?"

Storti grinned. "Counter-insurgency work resembles, in many ways, ordinary police work. Just trying to keep the people safe."

Cusack didn't much care for his partners and didn't much care for how they'd been brought into the show. Still, this was the job.

Parsons cut in sharply. "You still think you're being followed?"

"Here's the watcher from the mall," replied Cusack, pointing at Storti who shrugged.

"Day after tomorrow we're moving on the Washburn," said Beaupre. "I don't want these two projects to work against each other." She looked at Parsons. "Clearing out the Washburn with minimal force is the goal. It's the only one for me."

"What's the time frame with Tyler?" asked Cusack. The scope

of the project seemed to have been expanded but with no apparent center. There were two new partners and, in spite of the talk, Cusack saw only a periphery of assumed menace. It was no good.

Parsons shrugged, then ran a finger around the edge of his glass. "It's unclear now," he said finally. "Short term, a week, two."

Cusack leaned back and looked around the room. Parsons' time frame was bullshit. The man Cusack kept looking for, Parsons' minder, was still nowhere in sight. "We're hanging a lot on something pretty thin."

"Tyler is not what he seems, not the muddled professor, tied up in complicated philosophical conundrums. Don't fall for that. Ever since Matam, the agency has gotten particular and negative attention in certain circles. The Center for Disease Control still wants to get into those villages east of Matam. I've said this all before. Tyler taught in Lyon for several years, has friends there. The French ambassador in Mauritania, Senegal's neighbor, has asked the State Department repeatedly about the incident. Rumors of biological weapons, etcetera. A couple of Tyler's colleagues in Lyon are working now in the French ministry of culture. A student organization petitioned Human Rights Watch to investigate the incident and issue a report. Like clockwork, every six months for the last five years there's been some stink and the agency always gets mentioned. I want that to stop right here."

"We don't want to interfere in your operation," said Beaupre. "And we don't want to be tied in with it either. Just keep us in the loop." She signaled the waiter and when he arrived, ordered a filet steak and a half-bottle of house red.

Parsons ordered a refill on his Scotch and Cusack saw that as a dismissal and stood.

"This can work out for all parties concerned," said Beaupre.

Cusack wasn't reassured and didn't think she cared one way or another about all parties.

Parsons walked with Cusack across the room to the top of the stairs. "The agency hasn't been as helpful on this project as I'd hoped," said Parsons. "But we'll be able to show them something very soon, won't we?" Parsons put his hand on Cusack's shoulder. "Won't we," he repeated.

Cusack said, "Anything else?"

Parsons looked back over his shoulder and dropped his hand. He turned to Cusack, lifted his head and laughed a short, cold laugh. "Study hard," he said and started back toward his table. "Nobody grades on a curve anymore."

A block from the Moravia, Cusack thought he could keep on going. The man back in the bar had nothing on him. He was beginning to feel the shape of some sort of need and he didn't want to kill it. He wanted to give into it, something he needed, someone like Lauren maybe, and when he did then he would go on until maybe he stopped needing it or it turned into something else.

Saint-Georges had opened the future for him by making it look like the randomness of absolute chance and diminishing to zero the necessity of precautions. It was liberating, in a sense. This was his last job. There wasn't much else that was for sure but he couldn't walk away yet, not without securing one outcome. He had to be sure about the bystanders, that they came away untouched. It would settle a score, all his own, and make things as right as he could make them.

*We count on the future with the desperation of habit.*
*More than any faith, our habits declare our belief in*
*immortality.*

# Chapter 4

Morning two days later, Cusack struggled out of bed. Sleep had not brought him any satisfaction, only a bare minimum of rest and a headache when he awoke. He collected a couple pills and left the condominium early. The local merchants' bare sidewalk sale tables and collapsed umbrellas looked forlorn, like a scene from a science-fiction movie with stark, dissonant, background music and heroes set down in a town where everyone has mysteriously vanished.

He lingered at the coffee shop over his cappuccino and newspapers. The coffee helped clear his head. He had the measure of Tyler's workday. He would not come to the office so early, nor would he likely get many visitors so Cusack could start the day like this, like a day off. It was too cold to sit at the tables on the sidewalk although Cusack was tempted because smoking was banned inside. When he finished a section of the newspaper and looked up there was a crowd of students milling in the street. They had brightly colored backpacks and drank from large paper cups of coffee. Cusack remembered seeing a poster in Tyler's off and others around campus about a protest march. It was set to take place at the southern entrance of the Washburn, the site of the initial stage of the eviction. Beaupre had mentioned it at the *Moravia*. Placards appeared, *Build Houses Not Jails. Eviction = Oppression. Human Rights Not Property Rights* and the students practiced their chants but weren't loud enough yet to penetrate the glass next to Cusack. Some were smiling and laughing. It was an extracurricular activity. A lark.

A few minutes later, the street emptied out. The crowd was on the move suddenly like a swarm of gulls on a quiet plaza spooked by a running child. He recalled Beaupre's mentioning the mayor's preference for negotiation. Cusack walked out and turned in the opposite direction of the protesters. At the corner he looked to his right and, two blocks away, saw three large black vans with smoked windows. He leaned on the corner of the building and lit a cigarette. After a few minutes, a man stepped out of one of the vans. He was riot police, armored, helmeted and carrying an M-4.

Cusack turned and walked quickly south on University. Persuasion, that was Beaupre's term. Three blocks south, Cusack joined a sizable group of people, mostly students gathered behind the barricades the police had erected. Several cars with Department of Health and Human Service logos on the doors were parked inside the Washburn fence. The social workers, standing in small groups, looked tense.

Further to the south, across Third Street and behind more barriers, was a group of counter-protesters, also mostly students and mostly male. They had lawn chairs and signs propped against them, which said, *Squatters are Thieves* and *Eviction = Justice*. Occasionally, they sneaked a beer out of the coolers. Their boom boxes were turned way up. They looked primed for a scrimmage and the fun that came with it but Cusack guessed the squatters were going to go quietly. All that persuasion.

In the Washburn itself, school buses, modified by the State

Corrections Department, circled the ruined fountain. They were painted white and had steel grids inside the windows. The official Health and Human Services cars had been joined by a few police cars. The officers were out of their cars, some moving toward the buses, others toward the front door of the nearest building. They were dressed up with Kevlar vests and fully alert.

Cusack heard the thwop-thwop of an approaching helicopter. It came in just above nearby buildings and hovered. Cusack guessed it was loaded with cameras and transmitting the bigger picture to a police command center on the ground.

Standing next to one of the police cars Cusack recognized Deputy-mayor Beaupre. She was talking to a uniformed officer and gesturing back at the building behind her. Cusack gave her credit for being hands-on. Of course, it made for a nice politically useful photo opp, too.

Barriers were up all along the sidewalks on both sides of University Avenue. They formed a kind of getaway chute for the buses. There'd been some planning done, the efficiencies you get from being versed in the application of force. Cusack looked down 3rd Street and saw more buses wallowing along in his direction.

After a while, social workers began escorting people out of the building where they were met by police officers who took them to the buses. Several women held the hands of the first in a string of children that trailed behind them. A ragged cheer went up from the people around Cusack. The counter-protesters booed and waved their signs.

The squatters seemed to resent being stared at, cheered or booed and some looked angrily in Cusack's direction but there was nothing behind their anger. There was no significance there. They walked like refugees, like they'd been on the road for days and needed a rest. They lived in the exhaust of their own dreams, saw only what was right in front of them and what they saw defeated them.

"It seems like a lot of cops," said a young woman standing next to Cusack, "if they're just going to put them on buses and send them away.

She was the young woman who'd come up to Cusack and Lauren Tyler in the mall. She seemed to be talking to Cusack so he said, "It's the way these things are done. The calculated appearance of overwhelming force. That way everything is serene. No spectacles."

The woman looked sharply at Cusack as if he'd said something obscene or threatening, then swung a camera from a strap, stepped onto the street and snapped off a half-dozen shots of the squatters as they climbed aboard the buses. A policeman waved her back, and when she returned to her spot next to Cusack a series of sharp explosions occurred some distance behind the building that was being cleared out. Cusack looked in the direction of the explosions and saw a cloud of smoke, dust and debris rise. The woman seemed not to have heard the explosions, absorbed by the activities across the street. "They must be scared."

Beaupre had moved to the first bus in line and greeted the squatters at the door before they climbed the steps. Cusack wondered what sort of bullshit she was handing them but he gave her credit for having the balls to be there and look them in the eye. She probably found all the cops around her reassuring, too.

Two distinct clouds could now be seen above the nearest buildings. Cusack guessed the implosion experts were making quick work of the smaller buildings deep inside the Washburn. As Cusack recalled from an article in the local newspaper, the timetable to level everything inside the WRA was very tight. The developers were eager. The clouds of dust began to string out toward Cusack, the crowd of protesters began to break up and the cops pulled out masks.

That seemed wrong to Cusack. The protesters were giving up and leaving. What need of masks? He recalled the vans parked two blocks off University.

Cusack looked straight up and saw, for just a moment, a rifle barrel on the rooftop. He turned slowly and scanned the crowd of counter-protesters. Several men didn't look quite right. They weren't students. He moved away at a brisk pace in the direction of his place. Things were going to happen quickly and he couldn't be in the middle of it. Still, he was curious.

At the next block he entered an office building and took the elevator to the top floor. He found the stairs to the roof and made his way carefully to the roof door. He eased it open slowly. He didn't want to spook a sniper but the roof looked unoccupied. In a crouch, he made his way to the edge of the roof and sneaked a peek. Three buildings along the bus route appeared to have snipers on the roofs. He made his way around the air-conditioning unit and looked down toward the street. Barricades had gone up at the intersection of University and the cross street, was it Fourth?

Cusack sat down with his back to the wall. Snipers and riot police. One of the ways you'd know you'd need snipers and full-gear riot police was if you had good intelligence and an abundance of caution. If you had guys working for you among the counter-protesters who were going to provoke a riot, that was the other way.

By the time Cusack reached the street bottles were sailing through the air. It was impossible to see where they came from. Anti-eviction protesters' signs were torn out of their hands and smashed to the ground. The police established a line across the street and began to move toward the protesters. Suddenly, from the street where Cusack had seen the black vans, two dozen police appeared on University Avenue moving south toward the protesters.

The protesters now had few places to go. It was going to be a bloody beat-down. Tear gas canisters sailed through the air landing near the barricades where the protesters were now frozen in place by the two advancing lines of police.

Cusack made his way back to the condominium. He entered through the alley and took the stairs. Automatically, he checked the tape recorder and confirmed his estimate of Tyler's workday. No one had yet been to his office.

He called Parsons. "What have we been doing down here?"

"What do you mean?"

"There's a riot going on. The students protesting the removal of the squatters."

There was a long moment of silence. "That's police business. Nothing to do with us."

"Looks to me like someone's been priming the pump."

"Trouble was inevitable. It's what we told the mayor."

"The inevitable can be arranged."

"We're here to do a job. Period." Parsons hung up.

Cusack dropped the newspaper in a pile by the worktable. He took a beer out of the refrigerator and sat down to read his class notes. Unable to sit still, he opened one of the windows and caught a faint sting of tear gas. The recorder clicked on and he listened to the noises of Tyler settling into his office routine, a chair creaking, a file drawer opening and closing. The boom box came on, rolled out the low moan of an alto saxophone.

Tyler was confiding in himself. "What is this?" and, "I sent that. What is their problem?" Then, after a paper-tearing sound, sarcastically, "Perfect. Just perfect." Cusack closed his eyes. Tyler was sorting his mail. A few minutes later a chair was pushed back and Tyler began his pacing routine.

For a time the only sound was Tyler's barely audible shuffling and Cusack, curious, went to the window. Tyler stood in full view of Cusack at the podium near the window with his hands clasped behind his back and muttering to himself. Then he picked up a pen and began to write in longhand even while he continued speaking.

Cusack leaned toward the tape recorder just as Tyler raised his voice. "All right. 'To speak of being born again as if it were a good thing.'" Tyler turned away from the podium, disappeared and reappeared. He was carrying a thin sheaf of papers now and looking at them as he paced. "Wasn't once enough? Has anyone been evil enough to deserve ... what?" Tyler's rasping breath was like another question. "Deserve to experience the ultimate ...?" Another stretch of silence. "Okay." Tyler put his hands on the podium then scribbled away. "Ultimate deja vu."

Cusack returned to the worktable and picked up the Cioran book. While he read, Tyler's voice would come through the speakers intermittently and break his concentration. "A child playing alone is an absolute tyrant. Children are comfortable with tyranny, experience it one way or another every day. They are the object both of adult tyranny and the unregulated power of circumstance." A pause. "Unregulated power of circumstance." Tyler pacing. "What would that be?" Then, "Oh well, let's say, not tall enough to reach the doorknob and shown only the books chosen by others. Polish that later."

In his career, Cusack had eavesdropped on dozens of people and the variety of revelations exposed was extraordinary, from the banal to the grotesque. The banal was usually the more revealing. Sexual episodes in an extreme variety. Schemes to steal millions. Discussions, in gruesome details, of the plans for murders. No experience of eavesdropping, however, seemed quite as intimate as this. A man working around in his own mind, trying to explain his world, or understand himself. Cusack lit a cigarette and blew smoke rings.

"Not yet a captive of assigned inhibitions," Tyler said, his voice growing stronger, "the child is an encyclopedist of the imagination. He creates a story and is both narrator and actor. He directs himself and imaginary others. He moves easily in and out of assigned roles, unhindered by adult formulations. He observes and participates simultaneously, seeing no curb to imagination's power. He shuns narrow particularity, which is the adults' response to the challenge of complexity and contradiction."

There was quiet again for a time, the only sound the shuffling of Tyler's shoes across the floor. Cusack tried to remember if his childhood fit into Tyler's formulation. No, he decided at last, his own past could not be redeemed in that way. Still, he could see what Tyler was getting at.

"Now where is that book? Let's see, let's see," said Tyler. "Ekelund, I'm sure it was Ekelund, and the line was something like, 'more dignified ... something ... iron sky of infinite meaninglessness ... something, blind man's bluff.' Where the hell did I put that book?"

Cusack recalled that Lauren had mentioned, without enthusiasm, that her father was working on another book. What he was hearing sounded like work on the book and not on his lectures. Moving around his room, jotting down thoughts and muttering to himself. Cusack thought it was one way to get things right. Line up the thoughts one after another and see if they hang together. Change the order. Discard the losers.

"To hell with it. A little post-it here, for Lauren ... Let's see. Find the Ekelund book - my copy for class. All right."

Cusack tried to recall the Bob Dylan song he'd heard outside Tyler's office door just before he'd met Lauren. *Maggie's Farm*? What if Tyler had been able to listen to Dylan when he was kid like Cusack instead of reading Pascal and Nietzche?

"A man of fixed ideas," said Tyler. "The purity of his ideas is in his conceptions."

Tyler had thrown out lines about fixed ideas and fixed realities in his first class period. This, too, must be another way he tested his writing. He would try out his lines in the classroom, in spite of his apparent dissatisfaction with the young generally and, more particularly, a rejection of the effect of enthusiasm on their judgment.

"A man of fixed realities ... the purity of him is in his refusals."

Cusack was fascinated by Tyler's fractured monologue. Did reading aloud help him decide what needed to be re-thought? Was it like poetry, meant to be read aloud? Was his mumbling recital a sort of first draft? What might Tyler himself say of the technique, something about the importance of resonance?

A knock on the door and Cusack realized the door was Tyler's. An exchange of greetings, the visitor one of Tyler's advisees. Cusack went to his camera. The girl was blond and cute. They talked about her academic goals. His tone was avuncular, chiding. Was Tyler putting the girl on or was he flirting with her? Apparently, Tyler wasn't hostile to the company of all young people.

Cusack left the worktable and dug into the refrigerator. He spread mustard on two slices of bread, laid on thick slices of cheese and ham and opened a beer. He started reading the Ekelund book that Tyler couldn't find in his own bookcase. The book was a collection of extracts from various Ekelund books. Cusack had to turn repeatedly to the "Key Concepts in the Writings of Vilhelm Ekelund" section to make sense of it.

After Tyler concluded his discussions with the student, there was an extended period of quiet. Cusack finished his sandwich and beer and a chapter in his book. Curious about the extended silence, he walked to the window. Tyler was seated at his desk and holding the oxygen mask over his face. Cusack stepped behind the camera and zoomed in on Tyler's face and adjusted the focus. His eyes were closed. His shoulders lifted as he tried to draw in more oxygen. While Cusack watched he put the mask down and walked to the podium

Cusack heard a clear, strong voice, 'The opposite of ambition is not sloth but the radical compulsion toward self-negation; to aspire to be not the early bird but the early worm." A pause, then, "Yes, that's it."

Cusack thought of his mother and the psychology of the devout Catholic. Achievement through denial. Elevation through subjugation. His mother's ambition described exactly. It was unutterable crap.

Tyler restarted his pacing regimen, appeared and disappeared from Cusack's view, his mumbling so faint and garbled that the mic couldn't pick it up. He stopped finally and put the pen close to the page. "This one needs ... Let's see ... I think we can all agree that hell is likely to be customized for all of us who will be its occupants." Quiet again.

Cusack walked across the room and filled an olive drab duffel bag with clothes, bedding and towels. Just before leaving for the laundromat around the corner, he heard a commotion, Tyler wheezing, the chair creaking, the sound of one thing smashing, then something else heavier hitting the floor. Cusack was at the window in a moment, adjusting the camera. Tyler lay on the floor, only his legs visible. Cusack stepped across to the worktable and tucked the pistol into his jacket pocket, then rushed out and down the stairs. He dodged across the street, just missed being clipped by an Audi and burst through the front door of Tyler's building. He headed for the stairs and was breathing hard by the time he reached the second floor landing. When he burst through the stairwell door on the third floor his legs were wobbly. He leaned against the wall, his hands on his knees, a pain tearing at his chest as he tried to pull in some air. He pushed off the wall and stepped across to Tyler's office door. He knocked hard, got no reply and drew the pistol and held it against his leg. He pushed the door open, stepped inside and brought the pistol up quickly and covered the room.

Cusack stepped over Tyler and looked behind the desk. Finding nothing, he put the gun away, picked up the telephone on the desk and called 911. Tyler's eyes were closed and his chest was heaving with the effort to get air.

Cusack knelt down, "Professor Tyler, I've called the paramedics. They should be here any minute. Hang on." Somehow, at that moment, his not dying seemed very important to Cusack. If Tyler had to die, Cusack wanted it to be at some remove in time and space. Not here, not now.

Tyler opened his eyes but said nothing.

Cusack said, "Professor Tyler?" He did not respond and Cusack thought he'd died.

Then Tyler blinked his eyes, wheezed again, and began breathing noisily, a steady rasp in and out.

Cusack reached across Tyler and picked up the oxygen cylinder. He turned the knob at the top wide open and put the mask to his face. Nothing. He looked around the room for evidence anyone else had been there.

"Lucky you came when you did," said the paramedic, five minutes later, as they wheeled Tyler out on a gurney. Luck, thought Cusack, had nothing to do with it. As usual.

"Call Lauren," said Tyler who seemed to perk up when he was lifted onto the gurney. "Tell her to pick me up at the hospital," he added as he disappeared into the elevator.

"There's optimism for you," thought Cusack and saw the same thought in the paramedic's face.

A few of Tyler's office neighbors stood in the corridor as he was wheeled away. A tall redhead who identified herself as Brianna Martinson volunteered to call Lauren and tell her what had happened. She looked at Cusack as if she wanted to ask him something but didn't. When they all dispersed back to their offices, Cusack took the opportunity to search Tyler's office again, then called Parsons.

"Tyler's been taken to the hospital. Something with his oxygen tank."

"Mmmm."

"Did you arrange that?"

"First the riot, now fiddling with oxygen tanks. You've got me very busy. Where are you?"

"In his office. I called the paramedics."

"Good. That's good. This is a break for us."

"Did you fix the tank?" Knowing this became important to Cusack. Parsons had been too quick with the advantage to be gotten from the situation. It spoke to planning. If Cusack had left a minute earlier to do his laundry, Tyler might be dead. Cusack didn't like the way things were playing out.

There was a knock on the door and Martinson put her head in. "I got hold of Lauren and told her. She asked if you were coming to the hospital."

"The daughter will be grateful,' said Parsons. "There's our foot in the door."

"I am going to the hospital." Cusack said to both Parsons and Martinson.

"Good," said Martinson. "Lauren will want to talk to you. Get the details, you know."

"Keep in touch," said Parsons.

Cusack hung up.

In the car on the way to the hospital Cusack recalled the scene just after he entered Tyler's office, Tyler flat on his back on the floor wheezing and he, Cusack, with hands on his knees gulping air. There was a true picture for you and a good laugh. Two guys gasping at each other like fish out of water and not one decent lung in the room.

At the hospital, he stopped at the information desk in the lobby and was told that Tyler was in intensive care. Several family groups were clustered in the lobby. Low voices and an air of resignation. He overheard one of the nurses say, "The ER is jammed with students, some kind of riot. They're looking for volunteers for overtime."

He stepped into the elevator, rode it to the third floor and followed the signs. Lauren was standing with her back to him at the nurses' station and talking to the nurse behind the desk. He walked up and waited until the nurse looked at him. Lauren turned at the same time.

"Mr. Cusack."

"How is he?"

"They've scheduled a bunch of tests. Apparently he hit his head when he fell so they're doing a CAT scan. And of course, checking his heart. He'll be here for a few days."

Cusack noted that she had not answered his question. "Have you been in to see him?"

"He was very grumpy." She turned to the nurse and said, "Wasn't he?" The nurse shrugged. Lauren turned back to Cusack. "I'm going to let him rest for a bit."

"How about some coffee?"

"Sure."

They rode the elevator to the first floor and walked down a long corridor taking a left and a right. At the end, a steel accordion gate was pulled across the cafeteria entrance and a sign directed them to a coffee shop in the lobby.

*It is the action of the desperado not the serene contemplation of the wise man that we admire in this society. Yet the man of action can never be satisfied, can never escape from his ambitions for he is an invalid of hope while the wise man has found sublime health at his own motionless center.*

# Chapter 5

It began to rain as Cusack drove out of the hospital's parking ramp. He switched on the wipers and the resulting smear on the windshield put a halo on the streetlights and made everything seem flat and harsh as if the landscape was exactly what it seemed and yet incalculably diminished. At the first stoplight, he rolled down the window, put his head out and let the rain wet his face.

The traffic thickened as Cusack approached the center of the city. A van cut in front of him and braked suddenly. It was the same color and model as the one in the plaza at Saint-Georges. The brake lights flashed red again like in the plaza at Saint-Georges and Cusack felt himself standing there next to the crater where the van had been. Smoke in swirling gusts seemed to come from every direction, from the ground itself. One minute you couldn't see a foot in front of you and the next you were seeing everything, 360 degrees in a painful, opaline clarity.

He was trying to find Kristin Pedersen, trying to recall exactly where they'd been sitting. That was a starting point. He reverted to his orienteering training, examining the visual field methodically from left to right, recalling the terrain from memory, estimating distances and direction. What he could see, when he could see anything, was only wreckage and smoke and bodies.

The smoke cleared for a moment and the sun focused a brilliant light on the setting's chaos. A block away, the upper story windows in an apartment building were blown and the curtains billowed out. The gusts of wind made them curl and snap as if waving companionably to everyone in the plaza below.

For a moment it seemed as if everything he saw had been planned down to the last detail, like a movie directed by a megalomaniac. It seemed like everything, the wreckage, the breeze, the sunlight had been arranged for cameras just out of sight and waiting the director's call to shoot. Time had collapsed.

The smoke enveloped him again and added to it now was a baked, sulfurous tang. For a moment he felt completely lost, wrapped in an impenetrable white fog. The wind came up, whipped the smoke and he saw police and ambulance lights advancing along the street. It was hard to breathe and there was a piercing hum in his ears whose origin he wanted to locate and silence.

The smoke was making it increasingly difficult to breathe so he started walking and hoped it was away from the source of the smoke. When the air cleared again he found himself at the edge of the elevated outdoor patio, which served all the restaurants and bars on the plaza. On one of the bistro tables that inexplicably had not been touched by the blast was an arm without a shirtsleeve like some grisly entree. It was thoroughly burned with long shreds of

skin and biceps muscle hanging off the table. A patch of skin just
below the elbow bubbled gently. He looked at the hand and tried to
remember if Pedersen had worn a ring or a distinctive watch. It was
a ridiculous thing to think. Everything was ridiculous. He turned and
saw policemen and paramedics moving around the debris of cars
and tables and chairs.

Someone grabbed him by the arm and spun him around. The
man's jaw was working wide open; he was yelling but Cusack couldn't
hear a word. His face was blackened with soot and his jacket was
torn at the shoulder. He looked like he'd been hit with buckshot on
the left side of his face and neck. He dragged Cusack twenty feet
to a spot where part of the rear end of the van, the one carrying
the bomb, was lying on top of a man and woman. The man bent
down and tried unsuccessfully to lift the wreckage off the couple
then glared like a madman at Cusack. It was obvious to Cusack
that they were both dead but he helped move the twisted piece of
metal. Immediately, the man ran off after a paramedic and Cusack
wandered away. He was not looking for Pedersen anymore. Another
ambulance drove onto the plaza. Two men, blue-uniformed, hopped
out carrying bulky medic bags and raced toward the nearest bodies.

People strolled by Cusack with blood running down their faces,
oblivious to their injuries. He thought they might ask him for directions
to the nearest hotel or an antiques shop a friend had recommended;
their casual manner said they could have been tourists just passing
through. Smoke blew across the plaza blinding him and he walked
into the van's motor. It was tipped up with the front end driven
into the asphalt. Cusack thought he ought to find a policeman. This
was a pretty big piece of evidence and they shouldn't overlook it. A
tornado of napkins danced on the ground to his right.

A horn sounded behind him and Cusack came out of his reverie,
hands strangling the steering wheel. He stomped on the accelerator

and his car jumped through the intersection, slewing to the right on the rain-slicked street. The car reached seventy before Cusack noticed and slowed down. He didn't like it, the past taking over like this. The past belonged somewhere, somewhere else. A few minutes later he drove into the hotel's underground garage. The concrete walls and low-ceilings and fluorescent lighting together did no more than taint the air and gave off an atmosphere of rain without anything refreshing about it. He turned off the motor but stayed in the car for a minute.

His shoes smacked on the concrete like a warning as he headed for the elevator. Everything he saw around him looked like a movie cliche, half the lights burned out, dark shadows at every pillar, all of it a set up for the ambush in the parking ramp. What annoyed Cusack even now was his failure to spot Storti when he was parked outside Tyler's. It could have mattered. It was sloppiness and there was no excuse for it and now he had a gun on his hip, as if carrying it would somehow make him more alert. He was afraid he was losing the habit of seeing the options in every situation. Even if a job carried little hazard, losing the habit had no upside.

Cusack took the elevator to the lobby and inquired at the front desk .The desk clerk dialed Parsons' room and handed the phone to Cusack.

"I'm in the lobby," was all he said.

He walked to the door marked "Stairs" and pushed through. He looked over the railing, up and down. He went back through the door and made one circuit of the lobby before hitting the elevator. It was jammed with conventioneers, loud, happy and boozy. They gave him a pointed hat and a noisemaker and told him to visit room 2239. Open bar, someone said and then said it again.

"As long as it takes," said a man without a pointed hat but a bright red waistcoat. "That's our motto."

Cusack was the only one to get off at Parsons' floor. The conventioneers, speaking slowly to Cusack as if he were hard of hearing or mentally impaired, insisted that he not miss the party. Cusack reassured them that he'd be there.

The hallway was tomb-like after the noise of the elevator. His shoes sank into the carpet. Wall sconces every ten feet cast a benign light. Halfway down the corridor, two large vases on opposite walls sprouted native prairie grass. When Cusack tapped on the door, Parsons answered immediately, turned his back on Cusack and walked away. Cusack shut the door carefully and followed Parsons into a large suite with a sliding glass door on the far end that opened onto a balcony. The lights of the city below and more lights out to the far suburbs were framed by the glass door and made it all seem like a giant wall hanging.

"Help yourself," said Parsons as he sat on the far end of the sofa, gesturing at the bottles on the kitchen counter. The spacious room included the large sofa where Parsons sat, a coffee table, two brown leather easy chairs and, off in one corner, a desk and chair. There was also a table with four chairs near the sink, cupboards and a small refrigerator on the near wall. Through the open bedroom door Cusack could see the bed, its covers tossed back. Cusack poured himself a small drink and studied the paintings on the walls. One showed a mill on a stream, painted in a manner apparently designed to fit with the room's predominant colors. He preferred the condo. He dropped several ice cubes into the glass from an ice bucket on the counter.

"All right," said Parsons, "Let's hear what you know." He had a glass in his hand full up with an amber liquid.

Cusack tipped an inch of bourbon into his glass and offered his narrative, which Parsons interrupted repeatedly with questions. While he answered Parsons' questions, Cusack felt a remarkable detachment, as if he were watching Parsons through a camera from a great distance. It was a professional regression; it happened occasionally. A social interaction turned into a surveillance assignment.

A few minutes into his recitation, Cusack stepped across the room. "Stuffy in here. Mind if I open the door?" He slid open the balcony door and, standing in the doorway, shook out a cigarette but didn't light it. He looked out at the city and said, "What is this with DSM and the squatters?"

"When I got here I took in the situation and saw an opportunity."

"You brought them in?"

"They have something to offer."

"The mayor doesn't seem convinced."

"After today he might be."

"You mean the riot."

"At the least, the deputy-mayor is very open-minded." Parsons picked up the television remote control and punched a button. The huge television screen blossomed into stark colors. Parsons channel surfed until he hit a news channel. He killed the sound and turned back to Cusack. "The students are merely tools, as is usual in a case like this." He pointed back at the television screen, which showed students in handcuffs being put into police cars. "They can be useful to our side, too."

"The students were provoked," said Cusack. "They were set up. You know it."

"There are two kinds of reality, Cusack. The one in front of you and the one you create."

Cusack looked over at the food cart, dishes haphazardly stacked with the remains of a couple meals. He'd enjoyed his time with the Tylers, the professor's class and talks with the daughter. It hardly seemed hazardous. He must have been going soft on the family.

"What did the doctor say about Tyler?"

"The doctor didn't confide in me."

An aerial shot of the Washburn Redevelopment Area appeared on the television followed by one of the deputy-mayor talking with the squatters. The next scene was of a room in city hall, a podium with the mayor and the deputy-mayor. The mayor said, "Violence of this sort will not be tolerated. Those responsible will be found and brought to justice." Another cutaway to the street in front of city hall. The reporter said, "The police are taking statements and reviewing video of the incident to determine who was responsible for the protest turning violent. The president of the college, Arthur Hobbs, has said that the college is investigating and will take appropriate action if students are determined to be responsible."

Parsons rose from his chair, walked past Cusack and onto the balcony. "I'll say one thing for you, Cusack. You never look disappointed. That's something."

"It's a gift, all right," said Cusack.

"Could be, I suppose. But are you ever disappointed?" Parsons seemed genuinely interested in the question.

"It comes and goes."

Parsons considered Cusack for a moment, as if Cusack's remark had reminded him of something he didn't want to be reminded of. "You know after Senegal I was posted to a number of exotic agency offices. And since I've gotten back to Baltimore, I've heard that you're not well-liked. In the agency," he added.

"Could be." Sometimes you only got answers when you pissed people off. Sometimes you got no answer at all no matter what you tried. "Is that why you picked me for this job?"

Parsons leaned on the railing, looked out over the city and pointed. "Your place is over there, right?"

Cusack stepped to the railing. "Across University from the

Washburn Redevelopment Area."

Parsons lit a cigarette. "The Tyler daughter is a real looker."

To Cusack, Parsons' thoughts seemed to be wandering pointlessly though you could never be sure with Parsons. Cusack put another cigarette in his mouth and snapped his lighter. Was Parsons probing for weakness or just making conversation? "We could spend years here and not get anything useful out of that old man."

"Everyone can be brought around. You just need to find the right argument."

"I said this before, when I take an assignment, I like to see the full landscape. I'm not seeing that now." Cusack looked at Parsons and wondered if he was going to have to go down the road on him. It was a bad option but Parsons was on the wrong side of history. That's what Storti's involvement signaled but Parsons didn't seem to notice. In fact, he seemed to think it put a positive lock on the future.

Before responding to Cusack, Parsons made an elaborate ritual of extracting a cigar from his inside jacket pocket, clipping the end and lighting it. He hadn't smoked cigars in Senegal. In Senegal, Cusack remembered him as absolutely certain about every choice, every potential consequence. He'd been wrong there, terribly wrong. He was certain here, too, but Cusack had had time to think about things and was seeing things differently now.

"We only know what we know," said Parsons. "And we have to act on that no matter how imperfect it is."

They were generating a lot of smoke and it was being persuaded back into the room through the open door. Maybe, with any luck, the smoke alarm would go off and put an end to the meeting. They stood smoking in silence for a few minutes, then Parsons said he had to make some calls. He accompanied Cusack to the elevator. "We have to make this work. I've made some promises."

"What kind of promises?" asked Cusack.

"That's not your worry."

Cusack stepped into the elevator, turned and said, "Don't fuck me around on this. I wouldn't like that." He hit the button with the G on it and Parsons disappeared.

*To tell the truth without leaving a discernible*
*trace of yourself, not a single stylistic fingerprint.*
*To use words that become invisible and yet indelible.*
*To disguise your ambition from posterity*
*and thus insinuate yourself into the*
*soul of your reader."*

# Chapter 6

Lauren stood in front of the class, introduced herself and said, "Professor Tyler will be unable to provide his lecture this week. He has suffered what I've heard called a medical event. Nothing too serious," she added with a half-smile. "The doctors tell me he'll be back next week."

Her hair was down and framed the pale skin of her face in a way that made Cusack think of a painting he'd seen in a visit to a museum in Baltimore. A classic beauty from another age. Parsons thought she possessed some special knowledge; the widow of Philippe Ogbemudia was bound to know. For Parsons, it seemed now to be an article of faith.

She took a head count then looked out the window as if something there had caught her interest. "I will be facilitating the discussion this week although there will be one change to the order of things. The schedule has us talking about Pascal this week but instead we're going to talk about Ekelund. I've cleared this with Professor Tyler. It's a personal thing. Of the three philosophers we're studying this semester, my favorite is Vilhelm Ekelund.

"If you haven't dipped into the Ekelund book yet, what I have to say will point you at certain key concepts and important elements of his writing. If you have read some, I'll give you a little context for what you've already seen." Lauren stood perfectly upright and looked from student to student as she spoke.

"I like Ekelund best because of his lyricism and more than the other two, his outsider quality. His is an authentic voice. That's not to say that the others aren't. I just like the way he comes at his subjects. I like what he has to say, for instance, about poverty." She picked up a note card and read, "'Poverty is an endlessly long night, says some knowing man. No, he did not know the poor. It is a day, unfortunately: an endless, painful day with a sharp and piercing light that smarts in the eyes ... The matter goes deep and has an awesome reality. Utter destitution is a type of hypochondria that borders on insanity.'" She put the note card down. "He lived what he writes about. The lines I've just read show you a man who has been poor."

As much as he'd read of the three, Cusack preferred Cioran. Pascal was tarnished for having been put in his hands by Brother Christopher as a teenager, and nothing could change his status as one who'd been read young and dismissed. Cioran had an acid touch, and never relented; it was an appealing quality.

A woman sitting in the front row raised her hand. "I'm having trouble with as much of Ekelund as I've read so far." She stopped there but when Lauren said nothing, added, "I've read the assigned sections on him and I just don't see what he's trying to get at."

Lauren held up a copy of the Ekelund book and said, "If you

haven't already done so, look at the section at the front of the book titled, *Key Concepts in the Writings of Vilhelm Ekelund*, it might help. I say might because his concepts are interrelated and subject to a complex interpretation. We'll talk about that private lexicon of his a little later."

She continued to talk about Ekelund but by then Cusack was only half-listening. He thought of Tyler's file and the very few notations that made reference to her. There was her participation in political protests in college, then her marriage to Philippe Ogbemudia. Nothing else in the file about her years in Europe with her father except for her marriage. A single mention of her involvement with the political work of her husband when the family returned to the United States. The birth of the child, Sarah. The history seemed innocent enough, and then her husband was deported and killed. It made Cusack think that the file had been purged before being given to him or that Parsons knew something hidden and wasn't telling him. Cusack would be disappointed if that was what had happened. Disappointed but not surprised.

She had taken on a lot in her life and didn't appear damaged in any obvious way. Cusack figured she made up what was necessary, the answers to what came up when your life was bracketed by a murdered husband, a young daughter and a dying father. The consolation of philosophy; maybe Ekelund provided that.

At the end of class she caught his eye and nodded at him to stay. He met her at the door and they walked to the elevator. "Dad came home this morning."

"How is he?"

"Same as ever."

"You sound disappointed."

She laughed. "I worry about the doctors getting the diagnosis right. I think they look for the obvious answer. I don't know. Maybe in medicine the obvious is the answer most of the time. And anyway, it doesn't help them that Dad always plays the tough guy."

Lauren said that Tyler would like to see him, though she warned it would have to be a short visit since he was not back to full strength. Cusack hesitated a moment before accepting the invitation. He was still on the job and felt an obligation to go right to the end even as his intuition told him the assignment was a dead-end. Just before seven o'clock that evening, Cusack maneuvered his car to the curb in front of the Tyler house. He had gone from spy to guest in no time at all. A real professional. Mom would be proud.

Cusack picked up his phone, punched some numbers and Aanonsen answered.

"Well, things have been interesting around here while you've been gone. I was just brought in to do a series of scenarios. I haven't done that since you left to go into field work. Don't know why they brought me in. They have a good group doing scenarios two floors down. Everything on Tyler is with the Director. You want to know you have to go through him."

"Scenarios?"

"Yeah. I've been reading up about the history of the Washburn Redevelopment Area and the mayor and the governor and various protest groups and profiles of a few of the known squatters. Tyler shows up in some footnotes. Ditto his daughter and son-in-law."

"What are they looking for?"

"Seth, they're pointing at something. Step carefully."

Cusack snapped his phone shut. He opened the door to his car and stepped into the street. He made his way up the sidewalk and pushed the doorbell. He heard the ring and an echo from inside. Seconds later a small girl with the skin the color of an early summer tan and unruly black hair in pigtails opened the door. Cusack recognized her from her being picked up at school

"Come in," she said without smiling and disappeared back inside the house.

He walked into a small foyer, a built-in oak bench to his left with a hinged top and hooks on the wall above it. He dropped his jacket on one of the hooks and looked around the corner into the living room, which contained a sofa covered in a floral pattern and matching pillows. There were two small round tables, two unmatched easy chairs and three large dark oak bookcases that ran up to the ceiling, shelves jammed with books and manila file folders. A dozen framed black and white photographs hung on one wall. On the top shelf of one bookcase were four cameras, two that could have been antiques. Cusack recalled the statement in the introduction to one of Tyler's books, which spoke of Tylers parallel career as a photographer.

"Just another watcher," he said softly to the empty room.

He continued his inventory: a small stereo on a tall narrow table in the far corner murmured something jazzy and a red brick fireplace with a thick oak mantel above had a small fire going, flames of bright yellow blue and orange. He advanced into the living room and turned to the left into the dining room.

The dining room table was cherry wood and highly polished. One of its six matching chairs lay on its side under the window. A can of glue, a putty knife and a rag sat on a newspaper next to it. A small table in the corner held a telephone and a combination fax machine and copier. As he passed the table, Lauren came out of the kitchen.

"Hi. Where's Sarah?" she said.

Cusack shrugged. "She said, "Come in, and disappeared.""

"Well, come in."

He followed her into the large kitchen, windows on the left and right, a central island and pots dangling at a dangerous height above it. He smelled something sweet with a sharp tang he couldn't quite place.

"Dad is on his computer. He should be out in a minute." She looked back through the doorway into the living room. "Sarah was supposed to show you around."

There was a bottle of red wine on the central island and Lauren was winding the corkscrew down into the cork. "Would you get the wine glasses?" She gestured with her head at the cupboards to her left. "I'm afraid all I have is wine and cheese and crackers. With Sarah, dinner has to be at five."

"Wine sounds great." Cusack stepped across the room, opened the cupboard door and brought down three glasses. He looked around the kitchen, noting the location of the door that led to the backyard and the door to the right of that which must lead to the basement. He pulled out one of the high-backed stools at the island and sat down. To his left, a cluster of bananas hung from a banana tree. On the corner of the island was a rack of wicked-looking knives. A cupboard door across the room was ajar and bright yellow and red boxes of cereal were visible. A rawhide chew lay in the corner of the room and he wondered where the dog was being kept. It was a comfortable house, a house intended for reassurance. He could see its appeal. He was open-minded about other people's priorities.

"Just so you know," said Lauren. "I want to keep this short. Whatever Dad might think, what he needs is rest." She eased the cork out and filled all three glasses.

Sarah appeared in the doorway. "I told Grandpa we had a visitor." She crossed from the doorway, climbed onto the stool next to Cusack and glanced at her mother.

"You have a very nice home," Cusack said to Sarah.

She ignored the flattery. "Where do you live?"

"I have an apartment." Cusack saw the girl's purple school bag on the floor by the back door and next to it Tyler's walking stick.

"My friend Jackie lives with her mother in an apartment. It's a big building near the freeway. They have an indoor pool. Do you have a pool?"

"No." Cusack could see her disappointment. "I have a nice view of the city, though."

"Uh hunh."

Tyler entered the kitchen then and said, "Welcome, Mr. Cusack." They shook hands. "I believe I have you to thank for my still being here."

"All I did was dial 911."

"It was the necessary thing." Tyler rubbed his hand across Sarah's head and picked up a glass of wine.

Sarah tugged immediately at Tyler's sleeve. "Okay," he said. "A taste."

She held the glass in both hands, took a large gulp and smacked her lips.

"How long have you been teaching here, Professor?" asked Cusack.

"Enough," said Lauren, taking the glass from Sarah.

"Almost ten years." He stared blankly for a moment as if just then realizing the passage of time. "Longest I've been anywhere."

"Dad," interposed Lauren, "thinks academia is mostly a trap." It sounded like a dispute that had become routine.

"At a certain age, the idea of moving again gets to be too much to face. You accommodate yourself to the trap." He pointed at the oxygen tank on the floor by the refrigerator. "That doesn't help."

"How long have you lived in Baltimore?" asked Lauren.

"Seems like forever," Cusack replied and sipped his wine. There was a quality of ordinariness here that seemed impenetrable to him like the ordinary was a mystery and had to be taken on faith. "I peeked into a couple of your books at the bookstore," he said to Tyler. "What are you working on now?"

"Oh, no," interrupted Lauren. "We're not going down that road." Lauren set a small platter in front of them with a small half-wheel of cheese and a dish of chutney. She shook out two kinds of crackers onto a plate and put that out. She sliced the cheese, arranged them on the plate and laid the cheese knife next to the plate.

"I must admit, I am working on a book."

Lauren glared good-naturedly at her father.

"I think there were four in the series I looked at," said Cusack putting a piece of cheese on a cracker. "Is this one going to be part of that?"

"Yes," Tyler said holding up a hand, palm out at Lauren. "A summing up, I suppose."

"Mr. Cusack rents an apartment like Jackie's mom," said Sarah. "Grandpa, can we go to the pool at the college on Saturday?"

Tyler took a small drink from his wine and put the glass down. "Sure."

Sarah dipped a cracker into the chutney.

"Eat over the plate, Sarah," said Lauren.

Cusack had not been in such an unmitigated domestic atmosphere since his brother and sister and their families had all gathered four years ago at their father's home. He didn't like this sort of thing but you had to go through what you had to go through. His previous skin-on-skin work had all been in a work environment. That environment presented, he believed, fewer variables and a greater opportunity for straight-line progress. This scene offered, like the meager file on Tyler and Parsons' falsely reassuring bullshit, the likely prospect of an informational dead end.

"I told Mr. Cusack," said Lauren, "that employment prospects for philosophers were a little thin on the ground."

"Is this a mid-career move for you?" asked Tyler.

"Philosophy?" Cusack raised an eyebrow.

"I don't know," Tyler said, looking into his back yard, "if you expand the idea of philosophy to include self-help and motivational speakers, there might be quite a few jobs out there."

"Oh, that's what we need more of," said Lauren. She drained her glass. "Five minutes, Sarah. It's already past bed time." Lauren picked up a sheaf of papers from the counter. "And put these worksheets in your backpack. I signed them all."

Cusack said to Tyler, "I did a search of your name on the Net and one of the things that came up was an article about you and the CIA."

Tyler had a cracker in his mouth and held up a finger.

"That was about my husband, Philippe," said Lauren. She tipped more wine into her glass.

"The CIA?" said Cusack. "That sounds like a movie plot."

"Philippe came from Senegal," said Tyler. "Here in the States he worked with refugee groups and a kind of government-in-exile called the Front for the Liberation of Senegal and other groups fighting the dictatorship. The Senegalese government called them terrorists."

"It's the all-purpose smear," added Lauren.

Cusack sliced a piece of cheese and laid it on a cracker.

"We never found out exactly what the politics were for the U.S. government," said Lauren, "but they sold him out to the Senegalese."

Sarah was staring up at her mother who was making a shooing motion with her hands.

"Philippe's guilt or innocence was irrelevant to our government. He was convenient and useful." Tyler picked up another cracker and spread chutney on it. "Those were and are their moral touchstones," he added.

"What happened?"

"I accused our government of sending Philippe back to certain death."

"Then what?"

"Nothing much. Officially anyway. I suppose I have a file now in some super-computer at Langley. And a radio talk-show idiot spent a few days demanding the college fire me. The usual diatribes."

"Sarah," said Lauren, "Tomorrow is a school day. Say good night to Mr. Cusack."

"Good night, Mr. Cusack."

"Good night, Sarah."

When Sarah could be heard on the second floor landing, Lauren said, "Philippe was sent back and a few days later." Her face went blank. "His body was found floating in the bay at Dakar."

"I'm sorry."

She nodded.

"But that wasn't the end," said Tyler. "Oh, no, not at all. Lauren and Sarah and I went to Paris a year after Philippe's death and when we got back we were held up at Customs. Shunted off to a room, asked a lot of questions about who we met in Paris. This asshole in a pricey suit and a nice manicure asked me, "Did we know so-and-so?" Then, "Did I know that the editor of the magazine where I had my essay published was an ex-Communist?" Tyler looked up smiling. "I asked him if he knew his mother was an ex-whore."

Cusack finished the little bit of wine at the bottom of his glass.

"A refill?" asked Tyler.

"Sorry," Lauren said. "I'm cutting everyone off. I have two kids that need to get to bed."

At the door, Tyler took Cusack's hand in both of his and said, "Thank you."

"I'm looking forward to your next lecture," said Cusack.

"So am I," said Tyler.

"I'll be taking the class this week," said Lauren, patting her father's shoulder.

"Good night," said Cusack.

He was all the way down the sidewalk to the curb when Lauren said, "Mr. Cusack, how about I buy you a real drink? Saturday when Dad's at the pool with Sarah?"

"I can make that."

*Killing is just one of the prerogatives of a belief in the Absolute.*

# Chapter 7

Cusack sat at a bistro table on the patio of a bar called Benjamin's, looking at the late afternoon traffic on University Avenue in front of him and waiting for Lauren to appear and buy him a drink. He'd hesitated before leaving the condominium wondering if he ought to cancel. Play it as it lays, was Parsons' instruction. An iron railing separated the patio from the sidewalk. On the sidewalk, students hustled back to their dorms, while others hurried on their way to evening events at the college. There appeared to be a loose discipline to everyone's movements as if everything that happened was scripted and purposeful. After a few minutes of waiting, he ordered the usual, a bourbon and ice. The sun was down but clouds, low on the horizon, were brushed with light.

Happy hour had just begun and half of the tables on the patio were occupied. Some cars, only a few feet away on the other side of the railing, were taking people home from work. The drivers' faces were stiff and concentrated. Other cars were being maneuvered into spots so that the occupants might, in a little while, sit at one of the empty tables near Cusack or one at any of the other restaurants in the next block. It was the weekend and everyone was getting away.

When the waitress brought his drink, Cusack looked at his watch and then at the waitress as she walked back inside. Her skirt was short and very tight. He raised the glass to his lips and gave the other tables a look. Partially hidden by a large plant next to the double doors that opened onto the patio was a table occupied by Storti and Beaupre. Storti caught Cusack's eye and raised his glass. Cusack nodded an acknowledgment. Lauren was due any minute and Cusack didn't want to have to explain Storti to her.

Cusack reached into his jacket pocket and brought out the photo of Victor Ogbemudia. He wasn't sure what useful purpose it might serve. Showing it to Lauren would be good for provocation but that could lead anywhere unless you had a precise track laid out. Cusack doubted she could be persuaded to be useful in the way Parsons meant.

A breeze came up and the smell of gasoline from the clogged street lifted. It was replaced momentarily by the smell of beer and barbecue sauce from the next table which was littered with platters covered with the remains of chicken quesadilla, barbecued chicken wings, a pepperoni and mushroom pizza, glasses and two empty pitchers of beer. In spite of all that wreckage, the students appeared to be ready for more.

Cusack sipped his drink and felt the reassuring harshness at the back of his throat. He wanted a cigarette but thought he'd wait until after he'd eaten.

A line of trees just beyond the fence on the opposite side of the street gave the appearance of an additional barrier to the Washburn. However, there was gap in the fence that looked like part of a short cut from the interior to everything on University Avenue. The light on the horizon dimmed and the air cooled suddenly. The streetlights fluttered on and off for a minute before staying on and put the line of trees inside the fence into a steeper darkness. It made the humps of buildings inside look like elements of nature and the Washburn just another urban park.

A horn sounded as a car jumped away from the curb, the driver cut in front of another, then gunned his engine and shot through the intersection on the yellow light. The man in the car who was cut off leaned on his horn. Cusack followed the first car's trajectory down the block until it was lost in traffic.

Storti pulled out the chair across from Cusack and sat down. "Where is our girl?" He looked around as if she might be hiding somewhere on the patio.

Cusack looked up, angry that Storti knew about his meeting with Lauren. "Our girl?"

Storti flagged the waitress and ordered a Scotch on the rocks. He smiled at her and called her darling. When she left, he said, "Parsons has got a real hard-on for that professor."

"What are you doing with the deputy-mayor?"

"Business. Why?"

"DSM was involved in Senegal with us. That didn't work out so well."

Storti smiled. "Senegal was before my time."

"It was counter-insurgency work. What's DSM doing here with squatters? Business that hard to come by or did Parsons figure he owed you something?"

Storti examined the occupants of other tables before settling his look on Cusack. "I know what it's like for someone like Parsons, close enough to the top to smell it but not quite there and wondering if you'll ever make it. That's where he was before that disaster in Senegal. You were one of those on that helicopter that went down, right?" He smiled at the waitress as she put his drink in front him.

He tipped her big and called her darling again.

Cusack leaned forward. He thought he'd heard something new. Not the facts. Senegal was a disaster, for sure, but something else in Storti's tone.

"You're on the grid," Storti continued on his riff about Parsons, "you're making plans, you've got good sight lines out to some sort of a future and then, zap, you're off the grid and it's like you were never there. I know about that. Your agency isn't the only one that's taken some big hits because of Senegal."

"You've got my sympathy." Cusack wasn't going to be a sucker and the past was starting to jeopardize present options. He was trying not to hold it against Storti who was just working his side of the street.

Storti shrugged and emptied his drink. "It's complicated, why we're here. What we've got is something that could wipe the Senegal mess clean. Parsons wants to scoop up Tyler and the terrorist in-law. Add in the squatters, DSM and a successful civil disorder management program. It's redemption, that's what it is.

Cusack looked at his watch.

"Don't worry about Ms. Tyler," said Storti, icy and deliberate, "I'll be smooth. An old friend."

As Cusack looked into the darkness across the street, a series of detonations sounded from deep within the Washburn. He wondered how long it would take to blow up everything. A dust cloud became visible above the trees. It was moving straight north though and wasn't going to spoil anyone's drinking on the patio at *Benjamin's*.

Cusack wanted one more question answered. "Senegal was a disaster but it belonged to the Senegalese army. They hired us and DSM. What does Tyler have to do with it?"

"You seemed a little upset when we met at the Moravia."

"Finding out you worked for DSM. Consultant, wasn't that what you said when you dropped into my car at Tyler's place?"

"I figured there was some baggage attached to Senegal and I wanted to keep that out of our first meeting. Get a clear picture." With his drink finished, Storti seemed ready to go.

"Everything clear now?"

Storti looked to his right and grinned. "Look who's here."

Cusack saw Lauren as she stepped through the double doors, which opened to the street-side tables where they were sitting. He and Storti stood when she arrived. Cusack introduced Storti and pushed back the chair for her. When they leaned toward each other he smelled her shampoo, a complicated citrus scent and saw, as she bent over, the freckles on the top of her shoulders and across her collarbones. The boys at the next table glanced in her direction. They could have been former students of hers.

Storti said it was a small world and he'd looked up Cusack when he arrived in town. They'd worked together a long time ago. His agency and Cusack's had been involved in some joint projects. He believed Cusack's leaving the agency had been a real loss. He smiled a lot and said he was consulting with the mayor's office. He was just as good as his word, however, and left a minute later, catching up to Beaupre as she made her way back inside the bar. At the door Storti put his cell phone to his ear and looked back at Cusack.

Cusack ordered a second bourbon on ice, Lauren asked for a glass of pinot grigio and the waitress promptly delivered them. Cusack guessed that the waitress had adjusted to the loss of Storti and saw the two of them as a more lucrative proposition than the college boys at the next table.

"How's your father?" asked Cusack.

"The tests were negative." She took a small sip of her wine. "Or positive, depending on your point of view." She reached into her purse and brought out her cell phone. She looked at it for a moment and put it back. "The CAT scan showed no head trauma and the EKG showed no problems with his heart."

"That's good news." Cusack gestured at the platters on the table next to theirs. "Do you want to get something to eat?"

"No, just a drink. But you go ahead if you're hungry."

Cusack tried to think of something useful to put in front of her, something that would take her mind off her father but nothing came to him. He raised his hand and, when the waitress appeared, ordered chicken quesadilla.

"How's the reading coming along?" Lauren sipped her wine.

"Interesting, but I don't know what to do with it."

"I'm so used to kids talking about their career plans that I'm not sure what to say to someone who ..."

"Doesn't have any?" suggested Cusack laughing.

"I see," Lauren said pointing toward the sky and a low cloud of dust and sinuous floating debris, "that the beat goes on. Isn't there a curfew for blowing up things?"

Cusack looked where she pointed but didn't want to talk about things blowing up. "You spent some time in Europe when your father was teaching there. I've spent some time there for the agency. Vienna before I got laid off. Yugoslavia after the breakup. Development work. Our agency was called ... ever heard the expression 'quango'?"

"Sounds like an exotic bird."

"Quasi-non-governmental organization."

"Did you like it?"

Cusack grinned. "Not the work, not much. Vienna was okay. Bosnia, Serbia, Crotia." He shook his head. "Did you like it when you were there?"

She sipped from her glass and said nothing for a minute. "When I was six we went to Garmisch-Partenkirchen. The German Alps. We were there to go to Kitzbuhl, the highest point in Germany. Mom said we could look into four countries from there. It was a real trip. Not a trip for Dad to give a lecture or something connected with the university. A real trip. You know, a railroad runs straight up into the mountain there." She showed her hand fingers spread and turned it. "Ratcheted? What's the word?"

"Cog railway," said Cusack.

She raised her eyebrows. "You stop at one point just before you go into the mountain itself and this toothed wheel drops down onto the track and then you continue straight up. The lights in the train kept flickering on and off. At 8,000 feet we came out and still had a gondola ride through the clouds to the summit. What did you do in Vienna?"

"A series of conferences on data collection, security and analysis." Cusack sipped his drink. She asked a question for every one she answered. "Yes," he added, "it was exactly that boring."

The waitress arrived with the quesadilla and Cusack lifted a slice. More people crowded onto the patio and the conversational noise level increased.

Cusack leaned forward to ask her what was the opposite of her Alps experience.

"Dad took me to prison once to see one of his students who was convicted of murder." Something else left out of Tyler's file. The visit could have been innocuous enough but it seemed an odd choice for a father.

"He was serving time in a federal penitentiary in Minnesota. Dad thought the boy might like to see a pretty girl."

"Did he?"

"I don"t know." She looked past Cusack into the Washburn. "When the boy came into the day room, he was all worked up, his hands were shaking. He hardly noticed me. He kept saying his lawyer was selling him out. He talked so fast I could hardly understand him.

He was on something. Dad wouldn't let me go again."

"Oh?"

"The boy wasn't the problem for Dad. It was the guards. They took us into separate rooms and did a very thorough pat-down. When I came out, Dad asked me how it was and I said it was just like a date but without all the talk."

Cusack smiled.

"He didn't think it was funny and that was the one and only time I went to prison." She smiled. "Except to visit Dad when he went in."

Cusack nodded and looked out at the street. Traffic was thick and slow moving and there was an intermittent smell of ozone. Just then Storti and Beaupre appeared around the side of the patio walking toward the street. They stopped a half-block south and talked for a minute with Storti pointing across the street into the Washburn. They concluded their conversation and Storti took out his cell phone as he slid into the driver's seat of his car. Beaupre was parked behind him.

Cusack glanced at Lauren who was looking around the patio. He looked up at a noise from the street and saw Storti blowing through the intersection as the light turned from yellow to red. Beaupre's car stopped at the crosswalk

A squatter stepped into the street and stopped in front of Beaupre's car. He squirted the windshield from a water bottle and then stepped back and fumbled under his coat like he was getting a rag. He pulled out a blunt-nosed automatic pistol with a long clip, pointed it and fired. The driver's side window exploded, blood splattered the windshield and Beaupre fell sideways out of sight. The shooter fired one-handed and the gun climbed as he fired, the last few rounds going over the top of the car.

Cusack rose from his chair. His hand twitched at his jacket but the pistol was at the condominium in the work table drawer. Lauren was standing now, too, and he said, "On the floor," and pushed her down and covered her, never taking his eye off the shooter.

The boys at the next table went for the floor, too, and Cusack heard screams behind him, tables and chairs going over and glass breaking. He could see the driver of a car at the crosswalk with a cell phone at his ear and his face frozen.

Beaupre's car, with her foot off the brake, crawled through the intersection but the shooter wasn't finished. He walked alongside the car, took the gun with both hands this time and fired another burst through the door. The whack-whack-whack sound seemed absurdly loud to Cusack as if it had been piped into speakers especially for the occasion. Then it was quiet.

Cusack took in the burned gunpowder smell and let his breath out slowly. He was seeing everything now but he wasn't quite in it. It was stupid not to have kept the gun with him. If he had it now, there would be nothing fancy - the pistol out and up, a moment to settle the barrel on the shooter. Then two rounds at the center of mass. Or maybe four or six or the whole fucking clip. Cusack could feel the queasy beginning low in his gut. It brought him forward, made him aware of the danger. He wanted the gun. It was just one part of a whole world of false security, but it was what he needed just then.

Beaupre's car finished making its way through the intersection, climbed the curb, and put its nose softly into a concrete bus bench. There were more screams and orders to get down or get moving and the sound of people rushing away. The streetlight changed from red to green but the cars were stalled. A few car horns sounded from down the block, people too far back to know what had happened.

Lauren was muttering to herself, what sounded to Cusack like, "Can't be. Can't be."

The shooter held the gun away from himself, staring at it as if it were a live thing that had gone off on its own. He stood stock still for a minute and Cusack thought he must be very young. Cusack focused on details: the baseball cap, the hood and a paint stain on the shooter's cap, black leather gloves and a beard like a theatrical add-on.

The shooter turned suddenly and ran away, across the street, wide-legged, splay footed, like he'd wet himself and couldn't stand how it felt. He darted into a gap in the fence and onto the rubble-filled lot, then disappeared into the darkness between two buildings.

Cusack looked across his field of vision, in segments from left to right. There didn't seem to be a second shooter coming on. Not yet. He stood quickly and helped Lauren to her feet. Her mouth was working but no sound was coming out. He pushed her off the patio and up the street, moving at a right angle away from the intersection. Cusack thought they had a minute or two. He noticed on the periphery of his vision people getting up and moving out with the efficiency of fear.

A half block up the street, Lauren stopped and shook off Cusack's hand. She bent over and put her hands on her knees, like she was getting ready to puke. Her mouth was wide and he could hear her taking breath. He looked around and heard the first siren. There was no one near them. Car horns sounded. He wasn't going to wait for the police; he didn't want to answer questions just yet. He put his hand on her back and asked, "Can you go on?"

"I just need a second."

Cusack looked over his shoulder, not at Beaupre's car but everywhere else for some other guy with an automatic pistol. The front wheels on Beaupre's car were still turning, spasmodically, trying to get some traction on the curb. Another siren sounded and then another until they all blended into one indistinguishable  wail. He took Lauren's arm and urged her forward. Lauren stopped again. "We need to go back."

"We need to keep moving."

Lauren made no reply and let herself be led to the end of the block.

"Where's your car?" said Cusack.

She nodded at a dark blue Toyota further up the block and across the street and started digging in her purse.

"Is your father home?" Cusack wanted to put some other things in front of her, things that would keep her moving.

"At the pool with Sarah."

Their exchange sounded absurd at that moment, the small talk you shared in ordinary settings with people you'd known for years. Cusack flashed on the blast scene at Saint-Georges and the face of the woman who'd had a drink with him and died.

"We need to go back," Lauren said again, looking down the hill toward Beaupre's car.

"No," Cusack put his hands on her arms just above the elbow and looked straight into her eyes. "Sometimes there is a second guy. When the paramedics or cops show up there's more shooting or a bomb goes off. The woman in the car is dead. We can't help her."

Lauren was looking past Cusack down the hill. A police car and ambulance were there now, lights flashing, and in the air the woo-woo sound of other police cars on the way. "That's not right."

"You go home."

"And what are you going to do?"

"I'll call you later." Another line that sounded absurd in the circumstances, like what you'd say at the end of a first date. He pushed her into the car and watched her drive away.

She had looked at the intersection and the dead woman and seen things correctly with the precision of the naif when she said, "That's not right."

He didn't think what was right was going to matter in the long run. He wanted the gun. He could shoot someone; he was up for that now.

# PART III

*Begin with the premise that life is indefensible.*
*Do that and meaning becomes not merely*
*inaccessible but an affront.*

# Chapter 1

Cusack watched Lauren's car until it disappeared around the corner. He turned slowly, taking in everything. The street was empty of cars and people, too, as if the shooting had been a kind of dismissal. The shops across the street, vintage clothing, used books and a coin shop, were all shuttered. The sirens had run down but the police and paramedic lights, yellow and blue and red rolled and flashed up the street at Cusack. The effect made him think of 4th of July parades when he was a kid, fire engines in a parade. He was still amped up, his heart drumming against his ribs, and needed to sort out what he'd seen, to run out all the possible lines of consequence from Beaupre's shooting.

He couldn't stay where he was but he wasn't sure where to go. Everything, at least in the short run, was an unreasonable risk. Cusack stepped into the alcove entrance to an antique store and put his back to the door as a Jeep drove past slowly, the driver, unaware of what had happened, looking for a street number.

In the silence, the wash of colors from the emergency lights that painted the buildings across the street seemed now intended to reassure and not alarm. He could feel his heart slow. The benefit of every doubt came down to the shooting being a one off, an urban nightmare fluke. Cusack saw three men all linked together in a line of work and to the woman killed that made that the very last possibility he should consider. He headed for his car.

He approached it with caution, walked around it looking for something, he didn't know what, and finally got down on his knees and checked the undercarriage. There was nothing there and he drove off, careful at intersections as if the absurdity of Beaupre's killing meant anything was possible. He was only a few blocks from the condominium when he pulled to the curb to call Parsons. He left the motor running and as he reached for his cell phone an older man, with wild hair and shabbily dressed, crossed the street immediately in front of him. The man slowed, turned and stared into the car.

Cusack eased the car into drive, gripped the steering wheel, put his left foot hard on the brake and toed the accelerator with his right. He felt a terrible pressure in his chest. He was going to put the radiator into the man's chest if he reached for a water bottle. Instead, the man stepped onto the sidewalk and turned away, walking down 4th Street and occasionally looking into parked cars and tugging on door handles. Cusack let out his breath and dialed Parsons, who answered on the second ring.

"There's been some trouble. It's the deputy-mayor."

"Again."

"She's been shot." There was a long moment of silence. Everything from now on carried weight. What Parsons said and what he didn't say.

"How bad?"

"Dead."

"How'd it happen?"

"I was at a bar on University Avenue." Cusack wanted to leave Lauren out of the narrative, make her a bystander. It was simpler that way, at least for the time being. "Beaupre was there with Storti. He stopped at my table for a minute, we talked and then they both left. A few minutes later I saw her pull up at the intersection. A homeless guy or someone dressed to look that way, walked out to her car and started to wash her windshield. They do that a lot around here. The guy pulled out a gun, shot her and ran off."

"Then what?"

"Then nothing. I got the hell out of there." Cusack saw Beaupre's car rolling through the intersection again, the blood spray on the windshield and the shooter running off. Had he missed something in the prelim? Was there anything he could have done to prevent it? Others were going to ask those same questions.

Parsons said nothing for a minute. Cusack let the silence wind out. It was Parsons' play. "The shooting might have nothing to do with the Washburn."

Did Parsons think Cusack needed calm and bullshit would do the trick? Beaupre was at the Washburn when they took out the squatters and when the police thumped the students. Plenty of grievance there. "You, Storti and I and the deputy-mayor have been seen together," said Cusack. "She got shot in the middle of the street with a bunch of witnesses. A cowboy shoot. You need to start thinking that the rest of us could be targets, too."

Parsons' silence was an admission of uncertainty. "I'll alert the Director. Where are you now?"

"Five minutes from the condo."

"When you get there, sit tight. I'll get back to you."

Cusack snapped the phone shut, drove off but stopped again near the condominium at a spot where he could see the alley, the front door of the building and the windows to his place. He watched for fifteen minutes while several, innocuous looking student types and a woman pushing a small child in a stroller wandered past.

Time's up, he said to himself and slipped out of the car, hustled up the stairs, slid open the door and collected the pistol from the work table along with two extra clips and a box of shells. He picked up a small bag from under the bed that he kept ready for emergencies. He collected cigarettes, the fifth of bourbon in the refrigerator and the bottle of pain pills. He didn't like the spot he was in or much of anything just then. He gave the room one last look and slung the bag over his shoulder.

He drew the gun and used it to point the way to the ground floor. There were going to be questions and not just from the police. It was looking too much like Saint Georges, like everything had turned to shit. Back at his car, he settled in, put the pistol between his legs and smoked a cigarette. He watched the alley and the front door. When nothing happened for twenty minutes and he started the engine and drove off.

The Midway Motor Lodge was a mile away. He'd passed it on one of his tours of the area. It advertised cheap rooms in neon on a twenty foot pole. It was two story, cream colored stucco, built in the shape of a horseshoe with an open exterior walkway around the horseshoe on the second floor. The asphalt courtyard below had spaces for resident parking and a small swimming pool with cigarettes and a white sock floating on the surface. Summer was over. He slipped his car into a parking spot next to a late-model white Cadillac convertible.

Cusack walked under a Registration sign and pushed through a glass door with a steel grill on the backside. On the counter was an open pizza box with several curled, hardened pieces. A dusty rack to his left held tourist brochures with pictures of children enjoying a local water park and a theater performance with actors in period costume. A ceiling fan squeaked with every turn. A door to the left of the desk was open and gave onto a disheveled vista, a sofa with a bed sheet crumpled on it, a TV tray with a six pack of beer and a large television with silent zombies lurching toward the camera.

There is no place like home, thought Cusack as he tapped the bell on the counter next to the sign that said, "Ring for Service."

A young man with stringy, blonde hair peered around the door as if not quite willing to believe the bell. Seeing Cusack, he stepped quickly across to the counter and asked a series of questions as if he couldn't wait to get back to the zombies' story. He was furtive, couldn't look Cusack in the eye, as if he, and not Cusack, were on the run. Cusack paid cash for three nights and the clerk gave him a key and went back to his room, leaving the door ajar.

Cusack's room was on the second floor at one end of the horseshoe. Standing at the front door he had a clear line of sight at the entire parking lot, the street-side entrance to it and several blocks up the street. The drapes on the picture window next to the door were closed. He slipped the key in and pushed the door open. It was warped and he had to lean on it to get it to close. He twisted the lock in the doorknob and slid the deadbolt in.

He put his bag on the chest of drawers and laid the pistol next to it. The ceiling light was missing one of its bulbs. It may have been intentional; better lighting wouldn't have given the occupant a better impression. The walls were covered in a patternless off white, nubby, plasticized wallpaper. The desk and chest of drawers had a plastic walnut veneer. Everything in the room seemed to have been designed for cleaning with a minimum fuss. Still, the rug was filthy.

Cusack found the squalor bracing; he'd had it too easy lately. The whole project seemed more real now. When he turned on the television, it made a sound like plastic tearing. The local news people, whose faces started out with an orange tint, were all over the shooting. He flipped channels until he hit one that had Breaking News flashing at the bottom of the screen and a shot of Benjamin's over the reporter's left shoulder. The reporter recited the facts as reported to her by the police and pointed to the Washburn Redevelopment Area. The red and blue from the police car flashers strobed across her face.

Then the screen was full of scenes from the riot two days earlier. The reporter said she'd asked the chief of police if he thought there was a connection. Immediately, there was a cutaway to the chief of police in front of a bank of microphones and flanked on both sides by police officers.

"We've set up a task force and are pursuing all available leads. When we apprehend the suspect we hope to discover a motive. Finding the suspect is our top priority. We're not going to speculate on why he did it."

The next question for the chief of police was, "Are you planning on going into the Washburn to find the suspect? That was where witnesses saw him go after the shooting."

"Again, our plans are to follow the evidence and the leads we have wherever that takes us. I'm not going to talk about any specific action by our office.

Next question. "There's been talk of martial law being declared and the governor sending in the National Guard. Is there any truth to that?"

"Neither I nor the mayor have asked for the assistance of the National Guard. This is a murder investigation, not a natural disaster." The chief responded to every question in the same flat, toneless voice.

The reporter seemed excited by the atmosphere of violence. She recited a brief history of Beaupre's career. The family, husband and two children aged eleven and fourteen, were at the hospital where her body had been taken. At the same hospital, she said were several students recovering from injuries received during the altercation two days earlier at the Washburn Redevelopment Area protest.

The breeze blew the reporter's hair across her face and she brushed it away. Switching back to the Beaupre shooting, she said that according to eyewitnesses, the shooter did not attempt to rob the victim or hijack the car. To eyewitnesses, she said with a certain breathlessness, it looked like an execution. One witness said that the scene reminded him of reports of Mafia killings. Another witness said he heard the gunfire but thought it was firecrackers.

The police had cordoned off the area immediately around Benjamin's as a crime scene and put blockades at the entrances to the WRA. Because of the size of the Washburn, any search for the suspect in that area would not begin until the police had reinforcements.

Eyewitnesses to the shooting were working with a police sketch artist and the sketch would be broadcast as soon as it was made available. The police were warning citizens not to approach the suspect if they spotted him. The reporter promised more details, including an interview with several more eyewitnesses, during the regular 10 p.m. newscast and Cusack hit the off button.

He stripped off his clothes, which smelled of cigarettes, beer and sweat. The shower looked like it had been cleaned not too long ago. The complimentary bar of soap was the size of a credit card, just big enough to last the three days he'd be there. He stepped into the shower and let the water beat on him. The ceiling vent was noisy but ineffective and the room quickly filled with steam.

When you didn't believe in the future and the past was a horror show, you settled into the present, free of baggage but with limitations all the way around. Cusack used to think that limitations were, in their own way, the same as opportunities, or could be played that way. He'd been kidding himself but the words were fun to play with. He thought he might be getting the hang of the philosophy game where words were as good as actions for losing yourself, where words could be as opaque a screen as an expressed enacted purpose and as tangential and comforting in their diversion.

After drying off, Cusack found a clean glass upside down in a plastic baggy on the chest of drawers and tipped some bourbon into it. He lit a cigarette and turned on the television. News crews were still at Benjamin's. A reporter was interviewing the owner while they stood on the patio. In the far left corner of the picture was the bus bench that Beaure's car had ploughed into. Cusack put down half the contents of the glass in one gulp.

This wasn't the first time Cusack had seen on television, after the fact, a location where he'd worked a job. Those other times, seeing the place on television had carried no more resonance for him than a travel advertisement, as if the immediate past were racing away from him at incredible speed and taking all its connections to the present with it. However, Beaupre's death was still with him; she was smiling at a remark of Parsons, savoring a glass of wine and patiently explaining the mayor's position, vanishing in an explosion of glass and a spray of blood. Things seemed to work differently now and Cusack felt trapped in some sort of psychological, long haul accumulation.

Since Saint Georges, he'd begun to realize that he'd conceded too much as straight loss, like everything just disappeared down a hole. That ex-girlfriend had nailed it. But even conceding that, he still wasn't sure how to know what was bad habit and what was just inevitable fact. Protection was smart but if you were too ... what was Parsons' word, fastidious? ... then everything was gone before you ever had it.

Cusack thought he had to do something about Beaupre's death.

A significance of some sort would have to be established. There was no other way to get to the end of this. Do something about her and keep the bystanders well away. That shouldn't be too fucking hard, he told himself. He was a security professional, after all.

Cusack needed to see Storti. The bottle-throwers in that make-believe riot were almost certainly people from his own agency or from DSM or cops. It didn't matter which. Storti, however, impressed Cusack as someone who might be willing to share a few professional secrets, if asked politely. Whoever ordered the riot was gambling the mayor would jump the right way in response. A big gamble, thought Cusack.

Storti had mentioned that he and Parsons were both staying at the University Towers, across the street from the WRA. Cusack dressed and drove across town.

As Cusack stepped off the elevator a young man in a hurry clipped Cusack's shoulder on his way in. Cusack turned to look at him but he was turned away and concentrating on the console. He looked up for a moment as the doors began to close. Cusack moved toward Storti's room.

Storti did not appear surprised when he opened his door. "Drink?"

"Bourbon."

They stood in the middle of the room for a minute drinking in silence. Finally, Storti said, "Maybe, we should go for a ride." He meant the room was wired. Anyway, that's the way Cusack took it. In the hallway, Storti said, "Parsons is just down there," and pointed down the hallway. In the elevator he asked, "What have you heard?"

"The reporters," replied Cusack, "like the idea that there is a connection between the student riots and Beaupre's shooting."

"What do you like?"

"I like not being treated like a fucking moron."

The elevator doors opened onto a lobby with a contingent of blue-suited policeman standing near the front desk. Storti nodded to one of the suits and they went through the front door.

"The cops talk to you yet?" asked Storti.

"How well did you know Beaupre?"

Storti tilted his head when he looked at Cusack and pointed to the right. They went to the end of the block before Storti spoke. "You want to know if I was sleeping with her?"

"I want to know what kind of deal DSM had with the city."

"Here," Storti said, pointing to his car. Once inside, Storti started the engine and guided the car down the street. They rode for several blocks in silence.

"It was a contingency operation."

"You mean DSM got to play only if things fell out a certain way?"

"Close enough."

"Was Beaupre's death the contingency you needed?"

"Parsons told me about you," said Storti. "He takes his own angles, he said."

"What's going to happen next?"

"How would I know?" Storti shrugged.

"What about Tyler?"

"What about him?"

"I've read the file. I've met the family. I don't know what we're after here."

"I don't have insides on that. I'm strictly on the squatter project."

"You've been around Parsons a lot since this whole thing started.

"He's got something for Tyler. I can't say anymore. Does he have the clout to push this on his own? You work for him?"

"Yeah, I do." Cusack concentrated on his driving while he absorbed what he'd heard from Storti. Talking to Storti was starting to resemble playing with one of those black magic balls he'd owned as a kid. Shake it after asking a question and the answer would roll up out of blackness – yes or no but more often, try again, or nothing's for sure, you're lucky, goodnight or fuck you. Every answer was as good as every other answer.

"Is the mayor going to go with DSM?"

"Honestly? No. I mean the set up is right. We're making progress on setting up in the public mind that the squatters don't have rights, only needs and that makes them ... well, who knows? I think we could pull it off. Everybody wins. Pull over."

Cusack maneuvered to the curb. They were in front of the University Towers.

"DSM's civil reorientation program is better than SWAT and snipers. Beaupre was on our side."

"You think the shooter was just some college kid?"

"Why not?"

"What's going to happen to those people from the Washburn?"

"One way or another, they'll be taken care of." Storti stepped out of the car but leaned down and said, "Hey, be happy, it's not your worry."

Back at the motel, Cusack dragged a chair from the room onto the walkway in front of his door. He pulled a blanket off the bed, wrapped it around his shoulders and sat in the dark with his pistol in his lap. He went over in his head the chronology of the evening's events but could find no conclusion to settle on, no illumination. He sat smoking and taking occasional sips from his bottle of bourbon until he started to feel the muscles in his shoulders and neck lengthen and his stomach settle out.

A staged riot and a political assassination. Everything was in the flow now. There was no way to step out of it. It was going to take him and a whole lot of others wherever it meant to go.

A giant, orange, harvest moon rose over the Denny's Restaurant down the street. The air cooled quickly and he drew the blanket tighter. At some point in the aftermath of great violence everything gets telescoped down to an unredeemable present filled with a kind of serenity that comes from the vacuum created. What's cleared out is the bad outcome, which is beyond you, and the outward pressure has emptied everything and made what's left seem drowsy with the solemnity of it.

He finished the cigarette and pitched it over the railing. When he began to drowse, he looked at his watch. 2a.m. He dragged himself inside, curled up on the bed and fell off the world.

*If, for each of us, every second were its own discrete eon, a private unrecorded history, existence would be de-categorized, supreme and blessedly pointless.*

# Chapter 2

Late the next morning, Cusack awoke with a binding pain across his forehead. He was unsure of its origin - bourbon, concussion or both. He shuffled across the room to his bag, still unpacked on top of the chest, found his pills and took two. He found the television remote. The Beaupre shooting was still first place on the morning news but the Washburn student riot was a close second. There were conflicting stories of who did what to whom and when. The reporter totted up the number who'd been treated for injuries. The president of the university, the reporter said, had ordered an independent investigation. The university's spokesman said that the investigation was to be headed by an alumnus, a former U.S. congressman.

After the brief detour inside the student "riot," the Beaupre shooting occupied much of the rest of the news cycle. There was statement by a man who was identified as a representative of the

Beaupre family and one by the governor with the mayor by his side. An effusive litany of praise for Beaupre as a public servant and wife and mother.

Cusack showered and, when the pills kicked in and the headache faded, began to feel hungry. He walked to a steak house two blocks away and ordered a breakfast of New York steak, eggs over easy and hashed brown potatoes and lingered over a third cup of coffee and a scrap of day-old newspaper. It didn't have much to tell him but it was just enough to keep him from thinking about the mess in front of him. He stared through the window next to his booth at a light rain beginning to fall steadily out of a seamless gray sky. It reminded him of Seattle.

At the end of an assignment there he stayed on a few days with the wife of Chief Warrant Officer, Hal Reynolds, who he'd known in Iraq. Reynolds was a helicopter pilot. He'd flown missions with Cusack as crew leader and they'd been lucky a few times to get out with a whole skin. When Cusack called, Hal's wife, Teri, answered and said Hal was in Bremerton but to come on over anyway. Hal never showed. Teri said, "The two boys are with Hal. It's just me for now." Cusack wondered if Hal was really in Bremerton, not that after a couple hours at a local bar it mattered.

The second day, Teri talked Cusack into going ice skating at the local rec center. As a kid Cusack had played pick-up games at the ice rink next to the high school with other kids from the neighborhood. The rink had waist-high boards all around, a warming shed and a blandly encouraging retiree who tended a wood stove. The old man had played hockey in college and told anyone who'd listen that he almost made the U.S. Olympic team. What Cusack liked most about the games was taking an opposing player into the boards. It wasn't much of a skill, he never made the varsity and he hadn't been on the ice in years.

At the Community Recreation Center where Cusack and Teri rented skates, the main room was high-ceilinged and chaotically noisy. On one side of the building was a rink for "family" skating and on the other side peewee hockey league matches. The crowd circling the rink was a mixed group: teenage couples happy with an excuse to hang onto each other in public, older men doing laps and trying to turn it into a workout and young couples with very young children who spent most of their time laughing and falling on their butts. After twenty minutes Cusack's thought his ankles were going to snap and he was wheezing hard from the effort of keeping up with Teri. After several falls he called for a rest break.

They returned to the community room where they sat on plastic chairs near a table with two giant steel urns, one hot chocolate, the other hot apple cider. Cusack scanned the room. Nothing seemed to require his attention. It always took some time to ramp down after an assignment.

"That was fun," Teri said.

"Yeah," agreed Cusack, wiping sweat from his face.

"You're out of shape. I thought the CIA kept their killers in better shape."

"What the hell did Hal tell you? I'm not a killer and I'm not with the CIA," he said for the third or fourth time. "We're a security firm with some government contracts."

"Well, shouldn't you be in better shape if you're going to protect the country?"

Cusack began to envy Hal, that is, the Hal that was in Bremerton.

After finishing a cup of cider, Teri coaxed Cusack into another tour on the ice. The second time he didn't last fifteen minutes. For Cusack, the fun was over.

While he was unlacing his skates, the peewee scrimmage on the other side of the rink ended and the players and parents poured into the changing room. Cusack's ankles and legs ached and he thought he was ready to go back to Baltimore. The room was loud with players' excited chatter and parents' complaints. Where was the goalie on that shot? Where was the equipment manager? Where was the ref? The league coordinator had promised a ref. Teri was talking about dinner at some restaurant in Tacoma but Cusack had told his principal on the project that he was only staying a couple extra days in Seattle and that time was up.

"What the hell do you think you were doing out there?" yelled a tall man at a small boy sitting on a bench who was trying to get out of his hockey uniform. Both Teri and Cusack turned at the sound of the man's voice. The man wore a long black leather jacket and a watch cap with the Chicago Blackhawks logo. His face was red and he had a big gut.

The boy continued to pull off his game shirt and the man grabbed it and leaned in close. "Are you blind?" the man said. "You had an open shot. Why didn't you take it?"

Teri looked across at the boy and tried to catch Cusack's eye. Cusack was slow to get into his street shoes. His ankles still hurt like hell; he was ready to get out and go home. He grabbed his skates and was on his way out when he noticed a long line returning skates at the rental booth.

Teri walked across the room, stopped in front of the man and said, "Do you have to yell like that? Can't you see what it's doing to your boy?"

"What the fuck business is it of yours?"

Cusack moved slowly across the room until he stood next to Teri. He kept his hands at his side. The guy she was talking to was just under six foot and weighed maybe two-thirty. He seemed to have lost interest in the game and was breathing hard. Teri had gotten his attention.

Teri wouldn't back down and Cusack gave her credit. She said again, "You're scaring the boy."

"I say again, what the fuck business is it of yours?"

The room had grown quiet. Some people were staring at the four of them. Some were pretending nothing was going on.

"You don't need to talk like that. You need to calm down."

"Don't tell me, bitch, what I need to do." He leaned toward Teri.

Cusack was close enough to sense Teri's fear. He took a step just to her right and the man finally decided to notice him.

"You got something to say?"

Cusack never took his eyes off the man but said to Teri, "I think we can go now. He's been told."

"You gutless little shit," the man said, taking a step toward Cusack.

Cusack, up on the balls of his feet, took a half-step toward the man and brought his right fist up with tremendous speed just under the man's ribcage. He followed with a left hook high up on his cheek. The force of the blows sent the man back into the wall where his left foot slipped under him and he sat down hard.

Teri grabbed Cusack by the arm and pulled him away. "What's wrong with you?" she said.

"An ounce of prevention." Cusack had hit him exactly where he'd meant to. He could feel the punch all the way back into his shoulder. He guessed that the man was having a little difficulty getting his breath. It was a solid combination. Cusack was keyed up and kept his eyes wide to see if the man had a friend.

"Jesus Christ, you're as bad as Hal." Teri shook her head, one hand on Cusack's arm. "Swing first and ask questions later."

Cusack waited for the man to pick himself up off the floor but he was having trouble getting his feet planted right for leverage.

"You're crazy. All of you." She walked right out of the building.

Cusack had nothing to say to her. He was glad she'd left; it was easier that way. Cusack stood still for a minute looking down at the man on the floor but he never did get to his feet. Cusack took a taxi from the skating rink directly to the airport. He hadn't left anything important with Teri. Later, during the flight back to Baltimore he recalled the look on the boy's face after he'd punched his father. It was a look of pure understanding.

That was a long time ago and he couldn't recall ever seeing that precise look on anyone's face again. After breakfast at the steakhouse, Cusack stopped at a drugstore on his way back to the Midway Motor Lodge and bought cigarettes, two newspapers and a bag of peanuts for later. He slipped into his car and dropped the newspapers on the passenger seat. He activated the phone and dialed up Parsons.

"Where are you calling from?" asked Parsons.

"Did they find the shooter?"

Parsons said nothing. Cusack had not stayed at the condominium as instructed and Parsons' question implied that he knew that and was weighing the intention in Cusack's move. Finally, Parsons said, "The police have been here. We enlightened them as to our professional relationship with the deceased. I think that's the way it's put."

"Operational containment is job one, right?"

"Of course, once they talk to Storti they are going to want to talk to you." Parsons covered the phone and spoke to someone in the room. A minute later he was back and said to Cusack, "By the way, I'm at the University Towers."

Cusack pretended it was news to him. "Right across the street from the Washburn Redevelopment Area? A nice view."

"Urban charm. The occasional sound of dynamite and the rattle of windows. Rubble growing like corn in Nebraska as far as the eye can see. We decided we needed to be close in. I informed the director about the incident and he's sending a man out."

"How's he going to help?"

Parsons ignored the question. "The man will be flying in late this afternoon. We'll get him settled here." Parsons was being generous, had decided not to make an issue of Cusack's relocating. "Nine o'clock. Room 1803."

Cusack snapped the phone shut. The killing would complicate, at the very least, the Tyler project because that's what killings did. Cusack wondered if Parsons, like Storti, could see an advantage in that complication. Cusack couldn't see one.

Parsons always carried a sense of what he was owed and usually put it out there. During the interview when he'd offered Cusack the Tyler job, he made reference to the disaster in Senegal with Cusack and his team. Parson's recollection of certain aspects of the operation was vague and noncommittal but Cusack's memories were distilled and clarified. Cusack recalled the helicopter going down hard outside Matam. Matam was located on the banks of the Senegal River on the northeast border area with Mauritania. Parsons made a point of talking about all that he'd had done to get Cusack out and Cusack who thought he was going to die, just kept himself from saying, "You were the fucking one who got me into that fucking snakepit."

Cusack wondered why it had taken him so many years to see the wheels within wheels that constituted every one of Parsons' enterprises. Early on in his association, he'd been blinded by Parsons' brilliance and charm. Now, other things were in play. Brilliance and charm weren't on the report card. That was the past.

Now, Cusack carried the unread newspaper to a coffee shop where he would kill time until his meeting with Parsons. The coffee shop offered free Internet connections and there were three unused PCs on the far wall. The shop reeked of a dense coffee smell. There was only one customer, Victor Ogbemudia, who was seated at a table under a small blue light. Well, well, well.

Cusack was third in a line of three at the counter. He ordered a cup of coffee and watched Victor who was reading a book and had an intense look on his face as if the book were arguing with him. It was, perhaps, the sort of book he preferred.

To Cusack, it seemed to take an extraordinary amount of time to assemble a simple cup of coffee. Finally, he was handed a mug, carried it across the room and slipped into the chair across from Victor. He was staring at his cup and running a finger tip around the rim. He looked up when Cusack pulled out a chair. "Russo?"

"Victor. Nice to see you again."

"Are you still looking for a place to stay?"

Cusack raised an eyebrow and sipped from his cup.

"I have only short-term rentals available now." Victor smiled not at Cusack but toward the street and nodded his head as if the joke were bigger than either of them. Victor was serene; his manner said he could handle whatever was put in front of him. He made you want to trust him.

"The woman that got shot," said Cusack. "I saw her just before she was shot."

"The deputy-mayor, yes. Very sad." Victor shook his head.

"For some people, yes; for others, no." Something in Victor's tone made Cusack think, was Beaupre shot to provoke a confrontation? Had the mayor's social worker gambit worked too well neutralizing the squatters? Had it been the solution, the last thing some people wanted?

"Inevitable, I would say."

"You knew the victim?"

"Not at all. I was speaking of the shooter. A man determined to kill will kill eventually, no matter what. Violence has its own irrefutable logic."

"What logic is that?"

"He didn't rob the woman, didn't take the car. She was a public official. It was an assassination then, yes? They happen all the time where I come from. In America it is more ... what is the word? Unusual?" Again, Victor smiled.

"And where do you come from?' said Cusack.

"She was killed because she was in the way. That is the logic of killing."

"In the way?"

Victor looked at the street again. "That first time you came into the Washburn, you were lucky."

"Lucky?" Cusack picked up his cup.

Victor smiled. "Some people living in the Washburn seeing a stranger might have been less ... open-minded."

Cusack sipped his coffee. "I'm not the law, if that's what you're thinking." He kept his voice low but no one was paying them any attention.

"I don't know the shooter if that's what you think. In any case, I am only concerned about my friends."

"You should be concerned." Out of the corner of his eye, Cusack saw four young black men crossing the street headed for the coffee shop. "The cops are going to go in there real hard." Cusack wasn't sure about that but he didn't believe DSM would get taken up on its civic disorder scheme. The Washburn was like a nightmare that had been disassembled and all its parts scattered. Sweeping up the mess wasn't going to be simple but old-fashioned people in power had a tendency to look to old-fashioned means of re-establishing order. Force and lots of it.

Victor leaned back in his chair. "What is it your Bob Dylan says, 'When you ain't got nothing, you got nothing to lose.'"

Cusack was annoyed to hear an echo of his exchange with Parsons only with him in the Parsons' role. The black men from the street entered the shop and occupied a booth near the table he shared with Victor.

Cusack put his hand on his leg next to the holster. The prospect of violence opened up for him like a flower. Three of the young men settled into the booth while the fourth went to the counter. Victor did not acknowledge them. "Nothing to lose?" said Cusack. "You start with that, Victor, where do you end up?"

"You tell me."

"Senegal?" said Cusack.

Victor's eyes widened slightly. "Comparisons are always ..." He held his hand out palm down and waggled it.

"What makes them ready to fight?"

"What makes anybody ready to fight? They think they can win." Victor tilted his head to the left. "Or losing is impossible to consider."

Cusack thought of the window washer's automatic pistol. "They can't win," he said but a car full of ordnance like the window washer's could make the Washburn a vast killing ground.

"You know that," said Cusack, "but for them it all depends on what you mean by winning."

Cusack had been in many places standing next to people like Victor and looking at the train wreck their country had become and calling it a revolutionary success or the beginning of a grand national experiment or a fucking tourist site, as if you could bring definitions in after the fact and assign them to any words you had close to hand. "I'm taking a philosophy class at the college from a Professor Tyler. Have you heard of him?"

Victor shrugged. If Cusack didn't know better he'd have thought Victor hadn't heard of Tyler.

"I haven't read everything of his," said Cusack, "but I bet he has something to say about the meaning of winning. He just seems like that kind of guy. You should look into that, what winning means."

"How do you spell his name?"

Cusack stood up. "You have a nice day." The young black men at the nearby table ignored him.

*The opposite of ambition is not sloth but the
radical compulsion toward self-negation: to aspire
to be not the early bird but the early worm.*

# Chapter 3

Cusack parked the car a block from University Towers. The streetlights, white and gaseous, left everything at ground level vague and unfocused, hard to know for certain what you were looking at. The only car on the street was stalled in the intersection four blocks north, its headlights on and steam coming from under the hood. The owner had walked away and not another person could be seen in any direction.

The intersection he was staring at could have been the same intersection where, earlier, he had watched the social workers bring the squatters out to the waiting buses. Now, there was no evidence of that. The street and sidewalks were cleaned up; even the barricades had been hauled away. The swarm of police made him feel something bad was inevitable. Not the ending to the student protest. That seemed like a prelude to much worse. The city seemed to have bottomed out now.

The light from the streetlight at the corner behind him was depleted when it reached the middle of the block, leaving Cusack to inhabit only a discounted grayness. To his left, beyond the fence that bordered the Washburn, was a line of shrubs and trees, their leaves gone and exposing the wreckage beyond of brick and pipes, smashed bath fixtures and doors that looked brand new. These mountains of refuse had apparently come from the recently downed buildings. The city's trash haulers wanted armed escorts now before they'd go into the Washburn. Everything got harder.

Cusack saw movement among the wreckage, a man, furtive and uncertain. Whoever it was became still and invisible as if suddenly made aware of Cusack's attention. Whatever he was looking for seemed, to Cusack, a futile exercise. Blown up and bulldozed, there couldn't have been much useful left to salvage though hope and desperation were habits hard to break.

On Cusack's side of the street, there were neither bars nor restaurants, only a drug store, discount tobacco, adult video and liquor. stores with heavy bars on the windows and doors. Cusack stepped out of his car and locked up. The absence of entertainments along the block might have been accounted for by the dismal view across the street. There would be no paying customers coming out of the WRA and the paying customers who did come to this street wouldn't much like what they saw or the people they were likely to meet. Cusack's shoes smacked the sidewalk, disturbing the unearthly quiet of the street.

He pushed through a revolving door into the Towers and its vast lobby. An enormous chandelier in the high ceiling lit up the room. Built in the 1930s, the Towers had clearly had a recent clean up. Art Deco designs and furnishings in the lobby had been polished or replaced. Someone was betting the WRA was going to get fixed up in a big way. The bar on the far side of the lobby had an appealing glitter but he headed for the elevators.

The walls and ceiling of the elevator were mirrored and that reminded him of a trip he'd taken while in Vienna. Brochures in his hotel offered tours to the Vienna Opera and the Salzburg Mozart festival. Cusack chose a tour to Hitler's Eagles Nest. Turned into a tourist site, the elevator there took visitors up through solid rock. It had highly polished walls, which gave the illusion of a much larger compartment, an antidote for Hitler's claustrophobia. The view from the top of the river valley was extraordinary but Hitler visited only once. He was afraid of heights which, to Cusack, made the entire enterprise seem ridiculous.

Cusack stepped out of the elevator and moved to the left toward Room 1803. Parsons answered the door and led him into the suite. Storti was standing next to the drinks cart and putting ice cubes into a tall glass. Beyond him was another man with his back to the room.

The man turned and walked across the room and extended his hand. "Cusack? I'm Deputy Director Merriwether. Parsons told us that you were a witness to the shooting. What happened?"

Cusack went to the drinks cart and poured himself a bourbon and dropped an ice cube into it. He turned back to Merriwether. "A squatter or someone who was supposed to look like a squatter came out of nowhere. He pretended to work the deputy-mayor's windshield then pulled out a small automatic pistol and emptied the clip into her car." He tipped half the contents of his glass into his mouth.

Merriwether was looking down at his drink. He looked up and settled his eyes on Cusack. "Why do you say, 'supposed to look like a squatter'?"

"Because we don't know. She was shot and a squatter would be convenient."

Merriwether seemed to give this some consideration then changed direction. "We can't be sure how this will affect our position. Will the mayor have a change of heart under these circumstances? The question is will he take the more measured approach to resolving the situation using our and DSM's expertise or go the way of SWAT teams and snipers and APCs?" He paused and looked abruptly at Cusack. "What are you saying? Convenient for whom?"

"There's got to be more than one reason she might have been killed."

Merriwether addressed Parsons and Storti. "Politically, I think our proposal is dead or, at the very least, on life support. You don't negotiate with the people who assassinate your deputy-mayor. There's no proof it was a squatter but that's what it looks like now and if the mayor continues with negotiation he will appear weak even cowardly."

"Our tactics take time and, at least, the appearance of negotiation," said Storti. "We'd need to get our hands on some squatters, a dozen say, plant our devices and return them to the Washburn. That takes time and I'm not sure the mayor can resist the pressure to do something right damn now."

"Don't forget there are women and children in the Washburn," said Parsons. "I told the mayor that no one wants another Waco. We're still in this." On that note, everyone refreshed their drinks.

To Parsons, Merriwether said, "What's the latest on the squatters?"

"We've inventoried every building that shows evidence of occupation. We have structural blueprints, heating and vent systems, electrical and plumbing. We have equipment in place, thermal imaging so we can track every single soul in any building. We have a data base with almost everyone in the Washburn."

"Almost?" said Merriwether.

"The population is somewhat fluid. There are a few residents we have not been able to identify. We're working on that. We do have personal histories."

Storti jumped in. "Following up on Parsons' cautionary note about Waco, I made another pitch to the mayor's Chief of Staff. What DSM can offer in partnership with your people."

"I'm going back to my room," said Merriwether. "I have all your reports." He turned toward Storti. "Send me the DSM protocols. I'll be talking to the Director later. Let's meet for breakfast and we'll set ourselves to finish this project. And Tyler," he added almost as an afterthought with his hand on the doorknob. "Where are we with him, Parsons? I'll need to be up to speed on that, too." He tilted his head as if he'd just heard a sound he liked that no one else could hear. "The Director doesn't like surprises. Like me, he wants to see the entire feature, not just the trailers." He smiled at his phrasing and let the door fall shut after him.

Cusack pushed open the sliding door and stepped onto the balcony. Merriwether reminded Cusack of one of the four guys Parsons recruited up for the security detail on the helicopter ride that ended so badly in Senegal. The guy that looked like Merriwether was Irish, probably ex-Irish Republican Army. There was a Dutchman who looked like an Olympic weightlifter. The South African hardly spoke at all. The last was an American but not an agency man. Cusack thought nothing of it at the time but later wondered why Parsons couldn't have brought his own agency professionals or why the Senegalese army didn't provide an escort for one of its own diplomats. Did they suggest a bad ending and didn't want their people involved? Was Cusack's presence on the team enough to settle any worries for the rest of the crew? Cusack didn't like what he was thinking.

They met in the hotel and rode out in a Mercedes stretch limo from the hotel to an army post on the northern edge of Dakar. The diplomat, who'd been introduced to Cusack as Mr. Seku or something like that, was talkative.

"First," he said, "we talk about a ceasefire, a truce. It will take them a little while to get used to the idea of surrender."

"You're very confident," said Cusack as he checked the magazine on his M-4.

"We showed them toughness."

"I heard two villages were wiped out. Men, women and children."

"Rebel propaganda," he said dismissively. "We don't kill women and children."

They were stopped at the entrance to the post. A soldier leaned in and Seku spoke sharply to him. He stepped back and saluted. The bar was raised and the car glided forward.

There were several helicopters behind a large hangar. Inside the hangar, lights showed mechanics working on several old jets. Two soldiers stood at attention next to one of the helicopters, theirs. When they settled in, it was another ten minutes before the pilot and co-pilot arrived. Seku raised his voice in a brief tirade. A few minutes later, the helicopter lifted off, banked hard and turned toward the north.

As they approached the meeting location, the helicopter reduced altitude and slowed and just then they were hit by small arms fire. They made it another half-mile before the helicopter crashed in a small clearing. Cusack was thrown clear of the wreckage, broke his right wrist and collarbone and was knocked out. When he regained consciousness, the helicopter was completely engulfed in flames and he knew everyone left inside was dead. He managed to get to his feet and make it into the trees. Forty-five minutes later the rebels arrived and celebrated by firing their weapons into the air. They walked around the wreckage peering inside and seemed satisfied with having knocked down the helicopter. They conducted only a cursory search for survivors, then spent some time knocking off the rear rotor. A trophy, Cusack guessed.

Cusack had used his belt to keep his shoulder stabilized. He dozed fitfully until dawn when he heard the helicopters, three of them, one transport and two gunships. The transport settled down fifty yards from the wreck and a rescue team of six hopped out. When Cusack staggered out from the tree line, they nearly shot him.

Parsons opened the door behind Cusack and joined him on the balcony.

"I'm not clear now on our approach with Tyler," said Cusack.

Parsons drew on his cigarette and exhaled slowly. "We're going to have to become obvious sooner with him and his daughter."

It struck Cusack then that this might have been what Parsons had wanted all along: to become obvious to Tyler. Parsons may never have been interested in the subtleties of intelligence gathering. Cusack pointed out toward the city below. "Have you seen that? Those National Guard trucks? What do you think they're for?"

"The mayor's putting a hard perimeter on the Washburn."

"He's going in the hard way. SWAT teams, and snipers and armored personnel carriers. We're finished here." Cusack stepped back inside, went to the drinks cart and poured himself a cup of coffee. He tore open a thimble-sized container of cream and tipped the contents in.

Parsons said, "You don't know that." Then he went back to the subject of Tyler. "Whatever you think about the Washburn, Tyler remains, and you know, he's not just a troublesome little man. He's dangerous."

Cusack sat on the sofa and looked up at Parsons. He was trying to figure out what, in precise tactical terms, Parsons meant by "getting obvious."

"Ever since his son-in-law was deported he's been doing his utmost to fuck with the agency. One of his colleagues when he was teaching in Lyon is now in the French diplomatic corps. The French ambassador to Mauritania gave our State Department a load of shit about those people killed around Matam. One of Tyler's former students works at the Center for Disease Control. The CDC said they wanted to send a team into Senegal to find out exactly what killed those villagers. That turned into another publicity hit for the agency. You know the agency wasn't to blame for what went wrong in Senegal."

Cusack turned to Parsons. "Why did the rebels shoot down our helicopter?"

"Desperation. Maybe one of their units went rogue just to show the government how tough they could be."

"They thought we'd killed the people in those villages, didn't they? With the shit DSM provided to the military, right?"

"The military thought if they showed the rebels how far they were prepared to go, they would agree to a cease-fire and negotiate."

"The military hired us to give them advice. What did we tell them?"

"They had their own ideas." Parsons sipped his drink. "The client is not required to take our advice."

Cusack wondered when Parsons had come to know what he knew. Was it before or after he sent Cusack and the others on that mission? Something Cusack had half-heard in the hotel before taking that doomed flight haunted him. It said something about Parsons' judgment. Parsons had been absolutely committed to the project in Senegal just like he was here on this project and that made Cusack uneasy and wanting to know the location of every exit.

"Forget the past," said Storti. "I'm trying to set up another meet with the mayor on how he can avoid a disaster."

"You can do that?" said Cusack.

Storti returned Cusack's smile. "The mayor's been told the risks in the use of conventional force. Dozens of women and children in the Washburn."

There was a knock at the door. Parsons looked at Cusack, then went to the door. He came back with two policemen, one tall and heavy-set who identified himself as Lieutenant Morrissey and Sergeant Winand, a reedy-looking man with dark wavy hair cut close to the skull and a thin mustache.

"What can I do for you, Lieutenant?" said Parsons.

Morrissey asked for names, then said, "Sergeant Winand and I are here about the Beaupre shooting. We have some questions for you, Mr. Cusack and you Mr. Storti. We can ask them here or downtown."

Parsons made it obvious he didn't like his tone but didn't immediately reply. "Ask away."

"You were at *Benjamin's* when the deputy-mayor was shot, right?" said Morrissey looking at Cusack.

"Yes."

"When were you going to come forward and let us know?"

Cusack looked him in the eye. "Eventually."

"That's an unhelpful attitude. Could get someone in trouble."

Cusack turned his back on Morrissey and sat on the sofa. He picked up his coffee cup and sipped from it. It was cold and tasted like shit.

"And you, Mr. Storti?"

"I was gone before the shooting occurred. I don't have anything to add to the picture."

"You were," said Winand, "the last one to talk to her before she was shot. What did you talk about?"

"Security issues. The Washburn. I'm a consultant. That's why I'm here."

"Consultant," Morrissey repeated derisively.

"Lieutenant," said Parsons, "Mr. Storti was not an eyewitness and

Mr. Cusack was first of all concerned for his own safety and, under the circumstances, I believe you can see how that's understandable."

Morrissey seemed to consider Parsons' remark before responding. He looked back at Cusack. "Why don't you tell us what happened."

Cusack put his cup on the table. Neither Morrissey nor Winand had a notebook or tape recorder. This was all between professionals. No need for tedious precision, for punctilious record keeping. Finally, he said, "I was having a drink with someone from the college. I'm taking a class there. "

"Who was the person you were with," asked Morrissey, who took one of the chairs across from Cusack.

Cusack guessed that Morrissey knew the answer. Cops and lawyers; they only asked questions when they knew the answer. Sometimes Cusack saw it their way, as professional discipline but other times as a simple absence of curiosity. He could go either way with Morrissey. "Lauren Tyler."

"Her father, that professor?" said Winand in a tone that suggested he knew Tyler and didn't like him. He moved across to the drinks cart and poured himself a triple shot of bourbon.

"Did you speak to Ms. Beaupre?"

"No."

Parsons said, "Lieutenant Morrissey, we're more than willing to cooperate with your inquiries." He put his glass on the cart. "However, we have a contract with the city, an understanding with the mayor and our own priorities."

Morrissey turned toward Storti. "What exactly was the nature of your conversation with the deputy-mayor?"

"We talked about the assistance DSM could offer the mayor and the police department in resolving the situation in the Washburn." Storti topped up his drink with an elaborate casualness that signaled to Cusack that something was wrong. What was he hiding? "On my way out I had a few words with Mr. Cusack."

Morrissey turned back to Cusack. "What happened after your conversation with Storti."

"Storti and Beaupre left and a few minutes later I spotted her car at the stoplight. A homeless guy stepped in front of her car and sprayed the windshield from a water bottle. Happens all the time. They come out at stop lights, spray your car's windshield, then get their hand in your face before they'll wipe it off."

"Yeah, we're familiar with that," said Morrissey. "Describe the shooter for me, would you?"

"Six foot. A beard. A purple watch cap and a long dark coat. Black leather gloves."

"What happened next?"

"The guy reached under his coat, brought out a pistol and fired a burst into the car. I hit the floor."

"What kind of pistol was it?" asked Winand.

"A small automatic with a short barrel and a long clip. A MAC 10 or an Uzi maybe. It happened pretty fast." The scene came back to Cusack, crisp and clear with color and precise sound effects. He had a good memory for details. "When he was done, the shooter ran across the street and disappeared among the buildings in the Washburn."

"Why didn't you follow him?"

Cusack expected the question. "This was supposed to be a surveillance job." He looked at Parsons. "Watching an old college professor and his family. I was unarmed. I thought I needed first to see to Ms. Tyler's safety."

"And your own." said Morrissey.

Cusack smiled. "Not all of us can be as brave as people who weren't there."

"All right," said Morrissey, "you talked to Storti and a few minutes after he and Beaupre leave she gets shot." He looked at Cusack like it was a question but Cusack ignored him.

"What else can you tell us?" asked Winand.

Cusack reached for his coffee cup. "The shooter was an amateur."

"How so?"

"He one-handed it. Got most of the rounds in the first burst on Beaupre but you can't keep a pistol like that on the mark with one hand." He held the cup for a moment, remembered how bad the coffee was and put it down. "The last few rounds probably went into the suburbs."

"That kind of weapon ... Maybe the squatters are getting organized," said Morrissey, as if talking to himself.

"I saw Beaupre with the cops when they went into the Washburn with the social workers and rousted the squatters," said Cusack. "That kind of high profile could have made her a target." Cusack wanted to needle the lieutenant who was a prick anyway you looked at it. "And maybe they are getting organized."

Winand said, "We stopped at your condo. Where are you staying now?"

"The Midway Motor Lodge."

"Nice," said Winand.

"First class," said Cusack.

After the two policemen let themselves out, Cusack walked across to the sliding glass door and onto the balcony. He lit a cigarette.

Through the open door Cusack heard Parsons say, "Beaupre's shooting shouldn't interfere with our work on the project. DSM or us. This can still be salvaged. The WRA, Tyler, Ogbemudia's brother. All of it." Cusack couldn't hear Storti's response.

A moment later Parsons stepped onto the balcony and pulled

the door shut. "Don't go off all wrong on this," he said.

"What if the shooter," said Cusack, "who looked to me to be strictly amateur, got it wrong? What if he got the wrong car, shot the wrong guy or only one of the targets he was supposed to hit?" Parsons was too calm about Beaupre's death. He should have seen how her shooting complicated the assignment. "What if the intended target was ..." and he gestured inside where Storti was refilling his drink. "I told you before, too many things have come together here. Storti represents DSM ... Senegal and Saint-Georges. Just like you and me. Maybe we're next."

"Do you think we can tie Victor Ogbemudia and Tyler together with the shooting?"

The eagerness in Parsons' voice was unexpected. "You think we can still put that package together?" said Cusack.

Parsons seemed lost in thought. Then, he said, "I'll talk to Storti."

"Why did you bring DSM into this?" Cusack thought he knew the answer but he wanted to hear it from Parsons. "A replay of Matam?"

"Everything's a circle," said Parsons.

"Is it?"

"You're the one taking a philosophy class from Professor Tyler."

Not for the first time Cusack thought the whole thing was beginning to look too much like a replay of Saint-Georges: pointless work, somebody he knew killed in front of him and too many questions from the wrong people. What was that Ekelund line? "There is no better compass than ... fleeing." But he couldn't go down that road just yet. There was the problem of bystanders.

Parsons seemed to be reading Cusack's mind and figuring a way to manipulate him. "You volunteered for this."

"You changed up the game."

"You're looking at it all wrong. It's an opportunity," said Parsons.

"It is that," said Cusack on his way to the door.

*Skepticism is a perpetual hesitation and, over time, causes a minor lesion in the mind. We become habituated to that frisson of rebellion though it ultimately precludes forever a certain kind of belief, the kind that is taken for granted.*

# Chapter 4

Minutes after leaving Parsons, Cusack stepped out of the elevator into the lobby. He looked around before moving to the entrance. It was too late to move back to the condo so he settled in again at the Midway Motor Lodge with Vietnamese take-out. There was an X-Files marathon on, and he propped himself on the bed, put his beer on the nightstand and dug into the kung pao chicken

Halfway through the box, he suddenly felt full and put the leftovers on the nightstand. He unwrapped the glass on the chest of drawers and poured in a couple fingers of bourbon. The ice in the bucket had all melted but the water was cold and he topped up the glass. He pulled his computer out of his bag and sat at his desk. The desk lamp had two bulbs but only one worked. He started looking for information on Merriwether. He was ex-CIA and had only recently joined Cusack's agency. That explained why Cusack hadn't recognized him. As a matter of fact, his first day was the day after Saint-Georges. Merriwether had worked in several countries; his work was defined as promoting development. Before the CIA he'd worked for Exxon. Before that he'd worked for a U.S. Senator from Louisiana.

Cusack keyed in Beaupre's name and went looking for a reason she had to die besides the one the media was pushing. She graduated with honors from the University of Wisconsin – Madison. Had worked for six years as a community organizer. A natural segue into politics followed; elected to the state legislature, three terms. Then deputy-mayor. No scandals, just a journeyman pol.

And then there was Tyler fronted as some kind of bogeyman. He was being linked to the WRA although his role in the protests was marginal. His link to Victor was familial, understandable. Parsons, Cusack mused, had a unified theory and Tyler was central to the theory. The Director and Merriwether appeared to buy it, too and that was a puzzle. It was a redemptive theory, at least for Parsons and had all the appeal that those theories possess. Cusack wondered if his philosophy class was rubbing off on him. Unified theory, indeed.

He closed his eyes, hoping for sleep and soon dozed. On his last visit to his mother, Cusack arrived at the nursing home some hours after she'd slipped into a coma. He joined his father, brother and sister in his mother's room. Her hair had been brushed and arranged around her face. A machine next to the bed showed her heartbeat. Two large vases filled with a variety of flowers stood on the narrow table on the wall opposite her bed. The smell was cloyingly sweet. Her hands lay on her stomach and a clear plastic bag on a pole was dripping something into the back of her wrist. A piece of clear tubing lay on her upper lip and pushed oxygen up her nose.

The drapes on the windows were open and he could see sprinklers working, water glistening on the grass and splashing on the sidewalk and the street beyond. There was no one on the sidewalk and no cars in the street. Outside, the temperature was in the 90s. The cabdriver who brought Cusack from the airport talked nonstop about the heat like it had never been hot before.

When he arrived, Cusack's father and sister told him what had happened that day. His mother had been in and out of consciousness then out for good. They had talked to her but she had not replied. A morphine drip was taking care of any pain; everything was being done to make her comfortable. It was just a matter of time.

Conversation lagged. Cusack exchanged perfunctory remarks with his brother and sister about work. Cusack asked about his nieces and nephews. His father said nothing and stared at his hands. Occasionally, a nurse would pass by. The intercom would come to life and announce meal times, the name of the movie being shown that night or a coded signal that someone was in trouble. The nurse came in and gave the occupant in the next bed her pills.

After one prolonged period of silence, Cusack excused himself. In the hallway, he asked a nursing assistant the location of the nearest men's room. He had no need for a bathroom except that it offered a door between him and everything else.

Once inside, he carefully depressed the lock button in the center of the door handle. He wanted an excuse not to leave for a long time. It wasn't a room made for comfort, however. There was no place to sit but on the toilet, no place to lie down but the floor. The walls were covered in a geometric patterned wallpaper with traces of red and green throughout. On a narrow, stainless steel shelf on the wall opposite the wash basin was a piece of paper, much folded.

He picked up the paper and, opening it, saw first names in a column on the left, the other columns apparently instructions of some sort. The paper was a photocopy, the writing in block letters, carefully legible. The headings were: Room#/ Name/ Mental Status/ Activity/ Meals/ Bath/ Restraint/ Sensory/ Cares, etc/.

Cusack read that Gert Baker was alert, well-educated, read a lot and was occasionally confused. Her bath day was Friday and she preferred a tub. She wore glasses. She was independent and should be assisted only as requested. She preferred to stay in her room. Cusack could see the appeal in that. The door handle rattled but Cusack ignored it.

He read that Eliz. Arendt was confused and only occasionally spoke, that she ate in the Dining Room and was a feeder. She required a tub bath, deodorant, please. She did not want dri-prides when in w/c. The nurse's aide should brush teeth after each meal.

Cusack looked down the list; his mother's name was missing. Was it an oversight or something more significant? Had they written her off already?

Bertha Fromme was sometimes alert and should be encouraged to join in. Wanted dri-prides when in w/c. Liked to be read to in the evening. Ate in the lunchroom. Preferred the shower.

Television game shows, dri-prides, oatmeal breakfasts, the company and kindness of strangers, putrid smells, the charade of family visits and the haunting face of death. Quite a picture.

There were two thumps on the bathroom door. Cusack folded the paper and shoved it into his jacket packet. Out of the bathroom, Cusack took a wrong turn, walked down a corridor and ended up in a dining room. Quieter in this room than the lobby, there were fewer residents and the atmosphere was different from what he'd seen in the dining room his mother used. Here, only a few of the residents, scattered widely at the tables, were eating, while the others were sitting at bare tables and staring vacantly into space. Zombies, thought Cusack. What was the staff thinking when they wheeled them out to sit at those tables? Was this their entertainment, staring at each other? The pungent odor of urine and disinfectant hit Cusack.

An old man wagged an admonitory finger and spoke sternly to a lamp. A woman, whose shock of white hair seemed to have been brushed with a two-by-four, snored loudly, toothless, lips flapping wetly. A round-faced man with gray face-stubble attempted with little success to bridge the distance from bowl to mouth with a shaky spoon; a sallow-faced woman's emaciated right arm moved like an egg whisk, her claw-like hand striking rhythmically the stainless steel tray on her lap.

Now, whenever Cusack thought of his mother at the end, he saw, not his mother looking serene, eyes closed, hands clasped across her stomach, but the other woman with the wild hair and the right hand like a claw striking the tray in front of her, moving it like a planchette on the Ouija board and looking for yeses and nos.

Cusack came out of his drowse and rubbed his face with both hands. He emptied his glass. He decided he'd had enough bourbon and crawled into bed.

The next morning, Cusack was drying off after a shower when there was a knock at his door. He moved toward his gun when, from outside came Morrissey's voice.

"Police, Mr. Cusack. We need to talk."

Cusack put on his pants and opened the door. "Come in." He walked back to the bed, picked up his shirt and buttoned up.

"We'd like you to come with us now."

"Why?"

"We want you see if you can to i.d. a body."

"Do you know who it is? You have a name?"

"He looks like your description of Beaupre's shooter."

"That was quick work."

"We got a tip," said Winand who was standing in the open doorway and looking around the room. After his inventory, he looked at Cusack.

Cusack put on his jacket and shoes and said, "Let's go."

Cusack rode alone in the back seat. Whoever the dead guy was, Cusack was convinced he'd been set up. Whoever had gotten him to pull the trigger was the one who made sure he'd never talk. It was neat. It was the way things were done.

The morgue was in the sub-basement of the county hospital. They took the elevator down two floors and walked into a corridor with harsh fluorescent lighting. It took several minutes to find someone who could show them into cold storage. The body was on a cart in the middle of a room with a half-dozen other carts also loaded up with bodies. There was a bad smell overlaid with a couple other smells that were less bad.

The attendant pulled back the sheet and Cusack looked at the face of a young man in his twenties with dark brown hair and a snub nose. The left side of his skull was pushed out and there was a dark hole on his right temple.

Well?" said Morrissey.

"He's the right height and build."

"That's it?"

"I told you he was wearing a watch cap and a hooded sweatshirt. He had a beard that looked like a Halloween trick. Did you find the gun?"

"Would you recognize that?" asked Winand.

"No. Did he kill himself?"

Morrissey nodded and the attendant covered the dead man's face. "Winand will take you back to the hotel."

Cusack couldn't say for sure that the dead man was Beaupre's shooter but he'd seen him before. He'd bumped into him at the elevator on his way to see Storti. The same floor where Parsons, too, had a room.

Back at the Midway Motor Lodge Cusack packed the car and

headed downtown to the condo. He drove the speed limit, in no hurry and noticed as he approached downtown the presence of National Guard trucks loaded with soldiers. There were four parked in front of a Dairy Queen as if someone had decided to take a break from fighting anarchy and get an ice cream cone or that ice cream had to be defended to the last man.

A block and a half from the condo he spotted Victor as he ignored the sale tables on the sidewalk and entered the hardware store. He appeared to be alone. Cusack parked the car where he could see the front of his building and the alley. After a few minutes, he left the car carrying his duffel bag. He moved quickly up the stairs. At the top, he noticed his door was partially open, stepped closer and shifted his bag to his left hand. He put his right hand on the pistol grip.

*Sometimes, I wish I could remember nothing.*
*Sometimes, I think the best thing would be to live*
*in a clean, amnesiac, perpetual present.*

# Chapter 5

Cusack held himself breathless for a moment but heard no sound coming from inside. He slid the door back and put a foot in the doorway. "Parsons ..." he said, then saw a young man standing by the work table and Lauren Tyler by the window. They both turned when he spoke. Cusack let his jacket fall over his gun when he recognized the man as the caretaker who had shown him around the condominium and given him the key. Cusack couldn't recall his name.

"Mr. Cusack," the young man looked surprised. "you're here."

"Is there something wrong?" asked Cusack. He stayed in the doorway.

Lauren had an uncertain look on her face though Cusack was convinced she had to know what the camera and tape recorder were for. She wasn't stupid. She said, "I was worried about you after what happened Thursday."

The shooting was Saturday, not Thursday. She didn't want the caretaker to know. She wanted to save it for when they were alone. She was starting to look edgy and her voice was strained.

"It could have been worse." Cusack looked back and forth between the two of them.

Lauren looked sideways at the caretaker. "Stan was a student of mine and I talked him into letting me in." Stan looked uncertainly at Lauren, then at Cusack.

Cusack started to breathe easier. "I think I'm going to have a beer," he said though he stayed in the doorway. "Stan? Lauren?"

"Thanks, but I should be going," said Stan smiling at Cusack. "I'm glad everything's okay." He let his eyes slide toward Lauren. "See you around, Ms. Tyler."

Cusack took a step inside and Stan edged past him. Cusack pulled the door closed. Nothing in the room appeared to have been disturbed. Stan had been standing next to the worktable. That would have to be checked but it was probably nothing. They couldn't have been there long. Lauren was frozen in place with one hand on the camera. She looked like she wanted to be anywhere but where she was.

"When I didn't hear from you, I called the Admin office," she said, looking out the window, then back at Cusack, her eyes gone flat and hard. "They had a phone number for you but it was turned off. Fortunately, they had an address."

"Fortunately." It was stupid to have given them the real address. Here he had no play to make, could only wait for her to give up and leave. Parsons wasn't going to like this but since the Beaupre shooting any kind of a clean finish to the project had become unlikely. He walked across to the refrigerator, took out a beer and twisted the cap off.

"I was surprised when I found you lived across from my father's office." She patted the camera. "Just the first surprise."

"You have to live somewhere." Cusack tipped the beer straight up and drank off half the bottle. He wasn't going to feel bad; it wasn't part of the job. This had happened before, his real identity exposed. But not quite like this.

"I came here because I was worried about you." She smiled at the floor. "Now I'm curious."

"I can see that." Cusack could see the end; he was already starting to close down, starting to look past this to the next assignment.

"Did you get any good pictures with this?" She patted the camera. She was asking a question but it wasn't the one she wanted an answer for.

Cusack took out a pack of cigarettes out of his jacket pocket and his hand brushed the photo of her and Victor.

"One."

"And the tapes? Anything interesting there?" She gave him a look of betrayal. He'd seen it before but it wouldn't play. It was a shitty job but it was what he did and the job had to go on until it was finished.

"I did catch your father talking to himself. His new book, I think. It sounds interesting." He took another deep drink from the bottle and put it on the worktable.

"Who do you work for?"

Cusack put the cigarette to his mouth, inhaled, exhaled, tilted his head and looked her in the eye.

"I should have been more suspicious," she said, shaking her head. "At *Benjamin's*, the way you handled yourself when everything happened. Getting me down on the floor, hustling me out and away from the scene. Like you'd been through that sort of thing before." She looked at Cusack. "Or maybe, knew it was going to happen?"

"I think we're finished here now. With your father. If that helps you at all." If she left now he could finish the bourbon. A suitable ambition now given what was left of the assignment. He was getting that feeling he'd had after Iraq, of just wanting to disappear.

"The guy who was with the deputy-mayor. Who was he, really?"

"An ordinary guy. Works for a pharmaceutical company." The sun had come around and the light fell on Lauren's face, bleaching out the features on one side and putting the other in darkness.

"People aren't supposed to get shot in the street for no reason." She hadn't moved from the spot that she had when he entered the condo. He wouldn't answer her questions but she wasn't going to be intimidated.

There was no point in lying, no point in telling the truth. It was a moment perfect for silence but the moment passed and Cusack said, "There could be a lot of reasons why Ms. Beaupre was shot." Saying her name made her death real, finally. He tried to think of something he could tell Lauren that might get her to leave. Nothing came to mind.

"Who's next?"

Cusack recalled the counselor who'd certified him fit to return to work and her question about how he felt about those who were killed at Saint-Georges. He had a better answer now but better answers always came too late. The better answer was he couldn't do any more for the living than he had for the dead. That's what he wanted to say to Lauren.

"A personal interest?" he said.

She bit her lower lip. "Yes."

"She was killed right in front of us and I don't know what that means."

"You're just trying to scare me," she said. That was why she stayed. She may have been afraid of him, but she had to know what was going to happen. It made sense to him that she'd be that tough. Her questions were just a way of keeping the fear away when what it was she wanted desperately to know was where her family stood in all of this.

Cusack again took out the photograph of Lauren and Victor in Tyler's office, stepped across the room and handed it to her. "You asked about interesting photos. Recognize this guy? I had a conversation with him not too long ago. His name's Victor and he's one of the squatters in the Washburn. I think you know him."

She looked down at the photo and back at Cusack.

"He's your brother-in-law."

"Victor? That was what this was about?"

"I don't have any answers for you." Cusack didn't care if she came to the wrong conclusions. She was a bystander and he wanted her out and he was leaning toward whatever it would take. "He's an illegal alien and a member of a group on the terrorist watch list."

"You people handed my husband over to a bunch of murderous thugs and now you're after Victor?"

"As I said, you and your father are outside the frame now. We're finished here." He was promising something he couldn't deliver on. It was a plausible lie but it could turn out to be the truth. The best possible lie.

Lauren looked at him for a minute as if debating whether or not to speak and then came down on the side of saying nothing. She pushed the camera over and started for the door. The camera cracked when it struck the floor, the back popped open and small pieces of black plastic went spinning across the room. She tugged open the door and disappeared.

Cusack walked across the room to pick up the pieces of camera scattered along the wall. He lifted the tripod, examined the camera. It was fixable. He had a fondness for high-quality equipment. He extracted the disk inside and slipped it into his pocket.

From his position at the window he looked at cops assembled down on 4th Street. They looked prepped to clean out the WRA with their body armor and helmets with smoked visors, automatic weapons with night scopes and lasers. Further down 4th were Humvees with antennae rising off the rear corner of their roofs. And at the very end of the block and probably beyond were several National Guard deuce and a halfs. A good guess would be that they were carrying National Guardsmen and not a social worker in sight. It was additional evidence that DSM had been pushed aside in favor of a more conventional approach to dealing with the squatters.

Cusack turned away from the window, took a draw on his cigarette and finished his beer. He packed the rest of his clothes. On his way out he locked the door and took the elevator. He'd taken the job because he could get lost inside the work and now he was afraid he'd gotten lost outside the work and that made him like just any other hopeless bystander. He could see his car from the lobby and waited for a few minutes before walking to it. He slipped the key in the ignition and looked in his mirrors.

A single Humvee was parked at the corner, a National Guardsman stood next to the open driver's side door smoking a cigarette. Another Guardsman opened a door on the far side. He carried his AR-16 at sling arms.

Cusack took the key out of the ignition and stepped out of the car. He walked two blocks to the hardware store. He examined the goods laid out on the sale tables on the sidewalk. There were socket wrench sets, candles in elaborate glass containers, kitchen utensils and 1950s retro toys. He picked up a slinky and let it waterfall from one hand to another and back again.

"Enjoying yourself?" It was Victor.

"The last time I saw one of these," Cusack said as he put the slinky back onto the table, "was in a high school physics class. The teacher was using it to illustrate some principle, which I never really got."

"Let's walk." Victor pointed up the street.

As they walked north on University Avenue, Old Main's clock tower appeared in the gaps between buildings. The mechanism of the clock was being repaired so the time was fixed at one-ten.

"Talk to your sister-in-law recently?" asked Cusack.

Victor seemed not to hear the question. "I hear they found the shooter, dead. Over there." He pointed at the fence across the street.

Cusack knew all about the shooter. He wasn't interested. "Why did you come here? I mean here," he added making a circular motion with his forefinger to take in the WRA. At the intersection the light was against them. Cusack didn't see any of Victor's friends from the coffee shop. He didn't think there was any reason to be worried.

"I was living in Paris," said Victor. "The French gave me, like my brother, refugee status. It was pleasant there. People were nice to me." He turned up the collar on his pea jacket. "But there are only so many rallies you can speak at, so many letters to the editor you can write. I decided I had to go back to Senegal. To the fight." The light changed and they walked across the street.

"Paris to Montreal to here then to Senegal. Kind of the long way around, isn't it?" Cusack thought Victor was believable. That didn't mean he was telling the truth.

Victor seemed to consider the remark a serious critique. "Yes, yes it is. But before I went back to Senegal I had to see my only living relative. It was just something I had to do."

"And so ..."

"I'm leaving tonight."

They had stopped on the far corner under an awning protecting the entrance to a bar called the *Lexington*. Cusack remembered what he'd said about the dangers for the police if they went into the Washburn. To Victor he said, "I think the police are ... agitated. What about the people in the Washburn?"

"I'm sorry, I have to go."

Cusack watched him cross the street and disappear around the corner.

Back in his room, Cusack put on a clean shirt and pants and poured himself a drink. It tasted like everything he wanted.

*For the human race there is no salvation in*
*perfect understanding - that would be Hell.*
*The definition of God is that He understands*
*everything and is in Heaven.*

# Chapter 6

Cusack called ticket reservation at the airport and secured a seat on an 11:55 p.m. return flight to Baltimore. That left four and a half hours to change his mind. He finished packing his bag, set it by the door and began reading the Cioran book, putting off the final decision. After twenty minutes, he stood up and stretched, walked across the room and took the second to last beer out of the refrigerator. He stepped to the windows and looked out. A helicopter flew in lazy circles over the WRA. They'd be smart to go in at night. The police and the National Guard would have superior night-vision equipment, superior numbers and weapons, and they'd have practiced for exactly what was going to happen. He went back to his chair and an hour later there was a knock on his door. He opened it and Lauren brushed by him into the room.

"Is he here?"

"Who?"

"My father."

Cusack opened his arms.

She looked around the room then went into the bathroom. When she came out, she stopped and looked around again as if not believing what she saw. "He's a creature of habit. He comes home every night at five, has a cocktail and then we have dinner. When he didn't show, I called his office. Professor Martinson said she saw him leave with a man. I thought it might have been you." She'd run out of things to say and stood there staring at the floor.

The phone rang and he guessed it was Morrissey with more questions or maybe some news about the identity of Beaupre's killer.

"I thought you might still be around." There was a hollow distortion in Parsons' voice as if he was speaking from inside an auditorium. "You want to leave, just walk away, don't you? This wasn't what you were hoping for when we met in Vienna, am I right? You wanted something clean and simple. Tyler cannot be redeemed."

Cusack was standing now at the worktable facing the windows. "I have a midnight flight to Baltimore." The sky was losing light but there was still enough to brush up the tone in the leaves still hanging on in the trees across the street.

"Is she there with you now?" Parsons said as if he'd included Cusack in his plans from the beginning and Cusack just needed a little reassurance about the time line.

"Is Storti with you?"

"Tyler is here with me." Parsons paused giving Cusack time to understand. "I thought it might advance the discussion if you brought the daughter, maybe even the granddaughter, here."

"What's the plan?"

"I want Tyler and Victor in a nice little package. Clean and simple."

Neither of them spoke for a minute.

Cusack said, "Where are you?"

"I think Victor can be reached. I don't think he is, as you say, in the wind. Not yet. And you have to understand, we have an opportunity here. We have to take it."

Cusack felt sick. Opportunity. He looked at Lauren and couldn't think of anything to say.

"Don't worry, Cusack, the old man is still kicking. All I want is the answer. He's the only one who can provide it."

"I need an hour."

"We'll be waiting for you in the Fitzpatrick Building on the south end of the Washburn. I'm looking at a busted up fountain. The police have cleaned everyone out on this end. Quiet as a tomb. A half-hour, Cusack. You work the daughter any way you like. I'm depending on your efficiency." Parsons cut the connection.

Cusack had been there and could picture the fountain, the police cars parked around it while the social workers brought out the squatters. He considered contacting Morrissey but the police had a routine and Parsons wouldn't get worked that way. There was no good option but if he went in alone, he had a chance to see what was what and it might not turn out so bad. He snapped the phone shut and lit a cigarette.

Cusack recalled the night before the helicopter ride north out of Dakar. Parsons and Cusack pored over maps in their hotel room and argued about the latest intel. The lobby had been full of soldiers when they arrived. The army top brass had taken over the top floor. The government minister who was going with Cusack on the helicopter to Matam was in the bar, waiting. Cusack mixed up his nightmares again, saw himself back in Iraq looking at Vasquez's face again, blood pouring out of his eye socket.

"Anything else?" Cusack needed a few minutes alone.

"Who was that?" Lauren asked.

"My boss. I was just telling him I'm catching a flight back to Baltimore tonight."

She gave him a look and walked out.

He put his holster on, tapped his two extra clips on the table and dropped them into his jacket pocket. He rummaged around in his bag until he found a flashlight. There was no time to set up any kind of a decent plan. Just go in, get Tyler and make it out with most of his skin. Maybe he'd get lucky.

He thought about Tyler's lectures and his precision when he spoke. Thinking about that now was no good. Cusack had to think the situation was salvageable and make it happen. That was the only ending he could work on. Parsons taking the angle he had meant this sort of thing could get stupid very fast. At the bottom of the bag he tipped up the lid on a concealed compartment and extracted a .32 Smith & Wesson snub-nosed revolver with an ankle clip. He swung his right foot up onto the chair, pulled up his pants cuff and wrapped the velcro strap above the ankle.

Cusack didn't need a trick to get into the Washburn. The cops weren't spending any time trying to keep people from getting in. Getting out, that was going to be a bitch. Parsons had a scheme and Cusack was either going to be able to talk him out of it or not. If not, well, he didn't want to think about that.

From the front door of his condominium, Cusack turned south on University. On the near side of University Avenue, halfway between two streetlights, he darted across the street and hopped the fence. He pushed through a scrim of undergrowth and litter until he came to Folwell Street, which was a block west and ran inside the Washburn parallel to University Avenue.

He sheltered in a doorway. The plywood sheet that covered the opening was full of graffiti. Mary figured in most of the obscenities. He remembered from his previous visits that the Fitzpatrick, a block or so from the hotel where he'd first met Victor, was an older brick building with a high-ceilinged first floor. He estimated he was still three blocks north of it. He started to work his way down Folwell and stayed in as close to the buildings, the ones left standing, as he could.

Suddenly headlights appeared to the south heading toward Cusack on Folwell. Cusack lay flat behind a low pile of bricks. Three Humvees drove by followed by three National Guard trucks. They were moving fast and heading north. Cusack lay still and, after a minute, the sound of their engines died away. He stepped cautiously out to the fence and looked north. The vehicles were stopped five or six blocks away with their lights out. Cusack retraced his steps to his hiding place and began to move toward the Fitzpatrick.

Suddenly, he heard automatic rifle fire from the north end of the Washburn, a kind of plastic sound. He looked up and could see to the north several helicopters hovering with spotlights directed at the ground. Then, there was an eruption of noise, both sides laying down an intense line of fire. There were lights in the sky now. From where he stood they looked like a second dawn but six blocks north it would be different on the ground.

He moved past one building, recently taken down, which lay in a pyramidal shape of brick, twisted steel beam and splintered timber. A twenty-foot long cable lay coiled along the edge of the rubble like a snake guarding its kill.

A full moon rose above the trees and added to the hazard for anyone on the move. The top floors of the buildings he was looking at would command a wide killing zone for a decent marksman. There were clouds and Cusack waited until one passed in front of the moon before moving.

A block north of the Fitzpatrick, Cusack slowed his pace. If Cusack's work in various locales around the world had taught him nothing else, it was that no landscape was innocent. Buildings and fountains didn't mean civilization and streets and stop signs didn't mean order. Anywhere could offer shelter for madness and an argument for savagery.

Cusack approached the open square in front of the Fitzpatrick with the fountain in the center. A building on the north side of the square had part of one wall still standing; he sheltered in its shadow and let his breathing return to normal. He studied the Fitzpatrick, which gave nothing away; there were only shadows on shadows. He knew that in bad light it was easier to pick up movement out of the corner of the eye than looking straight on. He took on the view from left to right but nothing showed up. He wondered if there was a point earlier in the game when he might have gotten Parsons to see things differently.

It was time to move in. He patted himself and felt the reassurance of the pistol in the holster under his jacket. Having it out would make his intention obvious. It was an irreversible signal. Cusack was edgy, didn't think Parsons was persuadable but it was too early in the day to be obvious.

"You're early."

Cusack just kept himself from hitting the ground. He took a deep breath and examined his field of vision for a minute without responding. Finally, he spotted Parsons as a darkness next to a doorway at the front of the Fitzpatrick.

"I'm coming across," said Cusack as he stepped into the open. Now was the bad time when everything got drawn up into itself, when there was no time if anything went wrong. He picked his way carefully across the street, the ground covered in broken pieces of brick and block. When he looked up again, Parsons had vanished. He skirted the remains of the fountain and arrived on the far side of the street.

"Over here."

Clouds shifted and in the glow from the moon Cusack saw Parsons outlined for a moment in a doorway at the center of the building.

He disappeared inside and Cusack walked over the remnants of the sidewalk to the same doorway. Cusack paused, hearing again a mix of weapons firing steadily. When he stepped through the door, Parsons said, "That's far enough. Where's the daughter?"

Cusack took a breath, said nothing and was careful to keep his arms at his side.

"Toss your weapon."

Cusack reached down, used his thumb and forefinger to pull out the Beretta and flipped it back at the doorway. Then he took a step to the left so that he wouldn't be haloed by the open doorway. It was a reflex precaution but if Parsons had the right kind of ordnance he could lay down enough fire to find him.

"Where's the daughter?" asked Parsons again. The sound of his voice echoed making it hard to pinpoint.

"Tyler has nothing to tell us," said Cusack. Inside the building the little bit of light from the moon didn't do much, offered only a perspective but no control.

"This could have been slick, Cusack. Am I going to be disappointed?" There was an edge to his voice, not anger, not fear.

"Is it just you and me?" Cusack gave the darkness a quick sweep but could make out no useful features. Parsons was keeping Tyler close but probably not right here.

"Are you worried?"

"I like to know who's on the team is all."

"Are you on the team, Cusack?" Parsons kicked a rock. He was talking while on the move and making it hard for Cusack to locate him.

"Even if Tyler knows something, it's too late now."

"Did you bring the girl?"

"Where's Tyler?" Again, Cusack heard Parsons sigh.

"We could have gotten it right this time."

Cusack wanted to put something in front of Parsons that would collect his attention. "When you sent me off with that team into Matam, how good was that intel?"

There was a long moment of silence and Cusack figured he'd asked the right question.

"That's ancient history. Isn't there a line from a song? 'History is just some people talking.'"

"I want to know." The first floor windows of the Fitzpatrick were all covered in plywood and the only light came through the open doorway. Cusack strained his eyes but couldn't pick up Parsons. He seemed to have stopped moving but even that was no help.

"Remember when I interviewed you for this job? I asked, if you believed that there was a moral dimension attached to everything we did. Do you remember what you said?"

"No." In the dark room now the darkness, instead of reducing seemed to add to the number of dimensions. It gave him a sick feeling.

"You said you didn't think it worked out along those lines."

"I said that?"

"I liked that. You didn't just agree with me in order to get the job. And I thought that when it came right down to it you'd do the right thing because it was the only thing to do."

"The only thing ..." Cusack repeated. He was thinking it was just the two of them and he was going to have to play it that way whatever the risks.

"I've given this a lot of thought, Cusack. You know how things work when you're collecting intelligence on someone. Ultimately, you have to act based on your best judgment. And your judgment, that's the thing that can be trained only up to a point."

"Parsons, agency records on Tyler ... there's nothing there. The French ambassador and the CDC, just coincidence. It's over."

"They looked but they didn't know how to look. Sometimes, you have to believe something is there before you can see it."

There it was, the escape into certainty. Evidence couldn't be trusted. Argument was futile. Everything moved through belief. Cusack heard a stone being kicked and figured Parsons was moving again, afraid, too, that he could be targeted by his voice. Cusack went into a crouch, lifted his pants cuff, eased the Smith & Wesson out of its holster and thumbed back the hammer. He took the flashlight out with his left hand.

"You think Tyler could carry on that sort of charade?" Cusack began to move further to the left along the wall away from the door and into a deeper darkness.

"You're a watcher, Cusack. You should know how easy it is to pretend."

Cusack thought he finally understood Parsons. His ambition corked his judgment, which made it all a crap-shoot for him. Tyler was the key to the past and the future and Parsons had gotten desperate when Beaupre's shooting and the agency's reinforcements didn't seal the deal with the mayor. It drove him into an absolute corner. He'd lost all patience. And from that place Parsons was going to keep tossing the dice until he broke the bank or crapped out. Whatever it took.

"Tell me where Tyler is."

"Hey, what the fuck do you guys think you're doing here?"

Cusack turned to see a figure outlined in the doorway. At the same moment there were two flat, smacking sounds and muzzle flashes and the figure in the doorway pitched to the right. Cusack got off two quick rounds in Parsons' direction as he fell to the left. He heard ricochets. Missed.

Parsons returned fire in Cusack's general direction but the two rounds were wide of the mark, high and behind him.

Cusack lay still, listening. Absurdly, what came to mind was a section in the Soldier's Manual of Common Tasks about determining the range of incoming fire. The flash to bang method. Sound travels through the air at about 330 meters per second. Watch the flash and count. There was the sound of rubble being kicked, once, then again. Cusack raised his pistol in the direction of the sound but held fire, unsure of the precise location of the sound and thinking of Tyler who might be close by. Cusack had cut his face when he fell and hit his right knee on a jagged piece of concrete. There was quiet for a minute, two, three. Cusack rose slowly into a crouch, testing his knee, turned his head from side to side straining to hear and see but there was nothing.

He held the flashlight in his left hand and extended his arm out to his left. He pointed it and the gun where he estimated Parsons had been, flashed the switch on and off. There was no Parsons, only a doorway and a room beyond. He doused the light and picked his way carefully in the direction of the other room across patches of smooth concrete and standing water that smelled very bad and soaked his shoes.

When he reached the doorway, he stopped to get his breath. He took a quick peek around the door frame but could see nothing. There was no easy way to do this and, on some level, this was exactly what he'd expected. From the moment he'd gotten the call from Parsons the good options were successively taken off the board. Now, he was going into a dark room against the man who'd taught him to be what he was. Cusack took another breath and went in low, rolled over and up onto his knees. He held his position for a moment and could hear someone else's labored breathing. Tyler? He risked a quick on and off with the flashlight and saw a figure lying on his back on the stairs twenty feet away. Parsons.

Cusack advanced quickly across the room, keeping the flashlight and pistol focused. One of his bullets had hit the mark after all. Parsons was lying on his back on the bottom three or four steps with his feet on the floor. The stairs were laid against the far wall, concrete with no handrail. As Cusack approached, he could see Parsons' eyes move. His head rested on the fourth step and his right hand was moving slowly back and forth searching with his fingertips for the gun on the step below. There was a large, growing stain on the right side of his shirt below the rib cage.

"Don't," said Cusack.

Parsons' face was messed with blood and he had a horrific smile frozen on his face. His fingers kept moving and they brushed the butt of the gun, paused and kept moving, then came back. He spoke, "He wouldn't talk. He's not scared, not yet. But it's not over."

Parsons' eyes glittered in the light from the flashlight and his fingertips touched the pistol grip and stopped this time. Cusack couldn't stand the look in Parsons' eyes and pulled the trigger. The impact of the bullet pushed Parsons up onto his left shoulder and he slid down until both his knees were on the ground and his face was turned to the wall.

Cusack heard a noise to his left, went down quickly on one knee and worked the flashlight around to the middle of the room. Tyler was strapped to a chair next to a pillar, slumped over but still breathing. Cusack knew he didn't have much time. He looked back at Parsons then ran the flashlight over to Tyler. He crouched next to Tyler while he worked the knots. A siren sounded not too far off. There was a floor drain with no cover at the center of the room. He stopped working on Tyler's knots and wiped off the pistol, then dropped it into the drain. He ran to the door, recovered his Beretta and ran back to Tyler.

Police lights came through the open door and around the plywood on the windows. Cusack finally freed Tyler and picked him up. It was like a bundle of dried sticks, like it had been with his mother. When he carried Tyler out, Cusack stepped into the opaline glare of police lights and a command voice booming at him a few simple instructions. On your knees. Hands on your head. Face down, arms spread.

Cusack rode in the ambulance with Tyler with a cop on the bench next to him. They raced up University Avenue and he saw to his left klieg lights from the police operation, which illuminated a wide area. Cusack thought about how he'd taken on the Tyler job to rehabilitate himself and how he'd ended up killing someone when he'd only come to save himself.

When the paramedic fitted an oxygen mask over Tyler's face, Cusack said, "He's got emphysema. I don't know anything else about him."

The paramedic nodded, then spoke into his walkie-talkie to the emergency room, describing Tyler's condition.

Cusack thought about Parsons and if what had happened was inevitable. The ambulance took a sharp right turn and Cusack just kept himself from falling onto Tyler. Cusack recalled Parsons saying that sometimes you had to believe in something before you could see it.

After the police had relieved him of the burden of Tyler, he offered them his ID and a brief memorized incantation, which kept them at a discreet distance. He gave them Lauren's name and an officer went to make a call. Cusack called Morrissey's office and left a message.

*The Last Judgment is announced like a threat when,
all of us desperate for the comfort of absolute certainty
know that, relief is the only honest reaction to its
impending arrival.*

# Chapter 7

The waiting area next to the emergency treatment rooms was noisy, with the sound of voices arguing, talking over one another and wailing piteously. The lighting was so bright that no one cast a shadow. The four policemen who stood at the nurses' station had come in with Cusack. Occasionally, one would look in his direction as if he'd suddenly made an interesting noise. They were relaxed and seemed to barely acknowledge where they were. After a few minutes, one of them took a call, nodded at the other three and they turned abruptly and left.

The scene looked, at first glance, like chaos but every one of the medical staff seemed concentrated on what they had in front of them and nothing else. The chaos was around them but they weren't in it. Cusack admired their lock on the moment. He was losing his own. A weariness was coming over him that felt like the aftermath of a beating.

The waiting area was four rows of hard plastic chairs and all were occupied. Those who were seated all seemed resigned and said little. Those with the energy to stand worked at making a nuisance of themselves, pleading with the nurses or tugging at the sleeves of doctors. Cusack sat at one end of the second row next to the wall. The place smelled of disinfectant and old sweat. He put his head against the wall and closed his eyes.

The emergency room doors that fronted the parking lot slid open to admit paramedics hustling in loaded gurneys. This process was repeated over and over again in seemingly endless succession as one paramedic team after another dumped the sick and wounded into the room. One doctor directed the incoming traffic, speaking to one of her staff as each gurney came in and pointing to where it should be taken. For forty minutes Cusack watched this and wondered where all the bodies were being put.

A nurse gave Cusack antiseptic wipes and bandages for his cuts. He took his time cleaning them then walked across the room to drop the wipes into the wastebasket. His knee still hurt but he didn't have the energy to fight a nurse for ibuprofen. He stood at the wastebasket and looked down the hallway to his left, which was lined with patients on gurneys. The ceiling lights haloed briefly and he knew one of his headaches was coming on. Some of the patients looked to be in bad shape and moaned convincingly but the doctors had seen them and left. What had the doctor thought when he saw Tyler?

Cusack returned to his seat and was hit by a second wave of intense weariness. It worked, surprisingly, to clear his head. He felt himself untethered, out at the extreme limits of the stalemate where he'd lived for too long. The present was an exhausted possibility and the future not just that same present brought inevitably forward but some undiscovered prospect. However, even with that, nothing was obvious and he felt, in spite of everything, that that was a good sign.

A group of National Guardsmen entered through the ER

ambulance doors pushing several gurneys. Nurses were telling those sitting in the waiting room that they needed the room for patients. Orderlies were ushering people outside, stacking chairs and moving portable beds and screens into place.

He picked up the paper cup full of coffee from the floor and took a sip. He'd gotten it from the machine at the far end of the waiting room. There was a greasy film on the surface and it tasted faintly of chicken soup, one of the other selections available. The combination of flavors set up a nauseous reflex at the back of his throat. He set the cup carefully on the floor.

Cusack felt his eyes closing and he propped his head against the wall. The moaning that came from the gurneys nearby hardly disturbed him at all. It seemed to him that he had just drifted off when someone nudged him awake. He jerked upright.

A tall black male nurse leaned toward him. "We need this space for patients, man."

Cusack nodded. "Okay."

"We're asking people to go the hospital cafeteria or the main lobby waiting room."

Cusack nodded again and headed for the open ER door and the ambulance bay and the lot beyond. He passed through the door and saw three ambulances turning toward the entrance. To his right Deputy Director Merriwether was stepping out of his car. Cusack waited for him.

"What happened with Parsons?"

Cusack rubbed his face, stood and said, "I need a cigarette." The two of them walked toward a paramedic van with its hood up and someone working on the engine. Cusack lit up.

Cusack had given some thought to the answer to that question.

"I was in there looking for Tyler. I'd gotten a tip he was there trying to get some sort of peaceful resolution."

"A tip?"

"A tip."

"So, when you got there, what then?" Merriwether scanned the lot and looked at the entrance where several of the Guardsmen were standing. Cusack followed Merriwether's look. The Guardsmen had done some shooting and looked like they had settled in.

"There was a dead man outside the building where Tyler was supposed to be. The first room was empty. In the second room, I saw Tyler on the floor and Parsons, who'd been shot, lying on the stairs. Otherwise, the place was empty. Parsons had been shot twice and was dead when I got there." There it was, the best kind of lie. A few true facts and a few plausible lies.

Merriwether turned away, too angry to speak but Cusack didn't give much of a shit. He put a cigarette in his mouth.

"Problem?" asked Cusack.

"I want this wrapped up tight. I can't see who's going to like this."

An ambulance wheeled in, its siren dying but its lights still flashing. A doctor and nurse hustled out of the emergency room as the medics hauled the patient out of the ambulance. A uniformed cop was standing next to the open door now staring at Cusack and Merriwether.

Cusack flicked his cigarette into the darkness and headed back to the emergency room. He had to move through a crowd and around several gurneys that were now being positioned behind makeshift screens. At the nurses' station he asked if they had any information on Tyler and just then a doctor approached.

"I'm Dr. Patek. You came in with the elderly man..."

"Tyler," said Cusack.

"What is your relationship with him?"

"Student."

The doctor's eyebrows went up. "I'm sorry. Mr. Tyler's heart, it couldn't take the strain. I understand he was involved in the trouble at the Washburn?"

Cusack stared at the doctor, giving him a chance to reconsider his verdict. Finally, he said, "His heart?"

"He was in here," the doctor looked down at a chart, "last week. Respiratory episode. He was seventy-eight. At that age..." the doctor's voice trailed off. "Does he have any next of kin?"

"A daughter. She's been called."

"Well, again, I'm sorry." Patek turned then and spoke to a nurse telling her to give the man in the second bed 200cc of something .

Cusack stood absolutely still as people moved around him. Tyler's death made him feel cleaned out and abandoned and looking at a vista but no horizon where options seemed like the dead end of everything. It was not where he'd aimed to be but it felt like the unknown trajectory in these events that had brought him to this place, where everything that had happened in the last few days had been driving him. A nurse touched him on the shoulder and he moved again toward the ambulance doors.

Lauren walked in from the main part of the hospital holding Sarah's hand and headed straight for Dr. Patek. She looked composed, ready for anything.

Cusack couldn't hear what she said. She wouldn't look at Cusack or anyone else. From the doctor's facial expression Cusack knew he was repeating what he'd said to Cusack minutes earlier. She betrayed no emotion. Sarah appeared stunned by the crowd and the noise. She never took her eyes off her mother.

Sarah appeared to ask her mother something about "Grandpa," then they disappeared down the hallway.

Back outside again, Cusack walked to the far end of an ambulance that had been parked against a concrete wall to the right. He shook out a cigarette and lit it. The lights on the wall above the entrance and the light poles on the edge of the concrete pad marked for emergency vehicles gave the air a chill quality and the feel of a rising fog yet with an absolute clarity.

He stood there and looked up at the sky but the city lights made the stars difficult to pick out. He wondered what he'd accomplished or where he'd gotten himself, having started out looking for work to lose himself in and a promise to get bystanders out. He felt that he'd worked through the available options instead of conceding some inevitability and that was something and was as good as it got. Still...

The double doors opened and Lauren and Sarah walked out. Sarah was crying, her face pushed against her mother's waist. They were surrounded by light from the waiting room. Lauren walked by without referencing him and he recalled his ambition to become a phantom, to be nowhere at all.

Right behind Lauren and Sarah came Morrissey. Cusack turned to watch Lauren as she moved among the cars in the parking lot. He thought he should acknowledge something, something finalized just for himself.

"Cusack? I have a few questions," said Morrissey.

Cusack had gotten most of what he wanted. He was invisible now but he was still Cusack.

"C'mon," said Morrissey. "It's cold out here."

Cusack started back toward the door and looked over his shoulder though he knew there would be no one there.

CPSIA information can be obtained at www.ICGtesting.com
Printed in the USA
BVOW070003171012

303126BV00001B/3/P